BILLIONAIRE BOSS

JULIE CAPULET

Our deal was simple. One night. Fake names. No strings attached.

Until it turns out he's my new boss…

I couldn't believe my luck when I got sent to a work conference in Hawaii. Living the dream after years of pulling myself up by my bootstraps.

The sand, the palm trees and the blue water were straight out of a romantic fantasy. So was the guy at the beachfront bar, let's be honest. Blue eyes. Broad-shouldered in his business suit but with a rough-around-the-edges swagger and a filthy mouth.

We laughed and had a night of crazy passion that enlightened me in every possible way. I understood what dreams coming true might actually feel like.

And then I left without saying goodbye.

That was two months ago and I've mostly been able to put him out of my mind. I've been busy landing my dream job in New York City.

Imagine my surprise when my new boss turns out to be Mr. Dirty Talking Swagger.

He's been thinking about me too, he says, his blue eyes dancing. He's been searching for me since that night.

And he wants to see me in his office…

Billionaire Boss is a steamy billionaire romance and the first book in the New York Billionaires series, starring the four Maddox brothers. Each book in the series is a complete standalone with a sexy fairy tale HEA.

New York Billionaires

BILLIONAIRE BOSS

1

Dusty

"THIS IS YOUR HOTEL HERE, DUSTY." My Uber driver, Earl, who I've learned on the twelve minute ride in from the Honolulu airport has been married to his high school sweetheart Marion for twenty-seven years, retired to Hawaii three years ago after Marion decided she could no longer handle the brutal Pittsburgh winters, has five grandchildren who visit for two weeks every Christmas and, as much as he loves seeing them, is always relieved when it's time for them to go. I even know their names: Huck, Brodie, Cassandra, Milo and Imogen. "It's the best hotel in Waikiki. No contest."

We pull up outside an unbelievably luxurious hotel with tall columns and a welcoming row of stately palm trees. The scene is as picture perfect as…well, as a life-long fantasy of being sent to Hawaii for a fully paid-for work trip can be.

Travel brochures and marathon binges of Hawaii Life don't really capture the neon turquoise of the water. Or the ideal temperature of the balmy, sea-scented air.

This place is unreal.

"Just wait until you see the views once you get inside," Earl tells me. "You're in for a treat. This is the oldest hotel in Oahu. The two towers on either side of the main building are the new additions, but the original hotel is where the charm is. The whole place is pure luxury."

"It's right on the beach?"

"Sure is. Best waterfront bar in Waikiki, hands down. An absolute magnet for love birds. I'm always giving rides to couples who are coming back to celebrate the place they first met, at least once a week. They're on their honeymoons, or they're here to celebrate their fifth, tenth or twenty-fifth wedding anniversaries. I once had this older couple coming back for their fiftieth. It's as if this place is spiking its drinks with aphrodisiacs and love potions. And you have that look to you." He winks at me in the rear view mirror.

"What look?"

"The starstruck one. The one that tells me your life is about to change."

I laugh lightly. "Oh, no, I'm just here for a conference."

"That's what they all say." He grins at me, then gets out to retrieve my bags.

I wriggle myself out of the backseat of the cab, no mean feat in the tight pencil skirt I poured myself into ten grueling hours ago. It was clearly the wrong choice for a hellish day of travel, but this is my first ever work trip and I was hoping to give the first impression of a put-together professional—a slightly crumpled one at this point, after a commuter flight from Austin to Houston, then eight and a half hours to Honolulu. I couldn't really rock up to the business class lounge in my usual jeans and cowboy boots, as tempting as that might have been. If I want to be taken seriously as a newly-minted financial advisor, straight out of college and fighting her way to the top of a dog-eat-dog, heavily male-dominated scene, I at least need to look the part.

I thank Earl, giving my best to Marion, Huck, Brodie, Cassandra, Milo and especially Imogen (who suffers from stage fright and has a piano recital next Thursday), immediately rate him five stars and give him a huge tip. "Bye, Earl."

"See you on your honeymoon," he winks.

I smile and wave as he drives away. Good old Earl.

As much as Earl might think of himself as an oracle, I laugh off his prediction. For better or worse, the circumstances of my life have made me a die-hard realist. Any romantic tendencies I might have been born with got trampled by ambition and circumstance a long time ago.

I heave my gigantic suitcase—because I've never been

on a work trip *or* to Hawaii and you never know what you might need—up the ramp. God bless the genius who invented wheeled suitcases, is all I can say.

Walking into the lobby of the hotel, I have to stop for a minute just to take in the breath-taking view.

Woah.

There's a giant banyan tree (thank you, three a.m. googling sessions) in the middle of a scenic, wide-open courtyard. A glittering pool sits to its right and there's a restaurant with a colorfully-lit stage, even in broad daylight, where a musician is singing a Hawaiian classic I recognize.

Somewhere Over the Rainbow.

You can say that again.

It's so beautiful I feel like I'm hallucinating.

The bar is perfectly positioned under the majestic tree. Beyond that, the golden sand of Waikiki Beach and the twinkling blue water are as idyllic as a fantasy.

"Pretty spectacular, huh?"

A man is standing next to me. He's dressed in a suit and has reddish, thinning hair and eyes so pale blue he almost looks see-through. He checks me out before his gaze lands once again on my face.

Um, no.

"Are you here for the conference? I'm Brad Channing. I'm with Rothwell and Dodd Financials."

"Oh. That's…nice."

I'm beyond grateful when two of his colleagues walk

over and hand him his key card. "Ogilvie wants to meet with us pronto," one of them says to him.

I take that as my cue to flee. "I better check in. Enjoy your stay." I make a beeline for the check-in desk before Brad can corner me with more chitchat. He glances back at me as he follows his colleagues outside.

Not a chance in hell, Brad. I'm definitely not here to get picked up by a junior assistant in a bad suit. My ambitions are on overdrive. Besides, I have way too much to achieve to get bogged down by a relationship, no matter what Earl might have joked about.

I wait in the check-in line. The hotel is busy with happy, relaxed people. Some are obviously here for the conference and are dressed in now-wrinkled business clothes, but most of the guests are wearing bathing suits and tropical prints. The more suntanned they are, the more relaxed they seem to be.

As I wait, I gaze out past the row of rocking chairs that line the deck, where people are reading books and sipping cocktails, to the beach and the cluster of surfers in the distance, catching wave after perfect wave. I'm already counting down the minutes until I can slip into my bikini and immerse myself blissfully into that blue, blue water.

I still can't believe this is *real.* I've flown business class to one of the most beautiful places in the world without having to pay a cent for any of it. In fact I'm being *paid* to be here.

Until a few hours ago, I'd only been out of the state of Texas once in my life.

The truth is, the struggles I watched my mother deal with my entire life have been implanted in my brain by now, and they motivate me to work like nothing else could, until the universe has no choice but to hoist me out of the rut my family seems to have been mired in for a long time. After my dad went AWOL when I was four years old, my mom and my older sister Skylar and I moved into our tiny bungalow in a lower-rent neighborhood (at the time, at least) of central Austin where my mother has lived ever since. She spent my childhood working day and night to meet our very basic needs. Both Sky and I started working as soon as we were old enough to help her.

And she did meet our basic needs. After searching for my dad but always coming up empty, she finally gave up. We later found out he'd changed his name—what a hero —then died in a drunk driving accident two years later.

So we made it work on our own, because we had no choice.

It was a struggle. We never had any extras. My mom used to make light of it and call it our no-frills lifestyle. We ate what we could afford, we had one pair of shoes each and we bought our clothes from thrift stores. When my friends took trips to Europe and vacationed in the Bahamas, I stayed at home with my paper route. When my classmates bought all the latest gadgets,

I watched them play with them. And as I did, I set goals.

I read somewhere that you're 43% more likely to achieve your goals if you write them down. The room I shared with my sister was so decorated with Post-it notes, she complained. I started a dog-walking business when I was seven. I got a paper route when I was ten. I got a job in a coffee shop when I was twelve, working under the table until I turned fourteen. When I wasn't working, I was studying.

UT was within walking distance to our house, so I started going to the library there when I was in sixth grade, skimming my fingers along the rows of books, watching the college students with their stuffed-full tote bags, their shiny MacBooks and their colorful Longhorns merch. I vowed I would not only get accepted into UT, but also put myself through college, graduate near the top of my class, and land myself a job that would pay me enough money to help my family and make sure we no longer had to struggle so damn hard every single day of our lives.

And I've *done* it.

The way the sunlight is sparkling on the white-capped blue waves is reminding me that all my hard work has finally paid off.

My new job might not be perfect but it's one step closer to the security I've always craved. My next goal: to land my dream job in New York City.

I visited my roommate from college in New York the summer after my freshman year and completely fell in love with the energy and the buzz of the place. I was enchanted by the look of it and the glamour. The opportunities to build something incredible out of your life had me hooked—that feeling that you're in the center of the world, where anything can happen. You could *feel* every lyric to all the songs that have been written about New York City. *Concrete jungle where dreams are made of. There's nothing you can't do. It's up to you, New York New York.* I wanted to be a part of it so badly I could taste it.

So I've been working my heart out every day since to get there.

"Next." The woman behind the desk smiles.

I step forward. "I have a reservation under Rose. Dusty Rose. I'm here for the Emerging Into Investments conference."

The receptionist types in my information. "You're here with Stellar Investments?"

"Yes, that's right."

"I'll just need your ID. The room is fully pre-paid."

She types in my info, sliding two plastic cards into an envelope. "Welcome to Hawaii, Ms. Rose. Your room is on the fourth floor. Number 417. Courtyard view, which is the best view, in my opinion. Here's your key and this card is a towel voucher. Swap it for a towel at the desk next to the pool and when you return it they'll give you a new card. Here's the finalized agenda for the conference, which is being held right across the street. And here's some information about the excursions and activities we offer if you have some downtime. Wi-Fi is complimentary and the elevator is right over there. Enjoy your stay."

"Thank you." My heart feels so full it might burst.

I find my way to the elevator, pressing the button for the fourth floor, charmed all over again by the surreal scene outside the open doors of the foyer, which leads to a bar area where a grand piano sits.

As the elevator takes me up, I scan the conference agenda. It's a two-day event with a jam-packed line-up of speakers, starting first thing tomorrow morning. At four-thirty each afternoon, the conference winds down, replaced by a cocktail hour.

My room is as beautiful as the rest of the hotel. There's a king-sized bed and tropical-themed art on the walls. Open French doors are framed by plantation-style shutters, leading out to a tiny Juliet-style balcony that looks out over the courtyard and beach. I can hear the live music.

After all the hours of studying, the exhausting internships, the working two jobs to pay my way through college: all of it—right here and right now—finally feels worth it.

For a second I just take it all in, wondering what it *would* feel like to come back here on your one-year anniversary, or your twenty-fifth. To revisit this magical place and reminisce about that one weekend where it all began.

You've got that look to you.

I laugh to myself.

Sure I do.

Putting on my bikini, I tie a pink hibiscus-print wrap dress over it and head for the beach.

2

Dusty

Bzzzzz. Bzzzzz. Bzzzzz.

Reaching blindly for my phone alarm from under mountains of plush duvet, I turn it off, stretching luxuriously. *Wow,* this bed is comfortable. Note to self: as soon as you can afford to, invest in good bedding.

From my pile of goose feather pillows, I grab the day's agenda and scan through the schedule I chose.

- 7:30: Tropical Buffet
- 8:30: The Magic of Compounding Interest
- 10:00: Index Funds and Why You Need Them
- 11:30: Diversify Like a Pro
- 1:00: Tropical Buffet
- 2:00: Keynote Speaker Ty Dyson: Managing Stockholder Expectations [Please note that

Mr. Dyson will be taking a few questions at
3:40 but will be unavailable after 4 pm]
- 4:30: Cocktail Hour Meet & Greet

The perfect day. Rung by bullet-pointed rung, I'm climbing my ladder. All the way to the freaking top.

I take a shower and put on the outfit I laid out.

I'm excited to see the keynote speaker, Ty Dyson. He's the CFO of a Seattle investment fund that was recently bought by one of my top three dream companies to work for in New York City. Invested Enterprises is run by three or four brothers who are investment geniuses.

My plan was to stick it out at my new job for at least a year before applying to New York companies, but now that I'm ready for my day, standing here on my little balcony with my view of the tropical blue sky and the ocean waves, I change my mind. Today, anything seems possible.

Why not apply now? If I could land a job in New York in six months instead of a year, I'll streamline my goals.

I decide to start applying as soon as I get back to Austin.

Checking my look in the mirror before I head downstairs, I pause for a few seconds. My two hours on the beach yesterday afternoon have already given me a sun-kissed glow.

Damn, girl, you look different in Hawaii than you do in Austin. You actually look like a confident professional. A CEO on the rise. A ball-breaker.

Which is good, except maybe for that last one. It's true that I have to be more than just self-assured in the industry I've chosen. A lot of my peers still see finance as a man's game, which in this day and age seems sort of ridiculous, but it's true. Today I'm going to need every ounce of confidence I can get.

I'm wearing an off-white skirt and a white silk top. It's professional-looking but also feminine. My curves aren't exactly being advertised but they're also not disguised. I can pretend I'm one of the guys or I can be exactly who I am: female, in a very man-heavy scene. I'm determined to make that a strength, not a weakness—which I've already learned plenty of men seem to think it is.

But I'll prove them wrong. I know I have enough grit to make it to the top or die trying.

By the time I get down to the restaurant, it's busy.

A buffet and allocated tables have been set up for the conference attendees. I help myself to some fruit and coffee at the buffet and find a small table at the far end of the terrace. The area is overrun by men in suits, laughing loudly.

There's barely a woman among them.

I missed the meet-and-greet drinks in one of the hotel's conference rooms last night, deciding to stay on the beach instead. After a life-transforming swim in the clear blue water, I laid on my beach towel for a while, just appreciating the sand on my skin, two slushy guava cocktails from the bar (to die for) and my book. I was so blissed-out I couldn't tear myself away.

But now, I realize it might have been a mistake to not spend at least some of my evening with the rest of the delegates.

I'm not easily intimidated, but the testosterone level on this patio is as thick as my Kona double espresso.

Being a recent graduate in a new job is never easy, but one of the hardest things has been being treated like a naïve, mindless girl who knows nothing about the complicated, old-school mechanics of finance, or—worst of all —like a clueless piece of ass.

A couple of guys get up from the table next to mine, glancing over at me, checking me out. "I heard the Victoria's Secret conference is being held at the hotel down the street," one jokes.

I smile sweetly. "Which is why I'm wearing my edible thong and diamond-studded wonder bra under my power suit." Jerk.

The other men roar with laughter and the pack of them wander away.

Whatever.

I eat my (amazingly delicious) papaya in silence, giving myself a silent pep talk. Not everyone is that rude. I'm used to being underestimated, which I can handle.

I'm young. And I know what I look like. Give me a couple of years and I'll be paying that guy's wages and deciding which one of his friends deserves a bonus or not.

To my relief, the day's workshops go better, only because everyone takes them seriously.

Each room I go into is full of people who are in fully-focused business mode. Ties have been straightened and new friendships put to one side as the sea of young and hungry attendees hang on every word of the speakers.

It feels good to be in a place where everyone has the same goals. I don't have to pretend to be unambitious or change my personality like I sometimes had to do in college. I can be the cool, corporate version of Dusty Rose, without worrying about being "likable" or "smiling more." I can focus on absorbing the kind of knowledge that will take me all the way to New York.

By the time I've sat through three back-to-back seminars and a keynote speech, my head is bursting with new information.

With the workshops done for the day, everyone heads to the beach bar. I'm about to join them when I see Brad and his friends. They're talking to the three guys who were sitting next to me at breakfast.

Wonderful.

And so I decide to pass on social hour. I've already done my research. The only New York companies with delegates here at the conference have sent their lower-level employees. Like me. This conference is for people on the rise, not the ones who have already made it.

I *want* to be social. But I can't quite face the brigade of loud-mouthed macho men dominating the bar right now who are already well on their way to getting inebriated on the company credit card.

So, instead of joining them, I head back up to my room and put on the bikini I splurged on when I found out I was coming to Hawaii. I bought a plain black one-piece that I thought would be more professional if I hit the beach with any new acquaintances, but I couldn't help myself when I saw the tiny leopard print.

It may as well be Victoria's Secret, for all the coverage it gives me. It shows off every curve I own and then some. But I'm in *Hawaii*. I want to make the most of it. My olive skin tans easily and I'm looking forward to a few more hours of baking myself happily in the late afternoon sun.

I throw a pink cotton sundress over the top for the elevator ride, grab a hat, slip on my flip-flops and head down to the beach.

My bikini is definitely too risqué for the hotel's pool, where I might run into Brad and Co. So I wander a little further down the beach to find a place to swim. I park my towel and pull out my book.

I can still hear the hum of conversation from the beach bar, laughter and the sound of glasses clinking. A guy with dirty-blond dreadlocks is giving a surfing lesson to two kids nearby while their parents watch.

I take off my dress and wander into the water, which is the exact same temperature as the tropical air. I float there for a while, feeling like the luckiest person in the world. Maybe one day, after I've conquered New York City, I'll come back here. Maybe I'll buy a little condo near the beach.

Maybe I'll come back with my lover to celebrate at the beach bar where we first met.

Sure. Earl has lot to answer for, planting romantic ideas in my head when I'm the least romantic person on the planet. After my father left, I watched my mother not-quite-date a series of losers throughout my childhood. She was always wary of bringing men into our lives and I was grateful for that. Not one of them seemed like someone I hoped would stick around. And they never did. They left my mother just a little more disappointed, jaded and broken-hearted each time, and I watched her motivation to conquer life slowly leak away. They killed her dreams and, little by little, she allowed it.

So it was up to me to figure out my own dreams. I always knew that only one thing would get me where I needed to go: my own hard work. And there's only one person I can rely on to get me there: myself. So there's not much point daydreaming about things that will never happen. If Brad is the caliber of guys on offer at the beach bar, I'll pass.

I wander back onto dry land and lay on my towel, letting the sun dry my skin.

A shadow darkens the page I'm reading.

"Hey."

Shading my eyes, I look up to see the surf instructor grinning at me. His eyes are green and his skin is deeply tanned. He looks like the ocean is his one and only source of bathwater—not that he looks especially dirty. Just… salty. Earthy. He's probably around my age. "Hey."

"You want a free surf lesson?"

"Um. No thanks."

I try to go back to my book, but he sits, reclining next to me like we're old friends, not caring that he's getting covered in sand. "You ever surfed before?"

I don't reply right away, half hoping he'll take the hint. The one in which I'm not interested in being ogled by an admittedly cute surfer—if you happen to be into the kind of guy who lives out of his van and chases waves for a living. If I'd lived a different life, maybe. But, as it is, I'm a million miles from this guy's wavelength.

He's still grinning, waiting for me to answer his question.

I finally relent. "No. Never."

"Where are you from?"

"Texas."

"I tried surfing in Galveston once. Wouldn't recommend it."

"Yeah, it's not really known for its surf."

"I'm Lucas." He holds out his sandy hand.

I take it lightly. It would feel rude not to at this point. "Dusty."

"You here on vacation?"

"Conference." I give a little nod toward the hotel, where the party at the bar is gaining momentum.

"You look too young to be at a work conference," he comments. "Is this your first time in Hawaii?"

"Yes."

"How come you're not hanging out with the stiffs?" His question is ironic, like he already knows the answer to that question.

"I wasn't really feeling the whole getting-hit-on-by-Brad vibe."

He laughs. "Fair enough. Just to be clear, *I'm* not hitting on you. I'm only offering to give you a free surfing lesson."

"Thank you, but no. I'm just enjoying the beach."

"You'd enjoy it a lot more if you were out there catching your first wave. It's absolutely required as part of the full Hawaii experience."

"Honestly, I'm not…dressed for it." This bikini really is sort of skimpy.

"You're in *Waikiki* now, Dusty. Skin is good. Trust me, you won't regret your first feel of the power of the ocean underneath you. It's a religious experience. Seriously."

I bite my lip.

"Come on, Dust. You know you want to. It'll change your life."

Am I considering doing this? "I'd fall off."

"Luckily, if you do, you'll land in warm, tropical water that's only around four feet deep until way, way out. Can you swim?"

"Yes."

"Good. Let's go."

"You must have other customers."

"Nope." Lucas jumps up and goes over to his surfboard, placing it on the sand in front of me. "Your life is never the same again after you catch a wave. It changes *everything*. Your Karma, the way you manifest the rest of your future, your entire path."

Damn it, he really is sort of convincing. I *have* always wondered what surfing would feel like. And when he puts it like that, how can I not? "Are you sure you don't mind? You don't have other appointments?"

"I'm done for the day."

He's still smiling. Maybe surfing makes a person blindly happy. I have the sudden urge to find out.

"Okay," I finally say. I climb to my feet, following him to his surfboard. "I'll pay you. You don't have to do it for free."

"The hotel employs me. I could sit on my ass all day and not take a single lesson and still get paid. This will be purely for my own enjoyment." He seems harmless, and he's persuasive. "I love helping people get their first surfing rush. Watching people's lives changing right in front of your eyes is about as real as it gets." I can see why the hotel pays him without worrying about a schedule. I can't imagine he's ever short of customers. "And I promise not to hit on you like Brad," he adds.

"I could do without that, thanks."

"This is a spiritual lesson and nothing more."

"Thank you."

"You're welcome. Now that we've gotten that out of the way, come over here and stand on this board."

"I've never even been near a surfboard before, so you might need to lower your expectations."

"I don't have any expectations, but if I did, you've already exceeded them. You're by far the most beautiful girl on this beach." More grinning. "Oh, shit, did I just break our rule?"

"I think you might have, yeah."

He shakes his head and his long dreadlocks swing. There are little beads on the ends of a few of them. "Okay. Sorry. Forget I said that. Now, watch me. Stand like this, in the middle, arms out but not too far. Feet like this. Get your balance. Everyone has the urge to lean back but I want you to do the opposite. Lean into it."

I spend the next hour learning how to get my balance. And then I follow Lucas out, paddling like he does. And then I proceed to spectacularly fail to stand on a live, moving surfboard as it jettisons me at what feels like a hundred miles an hour over open water.

I try a dozen times but it's much harder than it looks.

"One more," Lucas hollers from where he's sitting on

his own surfboard. "You almost had it that time. Do it again."

"Maybe I'm not cut out for this!" I holler back at him.

"You are! You almost had it. Get your footing. Lean into it. Here comes a good one. Go!"

I paddle as the wave approaches me and, just as it starts to crest underneath me, I stand up. I lean into it, getting my balance.

And just like that, I'm surfing.

I'm standing on top of the wave as it carries me along its rolling surge and Lucas was right. It's the best feeling I've ever had in my goddamn life. In this moment, I feel like the most powerful person in the world.

I can hear Lucas cheering as he surfs in behind me.

I lose my balance and fall off.

But as I climb onto my surfboard and let the waves take me back to shore, that taste of magic has transformed me. My limits have been obliterated. I'm as invincible as the forces of nature.

Whoa. Would you listen to yourself?

Lucas follows me back onto the beach and sets his surfboard on the sand next to mine. "That was awesome, Dusty. You're a natural."

I'm still buzzing and breathless. "You were right."

"Surfing's the source," he says simply, and I can't help sort of agreeing with him. "And now you can watch your life explode with good energy. I'd offer you another lesson tomorrow but I'm headed up to the

North Shore tonight to see some friends. Want to come?"

I laugh. "No. Thanks. I've got the conference tomorrow."

"Ditch the conference."

I wrap my towel around myself. Lucas watches me do this. For a split second, still riding my high, the thought flickers through my mind: I could cash in my way overdue V-card with a random surfer while on a work trip in Hawaii. I could attend my last day of the conference as a newly-experienced, take-life-by-the-(literal)-balls sex goddess, with adrenaline still spiking through my veins from both joyrides.

And never see him again.

Objectively, he's a good-looking guy—all dimples and bright eyes.

But there's no part of me that wants to jump the conference ship and sail away with Mr. Waikiki. If anything, catching that wave only ramped up my ambition. *I can surf.* Which means I can do anything.

I decide I won't ask Lucas to do me the honors. As nice as he is, I'm not feeling any real chemistry. Besides, I don't do casual relationships—which is part of the reason I'm still a virgin at the advanced age of twenty-three.

I had plenty of attention from guys in college. But most of them were only interested in partying non-stop and talking endlessly about beer and football.

My roommate Emma told me the first time is always

terrible anyway. Emma's advice was to rip off the band-aid with any random stranger and then find someone you're crazy about to help you get good at it.

But to me that sounded like terrible advice. I could never quite bring myself to follow it. I always felt like there should be something more to that first time than mechanics and just getting it "out of the way."

Or maybe I'm an idiot for making it into a big deal when it isn't. It's just sex, according to Emma.

The fact that it's been so hard to find any kind of genuine connection with a guy has made me wonder if something's wrong with me. Maybe I'm just too picky. There doesn't need to be fireworks and instant electricity, does there? I guess that's what Emma meant. A spark could turn into a bonfire, given long enough.

But I've never felt more than a flicker for anyone. Not even once.

Even now. "I can't ditch the conference, Lucas. But thanks for the lesson. Really."

"You'll remember me for the rest of your life. This is the day everything started to change for you. You'll see."

"I hope you're right," I laugh. "Have fun on the North Shore."

"You sure you don't want to come?"

"I'm sure. Enjoy those waves." He makes a sort of sad face and I smile at him, turning to make my way back to the hotel. "Bye, Lucas."

"See you around, Dust." He wanders up the beach to where his van is parked.

You should have gone with it. He was cute.

No.

I want to *feel* it. *All* of it.

I want to get totally freaking swept away.

Maybe it doesn't happen that way. Maybe you never will.

I guess I need to come to terms with the fact that it'll probably never happen like that for me. Maybe I'm just too focused on my career for any kind of relationship at all.

I head back up the beach toward the hotel's patio. As I get closer, I feel the heat of someone's gaze and I glance up at the raised table with the best view.

A man is sitting there. He's wearing a suit, and sunglasses. His tie is loosened and the top button of his shirt is undone. It's immediately obvious that his suit is expensive and beautifully cut. A far cry from the polyester Brad and his cronies favor. This guy's probably wearing Armani and it fits him in a way you can't help but stare at. There's something ideal about it.

There's something ideal about *him*.

My stomach does a funny little flip.

An iPad is in front of him on the table but its screen isn't lit up. His eyes are on me.

As I walk past him, he slides his glasses up, as though to get a better look.

"Impressive," he drawls.

At first I'm not entirely sure he's talking to me. I glance behind me and a smile quirks at the corner of his mouth. "Sorry?" I finally say.

"The surfing. Not bad for a first try."

"How did you know it was my first try?"

"Just a guess."

Was he watching the whole time?

"You didn't click with Surfer Boy?" His voice is deep and has a smoky husk to it that causes the tiny hairs on my arms to rise.

Wow.

He's all swagger. He has thick dark hair and eyes that match the color of the ocean water. His lashes are too long for a man, especially one that's so...*male.* They give him an almost romantic appeal.

He's sexy without even trying. He's got the cool, animal confidence of a lion surveying its territory. Big and cocky and fully comfortable in his own skin.

But I'm in too good a mood to be intimidated by him. "Oh, I clicked with Surfer Boy. He gave me the best ride of my life."

His low laugh does things to the low pit of my stomach...fluttery things that send little currents of warmth... lower.

I bet he smells good. I bet he's rough.

His handsomeness is rugged and seasoned. He might be in his late twenties or close to thirty. Compared to Lucas, this guy oozes *alpha*-ness on a level that's almost absurd. "I could give you better," he replies casually, his blue eyes dancing.

This makes me smile. "You think so?"

"I'm free tonight if you want me to prove it."

I laugh before I can hold it back. Talk about arrogant. "Thanks for the offer, but I'm busy tonight."

"Doing what?" His mouth is made for the kind of sin I haven't yet managed to get up close and personal with. I don't know how I know this, but I do.

"I'm afraid that's none of your business." *Cuddling up with Colleen Hoover in my California-king-sized helping of Egyptian cotton, thank you very much.*

"Have a drink with me."

I keep walking, flustered by the sheer magnetism radiating off the man. Something about the look of him, the slow smile, the Rolex—ugh, he's obviously loaded—are freaking me out. I know for a fact he's right. He *could* give me better. I don't know much about anything but even *I* know that. "Maybe another time."

My pulse flutters. A low heat simmers. Some sixth sense whispers: *him. He's the kind of guy you want to cash in your V-card with. Right there.*

I keep walking.

The last thing I need right now is a one-night stand with a smug, bossy ego-maniac who's probably got a wife and kids back in Connecticut.

I try to silence the voice of my inner sex goddess— who doesn't get the opportunity to make appearances very often but here she suddenly freaking is—and right now she's insisting: *what you need is to get thoroughly laid by that big, sexy tomcat.*

Shit. I'm getting…*hot.* Just from the heated gaze of a total stranger.

I feel…tingly and…*wet.*

Before I do something I'll wildly regret, I head toward the lobby, glancing back at him once more.

He's still watching me and he has a sort of dejected look on his face. Mixed with all that alpha gorgeousness, his disappointment is almost…cute.

I hurry inside to the elevator, pressing the fourth floor button.

I get to my room and order room service and a glass of champagne because I feel reckless and it's a better option than jumping into bed with the loaded Casanova downstairs.

Is it?

Yes.

I have a lot to celebrate.

I surfed today. I learned things.

I saw a real live alpha male in the wild.

I congratulate myself on my restraint. Of course I'd regret a one-night stand with a random stranger. Even if it was the first time in my life my body has *reacted* to a man like that, that doesn't mean I'm cut out for sex without strings. I'm a girl on a mission. I need to keep my eye on the ball.

I've made the right decision.

No, you haven't! He would have been an absolute BEAST in bed. How often do you come across men who have I WILL GIVE YOU LOTS OF ORGASMS practically tattooed across their forehead?

By the time I mentally shoo my inner sex goddess away and sit out on my balcony, glass in hand as I peek down at the table at the far end of the patio, Mr. Swagger is gone.

3

CASH

Fuck, I love this office.

Floor-to-ceiling glass on the nineteenth floor of a midtown skyscraper definitely has a way of making you feel like you've made it. And maybe I have.

My father might have been skeptical, but we've just received this quarter's financials and we are definitely going places.

I started this company without my old man's support and without his approval. Without his backing or his checkbook. And I'm already on my way to being worth more than he ever was.

I have a knack for investing, for zeroing in on a stock or a company that's about to take off and getting in at the right time. So do my brothers.

So did my father.

My point of difference is that I'm providing a service to young investors and taking a cut.

The Invested Enterprises platform was designed to have a gaming feel to it. Users create avatars, which they move through the different levels like they're playing a video game. Information is presented along the way and users have to solve problems and complete tasks and challenges to earn coins. Data is shown with interactive 3D graphics. Players learn the concepts as they complete the tasks, and each challenge they complete ranks them higher. There are incentives and cash prizes as they build their portfolios. They can choose to connect with other users and interact as they complete levels.

And I take thirteen percent of every penny they make. We now have twenty-seven million of them. Millennials and GenZers are competing against their friends. Word of mouth has taken us to crazy heights, not just among serious investors but also college students and teenagers. All those gamers sitting in their bedrooms across America and around the world are hearing about our platform. It's fun to use. It's social. They learn how to invest in the stock market and they make money. Sometimes lots of it. We keep it as low-risk as possible, making sure beginners are investing only in the safest bets. Many of our users have turned gaming the platform into their full-time jobs and they're raking in enough cash to easily justify that.

We're making a profit of seven million dollars a day.

I've been dreaming big for years but that number has exceeded even my wildest expectations.

New York was definitely the right place to base Invested Enterprises. We have a young, insanely talented group of coders, designers and finance hotshots from all over the world. We offer the kind of enticements that attract the best of the best. All the cool kids want to work for us.

Some of our perks include pool tables, a rooftop patio with an Olympic-sized pool and swim-up bar area, hot tubs, nap pods and a free cafeteria run by several celebrity chefs. One work week of every month is purely "creative." On these weeks employees can work from wherever they want—from bed, from Paris, from a bar in Key West, it's up to them. They're given a travel allowance, and we encourage them to explore and meet people who might be interested in IE. The goal: they recruit users and they present one new idea each month that we can integrate into the game.

This incentive is the best we've come up with. It gets us incredible talent. And it works.

We also own an apartment building and we offer many of our employees a complimentary apartment as part of their package.

We offer shares for employees who hit profit goals.

All of the above means we get hundreds of applications every day. I've hired a full-time recruitment associate whose job is to scour the applications for the stand-outs.

The sun glints off the Empire State Building and I glance up from my desktop, looking out over the city through the floor-to-ceiling walls of windows of my office. My prime view is intentional. The Empire State Building was my father's favorite New York landmark. The ultimate symbol of power and prestige. I figured if the reminder was front and center every time I looked up, it would remind me how hard I needed to work to make sure this company isn't just successful—since he never thought it would be—but one of the most profitable in the city.

New York was my dad's favorite place on Earth and it's where I've spent most of my life. A part of me wanted to move as far away from him as possible as I was setting up my business. But staying in Manhattan was the right move. The fact that my brothers stuck around too and wanted a part of what I was building gave me the confidence I needed, that I was making the right decision, even when my father insisted it was a terrible idea that would leave me broke and destitute.

As much as I hate to admit it, my father's insistence that IE was a complete waste of time motivated me like nothing else could have. He might not have built his own company from the ground up, but he ran it successfully for decades, growing the profits exponentially each year he was at the helm.

He was the one who taught me everything about business and investments, who schooled me in stocks and shares over science and Shakespeare. If Benjamin Maddox thought my idea was dead in the water, there was a very good chance he was right.

But in reality, my father was a dinosaur. What did he know about apps or gaming platforms? The idea of a tech startup was about as alien to him as showing anyone but my oldest brother Alexander any affection. He didn't know the market I was aiming for. He didn't understand the concept. But he still shot me down and told me I'd lose everything if I went ahead with it.

Maybe if I hadn't been so young and hot-headed, I could have explained it better. Of course I regret that the last conversation I had with my father was a full-blown argument where we both said things we shouldn't have said.

Sometimes I wish I could rewind time. Just to re-do that final day.

Anyway, it hardly matters now. Looking out over the iconic skyline reminds me that most of my decisions have been good ones. My father didn't understand why I wanted to game-ify the stock market. But if he was alive today, I know he'd be impressed by what we've done and how far we've come.

My office door opens and my brother Noah walks in, not bothering to knock. "We have a problem," he says, throwing his wide-shouldered frame into the leather chair on the other side of my desk. We're the same height but he has the build of a football player. If he worked out more, he could be seriously jacked, but Noah is too laid back to be competitive about things like that.

He's my CFO and the most perceptive person I know, with a built-in radar for detecting problems before they get out of hand.

Which is why his pronouncement gives me an ominous feeling. I stand up from my desk. "What's the problem?"

"A fucking serious one."

Business is all about problem-solving—endlessly—so I learned a long time ago not to overreact until there's something to overreact about. But my brother's concern gets my attention. "What kind of serious?"

"One of our employees has been suspected of insider trading."

"What?" My voice comes out in a low growl. I can't have heard that right.

"The SEC just called me. They noticed an anomaly in one of our reports."

"What kind of anomaly?"

"The kind of anomaly that means they suspect there might have been a leak."

"You've got to be fucking kidding me."

"Dude, I wish I was. I've spent the past hour trying to cool this off but it's gaining traction."

"Gaining traction where? With who?"

If the news has already spread, we're in big trouble. Our reputation is key. If this goes public, it would be an absolute nightmare. I've seen companies go bankrupt within weeks for insider trading.

I run a hand through my hair. "No one on our team would do this. They'd take bullets for this company. None of them would be stupid enough to jeopardize what we've built."

Noah shrugs. "Yesterday I would have agreed with you."

"Are there any clues? What kind of details did the SEC give you?"

"They're going to send through the full report this afternoon. We have until three weeks from Friday to respond to it and our lawyers have assured me they can buy us plenty of time. All the SEC has said is that the numbers that set off their alarm bells have to do with the Dyson Fund."

"The Dyson Fund? The ink's barely dry on that one."

"Yeah. And someone who knew we were buying it has potentially leaked that info. It preemptively set off a flurry of activity. Which is serious but not necessarily conclusive. Either way, they're considering an investigation."

"If word gets out, we're fucked."

"Yep," Noah agrees bleakly.

We're not the only company who's had the idea of game-ifying stocks and index funds, of course. We've just created the most user-friendly platform so far. But our competitors aren't far behind us. If we're in the headlines for fraud, users might jump ship. "We need to find out who's responsible for this."

"People do strange things when money's involved. I doubt it's personal. Someone might have seen an opportunity to make some cash, possibly very innocently. Maybe someone junior who doesn't know the implications."

"Everyone is junior in this team," I say gruffly. "We've made it a policy to employ young achievers."

Noah rubs his hand across his jaw. "I just spoke to Colton. Neither of us has any leads. Even if we did, it's not the kind of thing we can accuse someone of without concrete evidence."

My brain is lurching into disaster-planning mode. We'll have to do some digging to get ahead of this, but how can we do that when we don't know who we can actually trust?

I push the intercom that connects me to my assistant. "Hayley, get Colton in here, please, would you?"

Less than a minute later, Colton walks in, filling the room with his stormy energy. He's the youngest of the four of us and has always been the most rebellious. Now that he's 26, he's mellowed somewhat, but he still has an insolent vibe. All four of us are around 6'3" and built. Colton has always been the fastest. He moves like an athlete.

And he's as blasé as always. "Everyone needs to calm

down. Nothing's been proven yet. We can start by talking to IT. They'll be able to scan for unusual activity. Emails, screenshots, that kind of thing. Everything that's done here is on record."

"If we go to any single person, we're effectively tipping them off," Noah points out.

He's right. "We need someone we can trust absolutely," I mutter. "Unfortunately, the only two people I trust implicitly are you two assholes and you could hardly be mistaken for detectives."

"Speak for yourself," Colton protests. "We don't have to tell anyone exactly what we're looking for. The three of us should be able to figure it out."

I frown. "Yes, we should. But poring over every page of activity and transactions that have happened in this company over the last quarter would take weeks. Maybe even months."

Noah's the voice of reason, as usual. "The SEC said it was the activity surrounding our purchase of the Dyson Fund that raised a red flag. So we start there."

My brain is whirring. "Yes. We mine the report, listing all the people who contributed or had access to it."

"Almost everyone has had access to it, to some degree," Noah says grimly.

Damn it. Noah and Colton have as much blood, sweat and tears invested in this company as I do. Still, if we go under, it wouldn't be as much of a catastrophe for them. They could walk away with their pride still intact.

For me, this is personal. Invested Enterprises was my idea. I'm the one who distanced myself from our father's legacy to try to prove that I could do just as well—or better. Noah and Colton still do one day a week for Maddox Equities, where our oldest brother Alexander is CEO. I'm still on the Board, but other than that I've almost completely removed myself from the family business to concentrate on my own.

I've worked 24/7 for the past three years on this business, with no personal life and not a single vacation. I refuse to watch our company crumble to the ground because some jumped-up coding nerd thought he could get away with blue murder on my watch.

"Find out what you can today," I tell my brothers. "Do some more digging. I'll make some phone calls. We need to make sure this goes no further, publicity-wise."

My brothers nod just as a knock at the door interrupts us. I glare at it, willing whoever is on the other side to fuck off. Hayley would know not to interrupt me right now.

The door edges open.

"This better be important."

Rylee's face appears, her long red nails like blood-tipped talons as her fingers curl around the edge of the door. "Do you have a minute, Cash?"

I should have known. She's the one person who can get past Hayley.

"It's not a good time, Rylee."

"It's important, Cash."

Colton and Noah head toward the door. "We're done here anyway," Noah says.

"We're on it, bro," Colton adds. He pats my shoulder on the way out, feeling my pain, maybe, not just about the SEC bullshit but also about Rylee. My brothers happen to know that her inability to take no for a fucking answer is giving me some hell.

I grit my teeth, stopping myself from saying something extremely rude to Rylee as she walks into my office. The woman has a knack for terrible timing.

Rylee Winters and I had a very brief relationship around four months ago, right before she was headhunted by Noah. Noah didn't realize that the two of us had "dated" at the time he poached her from another company.

Rylee happens to be a savvy investor with a history of finding lucrative needles in hard-to-predict haystacks. Her grandfather was one of the early executives of a major hedge fund and she once told me that, instead of reading her bedtime stories, he taught how to read spreadsheets. Even I can admit she's good at what she does.

Rylee started working for Invested Enterprises right around the time things ended between us. I happened to be away on a work trip the week Noah hired her. By the time I got back, she'd already signed the contract.

My hope was that she'd forget about our brief and now-completely-over history, like I have.

Unfortunately, it hasn't worked out that way.

"Let me know what you find out," I tell my brothers.

Colton has a way of laughing off stress. Nothing really bothers him. And Noah's like a weathervane when it comes to reading a situation. If Noah predicts storms, then that's probably what we're about to get.

The fact that both of them look more agitated by this new development than they'd like to admit sets my teeth on edge.

Noah catches my eye before closing the door behind him, leaving me alone with Rylee. He's assuming she's come back here to beg. Which is probably true.

"What do you need, Rylee." It's more of an annoyed statement than a question. I don't have the patience for this right now.

I watch her as she moves across my office on six-inch heels. "I need to talk to you about something."

"Then get on with it. I'm busy."

"There's no need to be so rude about it, Cash." Instead of taking one of the chairs, Rylee perches on my desk, twisting her body toward me, tapping one of her long, painted nails on a pile of paperwork.

Here we go with the petty games. It was the reason I couldn't handle more than a few weeks of a relationship with her. She's a card-carrying bitch, is what it boils down to. Harsh but unfortunately true.

I must have found her borderline attractive at some point. She's got a reasonable amount of surface beauty. The long blond hair. The curves, which she's doing her best to show off. But her beauty doesn't go any deeper than that and it's a detail that, right now, is pissing me off.

"Do you ever miss me, Cash?"

"No. I don't miss you. And I don't have time for this today."

"You never have time for anything. Especially me. You never did." She didn't take our break-up well. She's been hounding me ever since.

I'm about to go to the door, open it, and order her to leave. But then it crosses my mind: is she *that* hellbent on revenge that she'd try to bring down the entire company? Just to get back at me for not wanting a relationship?

It seems too obvious. She's a shark but she's also very serious about her career. A move like that would get her fired. And no one else would touch her, after word got out. Gossip travels as fast on Wall Street as it does on any small town Main Street.

"Why do you have to be so uptight all the time?" she whines. "We were so good together."

I sigh heavily. "No. We weren't good together." There was no softness between us at all. It was all clashing egos and power-struggles. During the very short time we spent together, I was more unhappy than I've ever been in my life. "I'm going to politely—once—ask you to leave. Please. Leave."

She rolls her eyes. "I'm not asking for a commitment, Cash." She leans forward, adjusting her skirt, working whatever sexiness she seems to think she's projecting. "I just...I *miss* you, Cash."

"Look. I don't know how to make this any clearer. I've told you before and I'll tell you again: it's fucking over. Whatever we had fizzled out for me almost immediately and that's not going to change. Accept it and move on. This is getting tedious."

Rylee brushes her glossy tumble of hair over one shoulder, completely ignoring what I just said to her. She makes no move to get off the desk. "You look so tense, Cash. I could take your mind off whatever's bothering you. It would feel so—"

"Jesus Christ." I walk over to the door. As I do, there's a light knock.

I yank the door open.

"Mr. Maddox?" It's Hayley, who glances uneasily at Rylee. Rylee has that effect on people. She makes them nervous because she's steely and calculating and has the vibe of someone who wouldn't hesitate to stab you in the back.

Rylee smirks, sliding off the desk and straightening her clothes. She knows what this looks like. And she's enjoying it.

Hayley does her best to ignore the tension in the room. "Your car will be here in ten minutes to take you to the airport."

Airport?

Fuck.

I completely forgot I'm supposed to be going to Hawaii this afternoon for a business meeting.

"Should I book a…second ticket?" Hayley eyes Rylee, trying to be discreet. I have the urge to explain to Hayley that nothing has happened here. But it doesn't seem worth the effort.

I agreed to fly to Honolulu to meet with Ty Dyson. We've already bought his fund and the meeting was to discuss the closing. Considering everything that's going on, the last thing I need is to be five thousand miles from the office right now. Then again, I want to discuss the new development with Ty. To let him know what's happening, that we're aware of it and doing everything we can to mitigate the damage.

I have to go, no matter how shitty the timing is.

Maybe what I actually need is some distance. Everything will be done by phone and email anyway, and Noah said the SEC is giving us some time to respond.

Maybe some perspective will help. A few days in the sun to clear my head, to think things over. Nothing is going to be solved overnight, and those clear blue waters might give me a chance to figure out the best way to handle whatever the fuck is happening.

"No," I reply brusquely. "Could you call Marta and ask her to pack a bag for me? I'll pick it up on the way to the airport."

"Of course. I'll let you know when your car is here."

I nod as Hayley ducks back out of the office to call my housekeeper, leaving me alone again with Rylee.

"It could be perfect," Rylee suggests hopefully. "I could come with you, and we could spend some time together and talk things through."

"Not going to happen." I'm almost aggressively blunt but it can't be helped. My nerves are frayed and my patience is shot. I hold the door open for her. "Get out of my office before I call security."

She glares at me, hurt. "All I was doing was trying to comfort you, Cash. You don't have to be such an asshole about it."

That was part of the problem. This woman brings out the worst in me.

Unfortunately, most women do. Which is too bad. It's why my past love life is a debris field of one-night stands and failed attempts at something meaningful that always crash and burn before they even begin. Maybe I *am* an asshole. But I can't fake feelings. And I never *feel* as much as I wish I did. "You give me no other choice."

Rylee shakes off her disappointment and her expression shifts to one of cold fury. "Fine. I'm sorry to have taken up so much of your time, *Mr. Maddox*. You deserve whatever's coming to you. Enjoy your trip."

I narrow my eyes at the sudden formality but say nothing. *I deserve whatever's coming to me? What the hell does that mean?*

My brothers can hold the fort for a few days. The thought of putting an ocean between myself and Rylee Winters is suddenly just a little too appealing.

4

CASH

"THANKS FOR COMING ALL the way out here to let me know, Cash. I appreciate the heads-up." Ty Dyson shakes my hand.

"We'll do everything we can to set things right, Ty. If the accusations turn out to be true, we've got measures in place to make sure the individual is held accountable and not the entire business."

We leave the private meeting room and make our way toward the front door of the hotel. The place is swarming with tourists and young people dressed in cheap suits. Conference attendees, obviously. Ty mentioned he was a keynote speaker earlier this afternoon, at some junior professionals' seminar.

"I wouldn't have sold you my fund if I didn't believe in you and your brothers, Cash. I'm sure you'll figure this out. Keep me posted."

"Will do. We'll talk soon."

Ty gets into the car that's waiting to take him to the airport.

Once it pulls out of the hotel driveway, I head back inside. Hayley booked me into the hotel for two nights, but I really don't need to stay that long. I'll message her and tell her to book me on an earlier flight for tomorrow.

For the first time since I arrived in Hawaii hours ago, I take in the view of the palm trees and the beach.

And the bar.

Fuck, I need a drink.

I order myself a beer and a scotch on the rocks and take the drinks to a nearby table that's in the shade, at the beach end of the patio.

Taking a long sip of my beer, I watch a cluster of surfers for a while. It's the first time in a very long time I feel myself begin to decompress. When's the last time I actually allowed myself to relax for five minutes? I can't even remember. Years ago, it feels like.

A young woman walks past the row of hotel lounge chairs. She's wearing a short pink beach dress and sunglasses. Her long, thick hair is a lustrous shade of dark brown with streaks of auburn and dark blond that catch the sunlight.

Her legs are long and lightly tanned.

She wanders a little further down the beach, laying out her towel. She unwraps her dress to reveal a tiny animal print bikini.

Fucking hell.

The girl is stunning.

Her bikini barely covers her perfect curves. It's not a thong but close enough.

She pulls a book out of her bag and some sunscreen, which she smooths over her golden skin. Her long legs. Her toned arms. Her full breasts, which are barely concealed by that minuscule bikini top.

Fuck me.

My cock—which has *not* been enjoying its extended holiday from women, after the Rylee disaster—thickens.

She's fucking gorgeous.

And young.

She doesn't look deeply tanned enough to be a local. And she's not with family or friends. Unless they're off shopping or sightseeing, who knows.

I'm not the only one who notices her.

The surf instructor finishes up with a couple of kids and walks over, sitting down next to her.

She barely looks up.

I can tell by her body language she's not interested. But he's persistent.

For some reason this annoys the fuck out of me.

He says something that makes her laugh. He's talked her into a lesson.

I watch him teach her for a while, becoming more and more mesmerized by the way the girl moves and the taut smoothness of her skin.

She doesn't get too close to him and I'm relieved by this. I can tell this is the first time she's met him. She's giving off signals that this is a surf lesson and nothing more.

I have no idea why I'm so wildly relieved by this and I don't bother analyzing it.

She's cute as fuck and you haven't been laid in months. It's too long to go without. There's your fucking analysis.

She follows the surfer out into the water and I order another drink from a passing waitress.

The girl falls off a few times. I think Surfer Boy and I are both waiting for that tiny bikini to have a wardrobe malfunction but it miraculously stays in place.

I'm glad it does. I don't want to have to murder the surf punk.

What the fuck? Who are you murdering now? And why?

But then she's paddling again and she stands on her board. It takes her a few seconds to get her balance but she does. She's doing it. She's surfing.

I have no idea why, but I'm so…proud of her.

How many drinks have you had?

She's tenacious. Sassy. Determined. And mind-numbingly gorgeous.

My cock is fully fucking hard right now.

She falls off, then climbs back onto her board, paddling to shore with a huge smile on her angel's face.

Surfer Boy follows her. I can guess what he's saying to her. He's inviting her to wherever he's going tonight.

But she starts packing up her bag. She puts her short wrap dress back on but doesn't bother tying it.

She dismisses him, saying goodbye, making her way back up the beach to the hotel.

The guy stands there for a minute or more, watching her go. But then he accepts defeat and gathers up his surfboards, heading in the other direction.

As she walks closer, I get a better look at her face. And her body.

Kill me now.

She's a literal goddess.

"Impressive," I tell her as she walks by my table.

She looks around, like she's not sure I'm talking to her. "Sorry?" She's wary but not intimidated by me. It's refreshing to meet someone who has no idea who I am or how much money I have. I work so much, the only women I talk to on a daily basis are ones who are either working for me or wish they were.

"The surfing. Not bad for a first try."

"How did you know it was my first try?"

"Just a guess."

She doesn't reply but she's taking in the look of me. My build. My suit.

"You didn't click with Surfer Boy?" I ask, to tease her. And rile her. I want her to react to me.

Our eyes meet. Hers are a bright, variated green that basically slays me with the kaleidoscopic glow of them. It's a few seconds before she replies. "Oh, I clicked with Surfer Boy. He gave me the best ride of my life."

I find myself laughing at her sassy come-back. The little minx.

I want to eat that sweet pink mouth. I want to feed my big cock between those perfect wet lips, sliding deep until she moans. "I could give you better."

Her face gets pink but she finds this funny. "You think so?"

I'm seriously in lust. She's so fucking cute. "I'm free tonight if you want me to prove it."

Am I coming across as a prick?

The problem is, I don't know how to come across any other way. My job requires me to be cuttingly direct. It's been a while since I exercised any other muscle.

Say yes anyway, gorgeous. Please.

She laughs lightly. "Thanks for the offer, but I'm busy tonight."

"Doing what?" I can admit I'm rusty. It's been a while since I socialized with anyone other than my brothers or tech nerds.

She blinks long lashes. "I'm afraid that's none of your business."

"Have a drink with me." I have the urge to get down on my knees and beg.

Another smile. "Maybe another time."

She glances back at me as she walks toward the hotel lobby.

Damn it. Don't go.

My cock throbs hotly and my heartbeat feels dark and needy.

And I decide not to fly back to New York tomorrow.

5

———

Dusty

STARING at my reflection in the floor-length mirror, I'm amazed by how Hawaii has transformed me into a completely different person.

I look and feel…better than I can ever remember feeling.

I'm wearing a sea green sleeveless wrap dress that clings to my body. The color makes my eyes look light and my sun-kissed skin look even more golden. If I'm going to spend my final night drinking alone in a bar, I might as well do it in style, I figure.

My cheeks are flushed with a healthy glow.

From the sun.

From the lingering high of yesterday's surfing rush.

From the hot gaze of Mr. Alpha, who's probably long gone, thank God. On his way back to his loving wife in Stamford or wherever. I feel for her though, if he's coming on to total strangers on his business trips. I can't stand that type of man, even if he was hot AF.

Those burly shoulders. The dark look in those blue eyes. The sneer of that perfect mouth.

All I can say is that I'm very glad I was able to resist him.

It's my third and last night in Waikiki. I'll be back in Austin by tomorrow night, so this is my last chance to make the most of Hawaii. My plan is to spend the evening watching the sunset on the patio with a glass of wine or two.

By myself.

Which can't really be helped. It's fine. I'll get some dinner, listen to some live music and drink in the view, all on the company credit card.

I had seven dinner invitations, all from men at the conference, who did what they always do. Check me out and hit on me, seeing me as a less competitive distraction.

I politely declined and visualized my corner office with its view of the Empire State Building, with them as my coffee boys.

There's something even more special about the open-air beach bar in the evening. The sun is going down, an orange blaze on the horizon, casting its fiery glow across the water. People gather on the beach to watch the sunset every night in Waikiki, which I love.

Torches are perched on the sand around tables and there are festoon lights hanging from the timber frame over the bar. With the view of the setting sun, the gentle roar of the ocean and the warm breeze across my skin, it doesn't matter that I'm dining alone. This place is paradise.

I'm a little miffed to see that there are no free tables. And no free bar stools.

It's fine. I can order a drink and sit out on the sand for a while until something becomes available.

The bar is busy, crowded with people from the conference making the most of their last night by buying endless rounds for their packed tables. I smile and wave to a few of them but ignore their hollers to join them.

I've just managed to order a large glass of white wine when two spots free up at the end of the bar. I make my way over, slide onto one of the bar stools and take a deep sip of wine, feeling the icy tang relax me.

From this end of the bar, I've got a great view of the ocean and the beach. It's the perfect spot to watch the sun dip beneath the waves. A few stars are already out.

My phone vibrates in my bag.

I pull it out. My sister's name lights up the screen. "Hey, Sky."

"Hey, sis!" Skylar is sort of half-yelling and I can hear music in the background. She must be out somewhere. Which makes the conversation easy to predict. "How's freaking *Hawaii*?"

We spoke a few days before I left for my trip. She

always sounds upbeat, but her highs can mask some pretty devastating lows. If it's taken a few drinks for her to call me, I know what sort of day she's having. "It's so beautiful here, Sky. You'd love it. The color of the water is unreal."

I describe everything, down to the particular shade of the ocean, the way the waves foam up on the sand, the room service, and I give her a quick overview of the conference. Even Lucas gets a mention. Anything to take her mind off whatever's going on in her life right now. Her last boyfriend dumped her around six weeks ago and she's been having trouble getting auditions and gigs. Until Sky makes it big and can afford to have her own adventures, I'm living this for both of us.

"I'm so proud of you, Dust. It sounds incredible. You deserve all of it."

She's in auto-pilot mode, saying the right things, but her voice sounds hollow. I hear her order another beer.

"What's up?" I prompt, pressing my fingers to the bridge of my nose. Here it comes. I already know what she's going to ask, and I already know I'll help her. I always help. But the timing's not great.

"Nothing...I just..."

"Tell me."

"Oh, you know, it's just the usual. Things are tight at the moment."

'Tight' is code for everything has turned to shit. Sky doesn't ask for money unless she's desperate. In fact, she never really asks. She tells me how she's struggling and waits for me to offer. That's the usual pattern.

Might as well cut to the chase. "How much do you need?"

"I hate to ask, Dusty. We've just had the bills come through and this month they're way more than we expected. The hot water heater broke and my car needed some repairs. I thought we had a handle on things, but I haven't had a gig in a while, so we're relying on Mom's money and it's not going far."

Skylar's a musician. A hugely talented one. But she doesn't make a lot from the handful of gigs she gets each month. It's unfair that someone with her talent hasn't been snapped up by a major record label yet, but the fact that she's as good as she is almost makes it worse. If she wasn't anything special, it'd be easier to accept defeat and focus on a nine to five. But she's so damn good, it seems wrong to give up. She just needs her big break. If I can help her find it, I will.

"How much, Sky?"

"A thousand?" she mutters quietly. "Only if you can spare it."

Things must be bad. Usually it's just a couple of hundred here and there. Mom will be working her cleaning jobs, and Sky will be waitressing and busting her ass trying to get work, but some months it just isn't enough to support them both.

A familiar knot of guilt twists in my stomach.

The last thing I want is for them to have to move. It's our home, even if we've been renting for years. And Austin is getting more expensive by the day. I don't even know where they'd go if they had to move out.

From the outside, it must look to them like I have the perfect life. With my sublime view of the beach and a chilled glass of wine in my hand, maybe I do. But despite my job and its decent salary, my financial situation isn't exactly secure. I'm still on entry-level money with a massive student loan to repay every month and an apartment that has stretched my budget more than was sensible.

Once I landed my job, I decided I needed my own space.

I was manifesting when I signed the lease, trying to positive-mindset my way into being able to afford it, hoping the universe would come through. I'm due for a salary review next month. I'll get a raise, I'm determined. But at the moment, the apartment is a huge drain on my paycheck, especially when I'm bailing out my mom and sister every month or two.

"I'm sorry, Dust. I wouldn't ask unless we had no other option."

"It's absolutely fine." I take a deep breath and do my best not to exhale too heavily. "I'll transfer the money now."

Skylar doesn't hide her relief. "Dusty, you're the best. Thank you so much. I'll pay you back, I promise."

"When's your next gig?"

"I've got one in two weeks. I'm trying to get one at the Blue Lounge but Billy says they're fully booked for the rest of the month. For me, he might make an exception."

"Really?"

"He's…yeah. We're sort of…together now."

This is not good news. Billy is as slimy as they come. I have no doubt he'll be using my sister, promising her things he won't deliver on. Playing with her hope. "Be careful, Sky. Billy's no good."

"He's fine, Dusty. He's good to me. He wants to help me get more visibility."

"Just…please, Sky. Be careful."

"I'm always careful." Which does nothing to reassure me. "When do you get back?"

"Tomorrow."

"Have a great rest of your trip."

"I will. Have a good night, Sky. Be safe."

Ending the call, I open up my banking app and transfer the money to my mom's account, just to make sure Sky doesn't spend too much of it tonight when she's not thinking straight. But I text her to let her know it's there. I don't want her stressing too much.

"Another glass of wine, miss?" the bartender asks.

"Yes, please."

I pull out the company credit card and lay it on the bar as the bartender goes to get my drink.

Someone sits on the bar stool next to mine.

Someone big.

I look up to see…very blue eyes.

Oh no.

It's *him.* Mr. Alpha Freaking Swagger. "Hey, gorgeous." His slow, barely-there grin hits me…*there…* where I can feel a soft, warm pulse.

Holy hell. How does he do *that?*

He's not wearing his suit tonight, just a pair of dark gray pants and a white cotton button-down shirt that probably costs more than my entire wardrobe.

The man is absolutely drop-dead gorgeous.

Fate, for once, has dealt me an ace.

"Hey, Ace," I reply, not sounding nearly as breathless as I feel. *Ace?* I'm already feeling the effects of the glass of Pinot Grigio I practically chugged.

He grins at my greeting. "You're still here."

"Still here," I confirm.

"I was hoping I'd run into you again." His voice almost sounds like a purr, edged with panty-melting bass notes.

Get a grip!

I'm trying *not* to react to him but it's impossible. He exudes power. Confidence. I'm practically floating in the cloud of testosterone he's emitting. It's like breathing in a pure, uncut aphrodisiac. I can feel my heartbeat in the most intimate place imaginable.

Yikes.

The bartender delivers my wine and Casanova slides

my company credit card toward me, saying to the bartender, "Put the rest of our tab on my room, please. 700. And I'll have a scotch on ice."

"Yes, sir."

He's more handsome than any man I've ever seen. He has a strong, straight nose, a sharp jawline and thick, well-cut dark hair. I'm slightly in awe that anyone could be this good-looking.

"It must be difficult for you," he comments, that low, smooth rumble like velvet.

"What do you mean?"

"Trying to have a quiet drink when every man in the bar is watching you."

"Are they?" I glance around.

"Of course they are. Where's Surfer Boy?"

"Who? Oh, he left for the North Shore after he gave me that lesson yesterday."

"Well, that's good." Ace's blue gaze roves slowly over my face, like he's drinking in the details of me. The bartender serves his drink and he loosely holds his glass. His hand is tanned and strong-looking. *His grip must be punishing.* And there's no ring on the crucially important finger. Not even a tan line.

Don't even dream of being relieved, girlfriend.

"What's the accent?" he drawls. "Let me guess. Texas."

"Is it that obvious?"

"It's not a hard one."

"I guess that's true." Most people figure out I'm from Texas within the first five minutes of meeting me.

He holds eye contact much more easily than I do. I feel myself blush.

The way his clothes fit him hint at a powerful chest and an impressive build. The top two buttons of his shirt are undone, revealing a light pelt of chest hair. I've honestly never been in the presence of *chest hair* before. My father checked out early. And I was always too busy studying and working to hang out with random men. Broad, hair-dusted chests are new to me. My hands itch as I imagine running my fingers over the textures of him, to see what all that solid muscle would *feel* like.

This is completely unlike me. I've never had a reaction like this to a man in my life.

Damn it, girl, pull yourself together!

I take another gulp of wine.

He's ridiculously sexy. And he's tuning in to some buried female instinct that's—right now—waking up. Against my will, my body feels like it's opening to him like a flower seeking sun.

"I was hoping you might do some more surfing this afternoon." That lethal smirk again. His eyes never leave me. "I enjoyed watching you."

"I was a disaster for all of it but the last thirty seconds."

"It's not easy getting a ride on your first try."

Is it me or did he just say "ride" with a dark, dirty

promise behind it? God, I'm so bad at this. I don't even know whether he's flirting with me or not.

Whenever I've been hit on in a bar before, I usually make polite conversation for two-point-zero seconds and then get the hell out of there. But I'm pinned to my seat. The way he's looking at me…it's like he's put some kind of sex-spell on me.

Every alarm bell in my head should be ringing. He's too good-looking, too charismatic, too sure of himself to be anything other than trouble. But I can't move an inch, even if I wanted to. The thought of his muscular thigh accidentally rubbing against mine is keeping me locked in place.

"I'm definitely not cut out to be catching rides," I tell him.

Oh my god. Stop talking.

I feel myself blush, so I do my best to steer the conversation back to safe territory. "Have you surfed before?"

"Once or twice. In California." His eyes are an unusual shade of deep, dark blue. "It was a long time ago but I do remember it was a life-changing experience. Is this your first time in Hawaii?"

"Yes."

"Where are you from in Texas?"

I don't know why I do it. We're playing games, maybe. I want to keep him guessing and protect a small distance between us before I completely lose control.

Because I get the distinct feeling I'm going to. "Dallas. Born and raised."

"Had the best barbecue of my life there once." He's almost wistful for a few seconds. "So, you're here for the conference?"

"Yeah. I'm pretty new to my company, but they said it would be a good opportunity for me to learn more about how the industry works."

"And have you?"

I pick up a cocktail umbrella that he removed from his drink and start twirling it between my fingers. I need a reprieve from the intense eye contact with this man, who's already proving to be an absolute threat to my self-control. "The workshops have been great, really interesting, and it's been good to push myself out of my comfort zone."

"Where *is* your comfort zone?" He manages to spin the phrase into something absolutely filthy-sounding.

Definitely not being chatted up by the most gorgeous man I've ever seen at a beach bar in Hawaii.

Damn it, Earl!

I gently bite my lip and Ace watches me do this. "Uh, well, at work, I guess. That's where I spend most of my time. But being here has really opened my eyes to all the things I still have to learn."

He's watching my face and I feel myself blush again at the insinuation. I *do* have a lot to learn. Not just about work, but about…everything else. More than this god-like man could possibly know.

But something about the way he's looking at me makes me feel like he *does* know. Almost like he can read my mind.

He could teach me.

"You're not here for the conference?" I ask him.

"No. Not directly."

"On vacation?"

"Not quite. I had a meeting about an investment fund I just bought."

Bought? Then again, this doesn't surprise me. The man radiates wealth. "So, you're like a slightly hotter version of Warren Buffett, then?"

"*Slightly* hotter? Damn, Tex. You know how to keep a man's ego in check."

I laugh and take a long sip of wine, concentrating on how good the coolness feels as it slips down my throat. Anything to extinguish the fire this guy is igniting in my body.

He's relaxed and in the moment.

It's possible that he does this a lot. That fact alone should possibly be a huge red flag, but a part of me feels like there's a lot more to him than I'm giving him credit for. He's got a quiet, simmering depth that's intriguing me. Usually, I would already have politely excused myself by now, but tonight I'm in no rush to get back to my room.

"So you weren't leading any of the 101 workshops, then?" I definitely would have noticed him.

His eyes dance with mischief. "If I'd known you were in the 101 workshops, Tex, I would have been first in line to sign up."

I smile despite myself. "You're smooth, Ace. I'll give you that much."

He gently bumps his shoulder against mine. "Is that all you'll give me?"

"Yes. Because you probably wouldn't even remember me if you saw me again. I don't mean at breakfast tomorrow, I mean like if we ran into each other again on the street or something."

"Steady on, Tex. We just met and already you're inviting me to breakfast? I'm assuming that'll be room service."

"Very funny." I blush. "I was just wondering whether you'd recognize me someplace else, that's all."

"Of course I would. You're the most beautiful girl I've ever seen."

I laugh. "Now you're *really* laying it on."

"It's true." His eyes have barely moved from mine since the moment he sat down. They roam slowly over my face, lingering on my lips. I feel the heat as his gaze drops to my collarbone, grazing my skin, then lower, to my breasts, and back up again. It's as though a current of electricity follows his gaze, channeling itself straight to my core. Every single nerve ending in my body is standing on end. "Absolutely fucking stunning, in fact."

His crude delivery gets me instantly, shamelessly wet. *Oh Jesus*, if this man can get my blood pumping just with his eyes, how would his *hands* feel? *His tongue? His*—

"There, I think I've got you memorized now," he drawls. "Don't go committing any crimes. There's no way I'd be able to lie if the cops got you in a lineup."

"Right. I'll do my best not to break any rules tonight."

"I said don't commit any crimes. I didn't say anything about breaking a few rules." His husked teasing gives me goosebumps. "Didn't anyone ever tell you that life's too short to play by the rules?"

"Actually, I've found rules have gotten me exactly where I need to be so far." I really need to stop talking. I sound like some prim schoolmarm.

"Well, you need to get over that, Texas. You don't get anywhere in business by playing it safe."

"Maybe you're right."

"Of course I'm right. Tell me one wild and crazy thing you've done lately. I bet you can't."

"I surfed yesterday," I point out.

"Okay. Now how about career-related risks."

I think about it for a few seconds. "I bet on myself by leasing an apartment I can barely afford, to motivate me to work like hell so I'll get a raise. Does that count?"

He gazes into my eyes for a few seconds and there's a note of empathy there, maybe over my pathetic backstory.

"Yes," he finally says. "It does count. And I'm impressed. Betting on yourself is the hardest thing to do."

"Yeah. But there are no guarantees."

"Nothing in life comes with guarantees."

I sip my wine. "Well, I'll guarantee one thing," I nod toward the men behind us who are getting louder and more drunk by the second. "In only a few short years I'm going to be the boss of people like them. I'm on a fast track."

My grit seems to amuse him. "Is that right?"

Ace signals to the bartender who promptly brings us two more drinks. I'm wondering at this point if I should refuse another drink before my barriers are completely obliterated. "I should probably—"

"Oh no you don't, Texas," he cuts me off. "You can't leave me sitting here alone. One more, then we can call it a night if you want."

"I've got an early flight," I lie.

"Me too." I can tell by the quirk of his perfect mouth that he's lying too.

Our eyes lock again and this time I don't look away as the flutters in my stomach melt into a pulsing heat that spreads and concentrates. *Holy hell.* My body feels warm from my knees to my navel.

He's so damn gorgeous. And he's perceptive. He's reading that I'm considering...*him*. A hot one-night stand with this prime specimen of A-list manhood. I mean, *come on*. He's hot as hell and obviously doing well for himself.

He's also got the smug charisma of a man who knows he's a beast in bed. Considering I've never been *in* a bed with a man—beast or no beast—I shouldn't know this. But, somehow, I do.

Our thighs are almost touching. The heat between us is insane. Would it be so bad if I gave in to what my body is telling me to do?

One night. No strings attached. I'll never see him again.

I want to do it.

I want to cash in my V-card with *him*.

In reality, the last thing I need is to complicate this trip by getting laid by a total stranger.

Ace might not be like any other guy I've met, but he's still just working the charm offensive. Everything he's telling me could be bullshit.

Even if it was, why do I still get the feeling I'd have no regrets about spending the night with him?

Because he'd be rough. Those big, manly muscles would be hard and so would—

Stop drinking, you fool!

I drag my eyes to the skyline behind him that's now flecked with stars. "One day when I'm CEO of my own company, I'm going to come back here and stay in the penthouse suite," I say, maybe more to myself than to him. "Just so I can look at the ocean view and remind myself of where it all started."

His fingers entwine with mine and I let him do this. His hands are warm and strong, just like I imagined. "Do you want to see it now? It would be a shame not to get a taste of what you're working toward before you leave."

"I'm sure it's already booked. I heard one of the people at the check-in desk this morning say the hotel was at capacity."

"It is occupied." His eyes flash mischievously. But then he says, "Probably one of those rich asshole billionaires who founded his own young, hip startup company where they sit on yoga balls instead of chairs and have lunch breaks over ping-pong and kombucha."

"Exactly." Maybe it's the wine, but it takes me a few seconds to figure out he's describing himself.

Billionaire?

Something about the way he hasn't broken eye contact sets off another wave of those butterflies that are currently taking flight inside my stomach. I stare into his eyes as I say it. "He'll think he owns the world and can get whoever he wants."

He leans closer, whispering a low murmur close to my ear. "What he wants right now is to peel that little dress off the most stunning girl in Hawaii and get a taste of how wet she is for him. Are you wet for me, Texas?"

And at his mention of the word *wet*, my pussy softens and tingles and my panties get even wetter. I can feel my pulse *inside* and I have never, ever been this turned on in my life. "Are you trying to tell me you're in the penthouse suite, Ace?"

"Excellent deduction skills, Tex. You're definitely CEO material."

Sure, the effect he's having is doing ridiculous things to my body, but that doesn't mean any of this is a good idea. There's no way this can be anything more than a one-night thing, no matter how good-looking he is. I'm from Texas and he's from…somewhere else. Okay, there's no sign of a wedding ring but that doesn't mean he's not either a player or in a relationship with someone else.

"Are you married?" I ask him point blank.

"No. Of course not. Are you?"

"No."

"Are you in a relationship?" he asks me.

"You mean besides with my 24/7 job? No."

"Me either." He blinks and…*damn him*. He really is beautiful. "Now that we've got that out of the way, there's nothing stopping us."

No, nothing but the fact that he's a total stranger I've known for a total of one hour.

But what the hell. As Emma loves to point out, my first time doesn't have to be all rose petals and romance. It could just be about giving in to insane chemistry. And we definitely have that.

"The view from the penthouse is pretty good," Ace murmurs, reaching forward and skimming my cheek with his lips. "I think you'll like it." My pulse leaps at his touch as his whiskey-scented warmth skims the skin of my neck.

He slides off his stool and gently pulls me by the

hand. "Come with me, gorgeous. You don't have to stay. Entirely up to you. I'll give you the grand tour, and I happen to have a complimentary bottle of champagne I hadn't gotten around to drinking yet."

That would be a bad idea.

I hesitate, biting my lip. If I don't go for it with a man who's making my temperature sizzle, when am I ever going do it? I've got to be the lamest 23-year-old virgin on the planet to even be questioning this.

And I'm tired of wondering what "this" feels like.

One night. I'll finally cash in my V-card and get on with my climb up the corporate ladder, newly enlightened and ready to take the world by storm as an experienced no-longer-a-total-ice-maiden sex goddess.

I let Ace pull me by the hand, into the lobby of the hotel and straight toward the elevator.

6

———

Dusty

As the elevator takes us up, I can feel my heartbeat thrumming in my chest. And the slippery wetness of my panties clinging *very* intimately.

Am I really the kind of girl who sleeps with a total stranger on a first date?

Apparently…maybe.

My entire body is craving him like a newly-discovered drug. I never knew I could feel this *hot*.

"So," he purrs, still holding my hand. "Are we going to tell each other our real names?"

"No names." I sound emphatic about that so I must be.

Amusement flickers in his blue eyes.

"One night." I'm making this up as I go along. I mean, is there anything *wrong* with having one night of total abandon with an extremely hot stranger? I've been presented with the opportunity to cash in my long overdue V-card with a rich Adonis in his penthouse apartment that overlooks Waikiki Beach and—fuck it all—I've decided to take it. It's time to put my big girl pants on (or take them off, more accurately) and cowgirl up.

Then I can get on with my life, worldly and newly enlightened, and continue my gritty climb up the corporate ladder.

"No strings attached," I add. "And no regrets."

Stop talking! I sound like I'm reading from the cliché handbook.

"All right, Tex." A grin plays at the corner of his mouth. "Your call."

"Just so you know, I don't usually…"

"Fuck on the first date? Neither do I. But we're in Hawaii. And you're the most beautiful woman I've ever met. I might be in love with you already. I think we should go for it."

Okay, wow.

I lean up against the wall, my heart racing. Ace places his palm flat against the wall behind me, tilting his head just slightly like he's about to kiss me as he cages me with his big, warm body.

"I'm not looking for anything serious," I say. My brain is getting ahead of me. I'm desperate for this guy, but also terrified of how he's making me feel. I already know I could get addicted. "You're very charming, but I won't fall in love with you. Just saying."

A smile creeps over his lips. "Okay. Good to know."

"I mean, we don't know each other at all…"

He presses his body against mine, a knee pushing between mine to edge my legs open. "That's why we're here, Tex. So we can *get* to know each other. Really, really well." His mouth is torturously close to mine as he murmurs, "Besides, I know enough. I know you have one hell of a pretty mouth. I also know that it would look even prettier wrapped around my big cock, which is so fucking hard for you I'm already very close to getting you extremely…dirty. And giving you the kind of orgasm that might change your mind about me."

Help. "W-what do you mean?"

"You might fall in love with me after all."

In any other situation I'd laugh and call him out for being overly cocky, but I can feel his enormous erection pressing against my stomach and he's right. *He's really fucking hard.*

And big.

And hot.

He slides a warm hand round the nape of my neck as his other hand pulls me against his stunningly hard body, teasing me, grabbing a fistful of my hair as he tilts my head to expose my neck. Slowly, his lips press against my sensitive skin. His teeth skim, and his tongue draws a sensuous line, which makes me shiver. He lets out a low groan as he tastes me and the sound funnels into me like pure, liquid lust.

The pulse between my thighs is making me crazy and my need for his mouth on mine has become an overwhelming desperation. I need this man like I've never needed anything in my life.

I want all of him. I want to wrap my legs around his waist as he pushes inside me.

His fingers edge the hem of my dress upwards, skimming over the lace of my panties, skating over my clit. I moan at the feel of his fingers' warm, silky glide over the thin lace.

"Damn, Tex, you're so fucking wet, baby girl. You want me *bad.*"

It's slightly mortifying, but at the same time I don't care. I'm too freaking horny. "Please," I whisper, tilting my hips forward reflexively. I've gone crazy but I can't help it. I'm lost in a rising haze of arousal. "*Ace,*" I moan as his fingers slide my panties to the side. My voice is breathy, pleading. My body has never felt so purely physical. I don't care about anything except his strong fingers, which skate teasingly over the center of my universe.

He feels so good I exhale a soft gasp.

Oh my god.

This is already more intimate than anything that's ever happened to me.

If he keeps doing that I'm going to come.

He kisses me and I bury my hands in his hair as he thrusts his tongue into my mouth in slow, synced rhythm with his fingers, which slide barely inside me, gaining slow, slippery entry. It hurts a little, but in a good way. In a deeply hot, torturous way.

The combination of the heady, erotic taste of him as he plays my body is stoking a wildfire pleasure that's threatening to reach some crazy over-the-top peak.

I need to reach this peak more than I need my next breath. If he doesn't give it to me I might lose my mind.

"Perfect girl," he murmurs. "You're so gorgeous. How do you want me to make you come first? With my fingers, just like this? Or with my tongue fucking you slowly. You feel so fucking good, I know you're going to taste like the sweetest fruit on earth."

"*Ace. Please.*"

I'm vaguely aware of the ding of the elevator. "Patience, Texas. We have all night." His fingers slide free of me and he smooths my dress into place. Watching my eyes, he licks his fingers. "Come on, baby. We're here."

Ace pulls me by the hand into a private foyer. He swipes his key card and we enter the penthouse.

Even through my dazed lust I can still comprehend that it's the most beautiful, luxurious space I've ever seen in my life.

"Here's your view," he says, pulling me toward the panoramic window. The sliding doors are open to the private balcony, letting in the balmy breeze.

"It's so beautiful," I gasp.

It really is.

The midnight-blue horizon melts into the ocean and,

with no clear line between sea and sky, it feels like we're at the edge of the world. Like we're looking at an inky, velvet kingdom of waves and stars that's all ours. It's enough to take my breath away.

I expect Ace to stop, pour some drinks, to make small-talk for a while before we find our way back to each other, but he doesn't. He comes up close behind me, so close that I can feel the heat of his body.

The lights in the room are dimmed and golden, but just bright enough to cast our reflections onto the window. Ace touches my shoulders with his palms and lets them coast slowly down my arms. It's hypnotic, the slow movement and the feeling of my body coming alive under his touch.

His mouth lowers to the curve of my neck, where his lips graze my skin.

I lean into him, arching against him reflexively. His hands find my waist, caressing my hips, inching my dress up, his breath hot against my neck.

"Tell me what you want, Tex. I want to hear you say it."

"I want you," I whisper. They're words I've never said to a man before but I'm feeling them hard.

His hands move to my breasts, gliding over the fabric of my dress, charting every curve and pausing at every flicker of a response. His fingers slip under the edge of my neckline and his breath gets heavier as he discovers I'm not wearing a bra. My nipples tighten between his fingers as he plays me with rough, gentle fingers.

With one hand still teasing my nipples, Ace's free fingers slowly undo the tie that's holding my dress together. The feel of his hands on my belly, my hips, my waist, with no barrier between us, makes me writhe with need.

He turns me around, keeping my body close, and eases my dress off my shoulders so it falls to the floor. All I'm wearing is a pair of tiny lace panties and my heels.

"Look how fucking gorgeous you are. I've never seen anything so perfect in my life." His expression is intent and he growls another word softly. "Mine."

For tonight, yes. And only tonight. That's our deal.

I stare into those dark blue eyes and I force myself not to wish for more.

When he kisses me, I *do* let myself fall, just a little. Tonight it's okay to fall half in love with this stranger, considering what he's about to do to me.

His mouth takes mine, parting my lips with his tongue, stroking intimately. I take everything he gives me, lightly sucking on his tongue until he groans.

When his eyes meet mine again, they're blazing with desire. Currents of darkness and tenderness entwine between us.

I've never had anyone look at me the way Ace is looking at me now. Like every fiber of his being wants me.

A girl could get used to a look like that.

Ace lifts me carefully, as though I'm weightless in his arms. "Wrap your arms and legs around me," he commands, his voice low and gruff. I obey him and he carries me to the bed, laying me down.

Crouching over me, he kisses me again, and for the first time in my life I *want* to be dominated. Ace is forcing me to take his lead and I melt under the erotic hunger of his kiss. My pussy is tingling and softening. A fresh wave of wetness saturates my panties.

Yikes.

Slowly, he kisses a line down the delicate skin of my throat. He plumps my breasts to his mouth and sucks greedily on my nipples until I moan.

"That's it, baby girl. Moan for me. Tell me how you want me to eat you until you're screaming my name."

"I..."

"Say it." Ace peels off my panties. He stands over me, drinking in the sight of me. "*Fuck*, you're beautiful. You're so damn *wet* for me, Texas. My dirty girl wants my big cock *bad*."

"Give it to me," I breathe. "Please."

He hears my desperation in my voice and his dark, sexy smile sends me into a fit of giggles.

Give it to me? How have I suddenly morphed into a raging nymphomaniac?

"Oh, I'll give it to you, gorgeous. But first I'm going to

fuck you with my tongue until you're coming in my mouth. Then you can have my cock."

Okay, wow.

It's a crazy feeling, to be totally naked, exposed and vulnerable, while he's still fully clothed. I love how big he is and the hot, feral look in his eyes.

The huge ridge inside his pants is straining like it's threatening to bust out. *I* did that to him. And I want more.

I glide my fingers over his massive erection, squeezing lightly, fascinated by the hardness and the heat. The way it rears under my careful touch.

He fumbles with his belt buckle and his huge, heavy cock springs free.

Holy shit.

His gigantic dick is veined and hot-looking. He's so freaking *big*. In every way. I'm at this hot, sexy alpha male's mercy. But there's a power to this too. He's *so* turned on. His cock is rigid against his stomach and there's a slick of wetness at the broad tip that makes my whole body blush with anticipation.

Ace pulls his shirt over his head and tosses it aside.

Whoa.

His chest and shoulders are powerfully built. He's muscular and olive-skinned, with that dusting of chest hair that's so beguiling and foreign to me. A perfect wall of abs leads down to that delicious V. His hair is dark and his eyes glow like sapphires. The way he's watching me is tender, but also primal. Our chemistry is raw and charged.

This is a man who could have any woman he wanted. Right now he wants me. *He's mine.*

Never in my life have I lusted after a man like this.

I take his cock in my hands almost tentatively at first. This is the first time I've ever been so up close and personal with…anything like this and it's obvious there's nothing ordinary about him. I lean forward. Lightly, I kiss him, barely touching my tongue to his silky bulk. I carefully ease my lips around the head, suckling him in tentative licks.

Ace groans. "Fuck, Tex. I'm too close. If you do that again I'm going to come. Lay back. I need to taste you and fuck you with my tongue."

Oh god.

"You ready for me, Texas?"

Am I? "Yes," I gasp, hoping like hell that I can handle this.

He spreads my legs with his iron-strong hands. It's then that Ace licks me, tonguing my clit before settling in and sucking me with a hungry, deliberate rhythm.

I moan but he holds me in place as he eats me lustily. His fingers slide through the moisture as his mouth feasts in greedy pulls. There's a stretching burn. But more than that, there's a rolling burst of pleasure just barely out of reach that's wild and uncontrollable.

"Ace."

He feeds on my pleasure, forcing it higher, and higher, until it reaches an excruciating peak that's simply the most intense thing that's ever happened to me in my life.

The pleasure explodes. My whole body is coming. I buck against his mouth to try to deal with the overload of clenching, white-hot rapture.

"Fuck, my Texan girl tastes so fucking good when she comes," he murmurs.

How embarrassing. That literally took ten seconds.

His mouth sucks tenderly on my clit with just the right amount of suction, spinning my orgasm into another long, lush spasming rush.

Oooooh goooooddd. Aaccce.

I realize I'm moaning as the clenching bliss milks his fingers.

Ace teases the ripples further until they calm, kissing and licking my clit slowly, like he loves the taste of me and doesn't want to pull away.

Just when I think I might be about to come *again*, he removes his touch and climbs up my body.

His eyes are dark and intense and before I get chance to steady my rocketing pulse, he's crouching over me. My pussy's still rippling and his enormous cock is laying against my belly.

"Do you want more, baby girl? Let me hear you say it."

"Yes," I breathe.

"You sure?"

"*Please.*" I need more of what this god-like man can do more than I need air.

"Good girl."

He leans in and kisses me. It's strange but also erotic as hell to taste *myself* on his lips.

Ace reaches into a bag that's sitting on the floor next to the bed and pulls out a roll of four or five condoms. *Help.* My nervousness makes me giggle again. "I guess I like your ambition."

"If you think you're getting any sleep tonight, Texas, you're sorely mistaken. One taste of you was never going to be enough." He tears one open and puts it in my hand. His voice is rough now, gritty with his need. "Put this on me."

Now would probably be the time to tell him I've never done this before.

But something stops me. I don't want him to go easy on me. I want this alpha beast to give me everything. So I pretend like I know what I'm doing. I roll the condom down over his colossal hard-on, getting a feel for him as I stroke his hard length.

His breathing is uneven, his eyes dark. "Fuck, you're the sexiest girl, Tex." His voice is a low, thick growl. I can tell he's *very* turned-on. Another burst of moisture gushes into the tip of the condom and his cock barely jerks in my hands. He could come very easily now, I can sense this.

The thing is daunting.

It's also inflaming some crazy, animal need in me that's basically transforming me into a raging nympho.

It's mine. I want all of it.

But will it be obvious how inexperienced I am? What if he realizes I don't have a clue what I'm doing?

I'll mask my inexperience with enthusiasm, I decide. I grip his cock in my fist and cup him, exploring the feel of his outrageously enormous erection.

His eyes lock onto mine again and he looks so hungry, so desperate for this, I only hope he can't read my thoughts. Ace's head lowers to my breast again, and his fingers caress me between my legs, teasing my slippery clit until the pleasure wave starts to build again.

"I love how fucking wet you are for me, baby. From the minute I saw you at the bar, I wanted you riding my cock. You got me hard the second you opened that pretty little mouth."

How is he making me feel like this? It's not just his touch or his tongue, although, hell, he certainly knows what he's doing. He smells so good, all whiskey and man-spice and woodsmoke. I love his smile. The way he brushes the hair out of my face so carefully. I want him to fuck me like an animal and then hold me in his arms while we sleep.

His lips find mine again and as they do, my hips tilt upwards reflexively, inviting him in.

He eases the head of his cock barely inside me, groaning like his heart is breaking.

I gasp and close my eyes. It's way too much. I was expecting the first time to hurt, but it's the *pleasure* that's unbearable. My orgasm starts slowly. I'm riding a star-flecked wave. My inner muscles still ripple with the last orgasm he gave me, drawing him deeper.

"Tex. *Fuck.* You're so fucking *tight…so wet for me, baby, oh fuck, you're so beautiful.*"

Ace grips my ass and, using the rhythm of my own writhing body, pushes deeper.

I'm too tight, but the wetness and his thrusting force drives his huge thickness deeper. And deeper.

As he thrusts, his thick cock rubs against some wildly sensitive trigger inside me. Again. And again.

There are tears in my eyes because it hurts and because it feels so damn good. He thrusts again and that's all it takes. The pleasure explodes in a rich, crazy, over-whelming swell. I moan his name. Each ripple of my orgasm pulls him deeper and we move together, grinding, gripping, fucking, needing more. Until I'm fully impaled, barely surviving the hot possession of his huge, thick length. Aware of nothing but the astounding pleasure, my body grips him tightly and he growls like he's in pain. I know he's fully inside me now as my body squeezes him in rhythmic pulls. I feel his cock jerk inside me, and the hot pulse of him takes me over another edge, the rush of spiraling waves tugging him over and over.

We're coming *hard*, locked in a secret, throbbing, plea-sure-crazy dance.

It lasts a long time and we let it, working it, writhing and gripping each other like we're each other's life raft.

Wow.

I'm floating. My eyes are closed but I've never been so flooded with feeling.

I think I might be in love.

Is it possible to fall in love this fast?

With a total stranger?

It's one night only, Dusty.

Then why do I feel like I never want to let him go?

7

Dusty

My eyes blink open. Soft, golden early morning sunlight fills the room and I can see the view of the blue, blue water. Gauzy curtains wave gently in the breeze.

It all comes flooding back to me.

Holy shit.

I finally did it.

I lost my virginity.

Very, very thoroughly.

To a guy whose name I don't actually know.

I glance over at him, still sleeping next to me, his burly arm looped around my waist.

Ace.

I watch him for a few minutes as he sleeps. He really is a beautiful man. He's even more gorgeous in his sleep. Those sexy, masculine features are softer, somehow less severe. His dark eyelashes cast small shadows against his handsome face, and I can see the stubble of his beard.

The stubble that scratched against my tender thighs as he was making me come with his mouth.

I lost count of how many orgasms he gave me. Once we started, we couldn't seem to get enough. I can admit I went a little crazy.

We had sex in positions I've never even heard of.

Now, I move a little, gauging the state of my body and, yes: I am very, very sore. But the ache feels…good. It reminds me of the wild pleasure. More pleasure than I knew was even possible.

And I can confirm that my first time—and second and also third—was better than I could've imagined.

I'm glad I waited for him. "Ace" will always own a small piece of my heart.

Or maybe a big one.

Don't even go there, Texas.

We agreed. One night. No names. Now he can get back to his…life— hopefully not wife, but he told me there wasn't one and I believed him.

And that's as much as I can give him. Men don't stick around, I learned that a long time ago. My heart was broken by my father at the age of four years old and I never quite recovered. It was a heartbreak that was reinforced every day by my struggling mother. Hard work and independence is in my blood. I don't have it in me to get side-tracked by one beautiful—okay, the best of my life—night with my dirty-talking Mr. Swagger.

It's time for me to go.

Very carefully, I move his arm and wriggle out from under him. He stirs but doesn't wake. He's tired, not surprisingly. We probably didn't get more than two hours of sleep. We made love and we talked. We laughed. Those quiet murmurs while we were still connected at three a.m. might possibly be some of the best memories of my entire life. Which is sort of sad, but it is what it is.

Silently, I find my clothes and my bag. Checking my phone, it's 6:12. My flight leaves at 9:15.

Glancing again at his big body, those broad, tanned shoulders, the sheet low over his perfect washboard abs, I wonder what he would do if I slipped back into bed and woke him up...by taking his big, hard cock into my mouth...*drinking those throbbing, gushing bursts.*

I didn't quite get around to trying that. And it would have taken our level of intimacy one giant step forward.

I wish I'd done it.

Stop.

At least we used protection. I give myself points for being responsible, even if I did get down and dirty with a complete stranger...three or four times. Not including the things he did to me with his mouth.

How am I even able to walk right now?

God, he felt so freaking good.

What has this man done to me? I've lost my virginity

to a guy who has very possibly ruined me for all men. I mean, how can anything compare to Ace?

My face warms at the porn flick of fresh memories.

I let a stranger tongue-fuck me in the penthouse suite of a luxury hotel in Hawaii, then fuck me—several times over—as I screamed his name. Basically within one hour of meeting the guy.

Anyway, I can't regret any of it when he made me feel like a goddess. Like every inch of my body was the most beautiful thing in the world, designed just for him.

But I need to snap out of my Ace-induced haze. If he got me *this* lust-drunk after one night, imagine what he could do to me if I spent the day with him? Or another night? Or two?

The problem with Ace is that he has the power to break my heart, I knew that from the minute he sat down at the bar with me with those blue eyes and that dark smile.

The reality is: you probably don't get *that* skilled, *that* smooth, *that* irresistible out of nowhere. He's obviously done this many times. It's probably second-nature for him at this point.

I silently thank my lucky stars we agreed it was a one-time thing. No strings attached and no regrets. It's better this way.

And so it's back to reality for me. Even if it's a slightly new reality. One in which I'm no longer an ice maiden but a non-virgin sex queen who's had six or seven back-to-back orgasms and is still riding my killer endorphin rush.

Who even knew a person could come that much?

I glance at the clock on the nightstand and quickly tie my dress, pulling on my shoes.

Taking one final—long, lingering—look at Ace sleeping peacefully, I'm tempted to run my fingers through his thick, disheveled hair and kiss his perfect mouth.

But I don't.

I scribble a quick note, grab my bag and very quietly leave.

I sneak across to the elevator, hoping like hell that it doesn't wake him, and ride down to the fourth floor, making my way back to my room.

At record speed, I put my hair up and rinse myself under the shower, throw on a travel outfit, shove everything into my suitcase and order an Uber.

I step out onto my balcony, allowing myself one more adoring gaze out over my Waikiki view. *Bye, Hawaii. Thank you for the best three days of my life.*

Now it's time to put some distance between me and the to-die-for hunk who's still soundly asleep in his penthouse.

It was a one-time thing.

End of story.

But, wow, what a hot, beautiful, orgasmic story it was.

8

———

CASH

I REACH FOR HER, needing to wrap myself around the hottest, most beautiful girl on planet Earth. My gorgeous little hot-as-fuck Texan…

Instead, I feel only the cool, empty sheets.

I open my eyes. "Tex?"

Maybe she's in the shower.

Or out on the balcony.

I get out of bed, wrapping the sheet around my waist because I have a raging hard-on.

Not that she minded The Beast last night.

Fuck, that was a hot night. My cock is still on overdrive from the sweet, insanely beautiful perfection of her wriggling, nubile little body.

"Tex?" I'm not sure why but my chest feels tight with something that might be…panic.

She's not in the shower. *Or* out on the balcony.

She left?

She fucking left.

How could she do *that?*

Her bag is gone. And her clothes. She told me she had an early flight, but after the night we just spent together, I thought she'd at least wake me to say goodbye. *And give me her number. And agree to stay another night. Or two.* I could have convinced her to, I'm sure of it.

I look for a note and there is one.

> Ace,
> Thanks for an amazing night.
> xx Tex

That's it?

I turn the note over, hoping for a phone number. Or an email address.

Something.

Anything.

But there's nothing.

What the fuck, Texas?

Damn it! I don't even know the name of the woman who just gave me the best night of my entire fucking life.

And not just because of the sex.

Yes, the sex was phenomenal. But we also connected in a way that went beyond just physical—which, I can admit, has never, ever happened to me before in my life. Not even fucking close.

The little Texan stranger with the sassy mouth and the ridiculously lush body has just…I don't want to say she's ruined me for anyone else, but the thought flashes through my brain.

I don't like it one bit.

What I don't like even more is that she's gone and I have no way of tracking her down.

I turn on the shower, not bothering to wait for the water to get warm. I need it cold, to cool the raging heat of my body and my fucking rock-hard cock. The water pummels my neck and shoulders but I don't linger. The shower is huge, more than roomy enough for two, and my cock gets even harder at the thought of taking Tex in the shower. *Why'd you run, baby girl?* I'd be running my hands all over her hot, wet body, lifting her against the marble tiles, sliding inside her, making her come as she moaned into my mouth.

Fucking fuck.

I don't even get myself off because I don't want to take the time. There's a chance I can catch up to her and bring her back.

I turn off the shower and grab a towel. Throwing on some clothes, I shove the rest of my stuff into my bag.

The state of the bed makes it obvious what went on in here last night. I hardly care about appearances, but where the duvet has been rolled over, I notice on the sheet a streak of blood.

What the hell?

Surely not.

Tex was…a *virgin?*

She told me she was 23.

Who waits that long? And why? Especially when you look like a fallen angel and you have the most delicious body any man has ever seen or imagined. Damn, she was perfect. *So sweetly hot and hungry for my mouth and my cock.*

Goddamn it. Why didn't she tell me?

Was I too rough with her?

Did I hurt her?

I've never been so feral for a woman as I was for Tex last night. I simply couldn't get enough of her. I spent most of the night inside her, taking her again and again.

Is she okay?

Is she sore?

Is she regretting leaving me without saying goodbye?

I need to find her.

Does she want me to? Obviously not, if she left like that.

Is it best this way? What I need to do is think about this objectively. I'm not a good man.

Okay, I'm a good man. I'm just a man who's terrible at relationships of any kind whatsoever.

The wreckage of my past and especially the most recent attempt with Rylee—a name I don't even want to think about in the same sentence as what happened to me last night—proved to me a long time ago that I'm not cut out for commitment. I'm too distracted for relationships. My business consumes me and has for a long time.

I would have to take a step back from work to even consider having a relationship with someone like Tex.

What the fuck are you even thinking right now?

I grab my bag and punch the elevator button. I might be able to catch her.

What are you going to do if you do *catch her?*

Even if I was relationship material, she made it crystal clear that this was a one-time thing. She's a career-minded girl. I get that. I respect that. She's focused on her goals and doesn't want anything to get in the way of her plans.

But we were so fucking good together.

I could tell she was inexperienced, but whatever hesitations she had were no match for how hot she was for me.

As for my own raging lust, I couldn't have controlled myself even if I'd wanted to. Her surrender to her own desire was the most beautiful thing that's ever happened to me. We kept coming back for more until we collapsed with exhaustion.

My cock is thickening even more at the thought of how sweet she was as she kissed me with that lusty innocence. *Her mouth. The quiver of her squirming body when I made her come for the first time. The sweet taste of her candy-pink pussy as I fucked her with my tongue.*

Hell.

I adjust my briefcase because in a matter of minutes

I'm going to be in public and my monster erection is showing no signs of deflating.

The girl is an angel with a taste for the devil. Pure ecstasy. I've got an orgasm-hangover, but instead of feeling drained, all I want to do is feast on my dream girl again.

Now.

I get down to the lobby and it's crowded with people who are moving at a much slower pace than I'm used to. It's been too long since I've been away from New York. I sometimes forget that people can actually *be* relaxed.

I scan the lobby and the outdoor area for her, searching with a degree of desperation I don't even recognize.

She's not here.

Damn it, Texas.

Fine. Good. My one-night stand took off on me. Big deal.

How could you do that to me, baby girl?

I need to calm down.

It was just sex.

Than why did it feel so fucking good and real and intimate, in a way that's digging into me and won't let go?

She wasn't just sexy. She was also funny and smart. Cute and fun. The hint of nervousness slayed me and I was basically besotted from there on in.

I've found other women attractive, of course, but their appeal always quickly—too quickly—became overshadowed by the pettiness and the demands. The catty neediness. The grasping meanness.

Like with Rylee. I knew almost instantly that I could never love her.

What are you even thinking right now?

With Tex, it was like she *got* something about me. She wanted to please me, and when I pleased her, the most exquisite creature, it felt like the best fucking thing in the world was happening to both of us. She made me feel like the luckiest man alive and the king of the world. She made me feel invincible.

Fuck, I need to calm down.

I head for the desk.

"Checking out, Mr. Maddox?" the guy behind the desk asks me.

"Yes."

"Did you enjoy your stay?"

"Yes. Listen, a girl checked out just a short time ago. She's…from Texas. Brown hair with sort of golden highlights. A few freckles." *Listen to yourself, man.* "She was here for the conference."

I sound ridiculous but the guy is diplomatic. "I'm sorry, Mr. Maddox. There were four hundred conference attendees staying here this weekend and most of them have checked out this morning."

"Right."

"I hope you'll come stay with us again, Mr. Maddox."

I mutter something I hope is appropriate as I rush toward the front door.

My phone rings in my pocket and for a split second a flicker of hope pricks at the back of my soul—but it's impossible. She doesn't know my number.

It's Noah. "Hey."

"Hey, bro. How's Hawaii?" He sounds tired.

"It's fucking good."

My brother sounds almost surprised by my answer. "Must be if you decided to stay an extra night. Did you manage to meet up with Ty?"

"Yeah. He's fine. He trusts us, which is reassuring. If he does, others will too, hopefully."

"We've had a call from the Gleeson Fund," Noah says grimly. "They've heard a rumor about potential insider trading and they want a statement."

This is terrible news, obviously. But I'm distracted. I'm scanning the front of the hotel for Tex. "Have you given them one?"

"No. I wanted to talk to you first." Shit. Tex really is gone. "Cash?"

"Yeah?"

"What do you want me to tell them?"

"Tell them we're working around the clock to establish if there's any basis to these claims. We will cooperate fully with any investigations that the SEC warrant necessary—which we're confident they won't. You can be honest, but for fuck's sake, ask them to keep it quiet until we've isolated the incident and figured out if it's legit. We're innocent of the charges. If someone in our company isn't, we'll find them and prosecute them."

"Okay." I hear Noah scribbling down my words.

"I'm on my way to the airport now. I'll be back this afternoon."

"Colton has some ideas," Noah says. "Potential leads. We'll run you through everything tonight."

"So you think we really do have someone screwing us from the inside?"

Noah sighs. "It's looking more and more likely, yeah. The SEC doesn't generally make mistakes."

"Just focus on the investors. Reassure them that we're doing everything we can and this could just be an inconsistency in the report."

"You and I both know it isn't. That report was watertight."

"Yeah. I know. The most important thing is to make sure our investors don't lose confidence."

"Agreed." Noah takes a deep breath.

He sounds stressed. And tired. I shouldn't have taken the extra day away, but I can't regret doing it. It was the single most beautiful night of my life. Which sounds corny as fuck, but it was. If Tex hadn't bolted, I'd have taken ten more.

Still, I hate that I've left Noah to deal with all this. Sure, he's got Colton there, but our youngest brother tends to dedicate a lot of time to his bed-hopping schedule and he also tends to take life in general a lot less seriously than Noah and me.

"I'm sorry about the timing of my trip, Noah. I appreciate you holding down the fort. You've done a good job. As always."

"Thanks, bro. See you tonight."

The valet gets me a taxi and I check a few emails on the way to the airport. I respond to a couple, but I can't concentrate. It's an avalanche of demands that can wait until I get back to New York.

At the moment, she's still too close to me. I glance at the cars we pass along the highway.

Could one of them be her taxi? Is it possible her flight hasn't left yet?

For the first time in my life, the last thing on my mind is business.

It's terrible timing considering this issue has the potential to do us some real damage, but I still can't get myself to focus on anything but the memory of my Texan dream girl.

If only I'd asked for her fucking *number.*

What kind of idiot doesn't get the actual name of a woman he finds insanely attractive, doesn't insist she give him her number, and then make sure to find out where he can send her flowers the minute she gets back to Dallas?

I couldn't do any of the above because I was too fucking distracted, feasting on her in every way I could.

And now she's gone.

One night with her wasn't enough. The non-stop hot sex marathon and multiple simultaneous orgasms didn't get her out of my system at all. Very much the opposite, in fact. She dug herself into me with each fluttery squeeze and each delicate moan.

My need to see her again flares in me like a new addiction.

I need to fucking find her.

I start googling.

The name of the conference.

The list of companies attending.

The ones from Dallas.

9

Dusty

"I'VE FINALLY DONE IT, EM."

Even as I say it, I'm still not sure whether I'm about to tell my best friend that I've handed over my v-card, or that I've just applied for my dream job.

"Done what?"

I'm on my lunch break and I've wandered down to sit by the river, to make sure I'm not overheard by one of my work colleagues. Emma and I have sent a barrage of messages since I got back from Hawaii, but we're overdue for a phone call. "I've applied for a job. It's in New York."

"Yes! My bestie's moving in with me!"

"I'm not moving in with you." Emma lives with two other roommates in a tiny two bedroom in Greenwich Village. She's always telling me how cramped their apartment is and the only reason she's still sane is because she has her own bedroom and if she stands on a chair she can see a small piece of the Chrysler building from her small single window.

I want to tell her everything, but how do I do that without sounding clinically insane? It's easier to start with the job. Then I'll casually drop it into conversation that I had my brains fucked out by the hottest man on the planet.

"When are you coming?" she asks. "And why are you leaving a very good job after only a few months that, even last week, you were extremely excited about?"

"I don't even have an interview yet. But you know it's always been my dream to move to New York. And the timing feels right. What's that old saying?: 'nothing changes unless something changes'?"

Emma laughs. "I'm in the middle of a badly-realized zombie apocalypse, Dust. That's a little too deep for me right now." Emma works as a book editor for a publishing imprint that specializes in science fiction and fantasy. "If this is what you learned at the conference you should demand your money back."

"I think it was my mom who said that, actually."

"Well, I guess it's good advice. Have you told her you're moving?"

"You're the first person I've told, actually. But she'll be cool with it if it gets me closer to where I want to be."

My mom has always supported my dreams, and she knows better than anyone that I'm driven to succeed. She's the most encouraging person I know. It's why she never complains about working two jobs if it means Sky is one step closer to her big break.

But I know my mom and sister will both be surprised—and sort of devastated—when I tell them I'm leaving. I didn't really plan to look for something so soon, but being back in Austin after the whirlwind of my Hawaii trip has been harder than I expected.

It's been two weeks and I think about Ace constantly. I thought that once I was back in the office, all replays of Ace tongue-fucking me in his penthouse suite would stop, but it's a hundred times worse. It's like he's infiltrated my brain completely with all the things he freaking *did* to me and I'm powerless to do anything about it.

The amount of times a day I think about Ace…*about his mouth on mine…his rough fingers teasing my nipples…his greedy tongue licking my clit…his gigantic, glorious cock forcing its way inside me…*and about how much I sort of wish we could have had a little more time together are making me wonder if I've somehow managed to become a sex-addict after one single night with the perfect man.

I can't believe this is what I've been missing out on, all this time.

It's wildly distracting.

Maybe everyone feels like this. Do they? How does anyone ever get anything done?

What *else* am I missing out on?

This question, more than anything, is why I need a change. Besides, my company is already discussing other conferences. And the same one, for next year. I know if I stick around here, I'll be desperate to go to Hawaii again, just on the off chance he might be there. And that's ridiculous.

One night. No strings. No names. That was our deal.

No doubt Ace moved on with his life by the time I'd boarded my flight. He'll be back in Connecticut with his supermodel girlfriend or something. Or he's fishing at some other newbie conference as we speak.

The job alert for the position in New York landed in my inbox two days ago. It seemed like a sign.

"So, when's the interview?" Emma asks.

"If I get selected, it'll be in two weeks. I'm thinking that, even if I don't get shortlisted for this one, I've got a week of leave accumulated since I've been working over-time. I'm going to try to set up some interviews. New York is where I want to be."

"Wow, girlfriend. I mean, you've always been so focused, but I'm totally digging this whole new balls-to-the-wall energy. What's changed?"

I bite my lip, preparing to tell Emma I've had a sexual awakening that's changed my life. She's going to go ballistic when she hears this. She's also going to kill me because that was now two weeks ago and I still haven't told her.

I don't know why.

I needed to savor it quietly for a while. It changed everything about me and I needed some time to adjust.

"Getting away from home gave me some perspective," I begin. "I realized that if there's stuff I want, I have to go after it."

"That's not a new realization for you, Dust. You've always been that way. But I'll admit that flying to New York to hunt for jobs when you already *have* a good job feels like a big move. The right one, I'm sure. Just big."

"I guess it is. I might look at a few apartments when I'm there too. I've already started doing some research online."

"Never agree to anything until you've seen it, though. That's how you end up with a shower in your kitchen and a bed that doubles as a dining table."

"Okay. Good advice."

"You will absolutely stay with me when you're here," Emma insists.

"Are you sure, Em? I know you don't have a lot of room."

"I have my own room with a double bed and one third of it has your name on it."

I laugh. "Only if you absolutely don't mind. I can get one of those pod hotel rooms."

"You absolutely will not. I insist. Both my roommates got new jobs recently so they're hardly ever here. Plus, I'm a real New Yorker so I can show you all the best places to go. I also have contacts, which I'm going to start reaching out to."

"Thank you, bestie." To be honest, I haven't

completely thought this whole thing through. If I do find a job, I'll need to give my two weeks' notice soon. My apartment is on a six-month lease, which is coming up next month. Even though the job I've applied for has a much bigger salary than my current one, apartments in New York are more expensive and I've still got my mom and Sky to think about. Anyway, I've applied and now I've told Emma. The idea is gaining its own momentum.

"I can't wait!" Emma gushes. "I've got so much to show you. And we've got *so* much to catch up on."

Usually when Emma says that she means she's got a backlist of dating stories to tell me. She's really into her career, almost as much as she's into furiously swiping through dating apps. My friend likes to play the field. To "see what's out there," as she puts it, before she settles down. She doesn't have sex with all the men she goes out with, but she's much more worldly and experienced than I am.

We're so alike in so many ways but when it comes to our ideas about dating, we couldn't be more different.

"I've got a lot to tell you too," I say, knowing this will get a reaction.

"Like what?" I can already hear the curiosity in her voice. "Don't tell me there's a boy," she whispers, like she doesn't want anyone overhearing her.

"No." I draw another little heart on the hotel stationery I'm doodling on, pausing for effect. "Definitely not a *boy*." I wasn't really thinking when I grabbed the small notepad from the penthouse when I scribbled the quick note for Ace, but now I'm glad I did. There were two of them there, side by side. I left the note on one and I took the other. And now it's the one real thing I can look at and know that everything with Ace actually happened. Because without his real name or number or any other evidence that he actually existed, it sometimes feels like the whole thing was just a beautiful dream.

"*What?* Dusty, you *cannot* leave me hanging like this! Who is he?"

"Well, I met someone. And…we had fun."

"Does that mean you had *sex*? Oh my god, I can't believe it! Hallelujah, she finally got laid!"

"Would you stop."

"Who is he? Tell me everything."

"He's…older."

She whispers a scream. "How much older?"

"I don't know. Late twenties. Maybe thirty."

"Ahh! How did you meet him? Is he from Austin? He's not a work colleague, is he? Oh my god, don't tell me it's your boss. This isn't why you're moving, is it? It's not like…awkward at the office?"

I laugh. "No, it's nothing like that. I met him in Hawaii."

Another excited squeal. "When are you going to see him again?"

"I don't think I will. It was…you know, just a one-time thing."

"But do you want it to be more than that?"

"I mean…I don't really know, but even if I did, I don't think it could be more than that."

Emma pauses, letting the silence hang between us for a moment. "Dust?"

"What?"

"Are you okay?"

"Yeah, I'm fine."

"I think you should call him."

I sigh without meaning to. "I can't."

"Why not?"

"We didn't give each other our numbers. We sort of made this deal, on the spot, that we would just go with it. And it seemed like…" I don't know what it seemed like. It seemed like that was a good excuse to bone the guy into next week and not have to deal with the consequences. "…it seemed like a good idea at the time."

"Don't tell me you didn't get his last name."

I brace myself for her reaction. "I didn't even get his first name. We sort of…made up nicknames for each other."

"You kinky girl." Emma sounds almost impressed.

I laugh, glad she can't see me blushing. Yes, I offered myself to a hot stranger in positions I've never even heard of, basically transforming into a sex addict for one night only. I don't mention this to Emma.

"I'm sure we can find him. What company did he

work for? There must be clues. Give me every shred of info. Cyberstalking men is my specialty."

"I really don't know much at all." I shove the notepad back into my bag and wait until two joggers go past the bench I'm sitting on.

"What did you do, bolt first thing in the morning?"

"Yeah, kind of."

"Shit," she laughs. "Dusty Rose, you slut—and no, I'm not slut-shaming you. I'm wildly impressed. I'm sure we can find him. You met him at a conference. There must be a list of delegates, right?"

"They don't list them online, for protection. Anyway, he said he wasn't there for the conference. Not directly."

"It can't take much to just look up the companies that were represented and then research their employees. Do you know what company he works for?"

"No. We didn't discuss that." *We were too busy fucking like rabbits.* "There were over a hundred companies at the conference. Besides, he might not have even been with one of them. He said he was there to meet about some fund he was buying."

I can practically hear Emma's ears prick up. "He was buying a *fund*? Holy shit. Did he seem loaded?"

I bite my lip, remembering every detail. "He took me to the penthouse suite of the hotel, so, yes, I guess he did."

Emma squeals with glee. "Oh my *god*! Bagging the billionaire! I never in a million years saw my down-to-earth Dusty Rose going for that type, but I have to say I like this look on you."

"Emma. I didn't go back to his room with him because he seemed loaded. I didn't know he was in the penthouse until after we'd already decided to…go with it. It was more than that. He was just so…"

"So what?"

"So perfect."

Emma goes quiet for a few seconds. "Oh, fuck. You didn't *fall* for him, did you?"

"Of course not. It was one night. We just had a…" What to tell her? That Ace was the most beautiful man I've ever seen, with the perfect body, the perfect cock, the dirtiest mouth, *and* that he knew exactly how to use all of the above until I was moaning, begging and crying his not-quite-real-name? "…a meeting of the minds."

"Girl, we *have* to find him."

"I honestly wouldn't know how. Which means this is the universe telling me it's best this way."

"Do *not* give me that woo-woo bullshit," Emma scolds. "Trust me, perfect men do not materialize very often, if at all. *I've* never met one and I've looked under every rock in Manhattan. We need to search for him."

"Even if I did find him and we saw each other again, all it would do is shatter the illusion. No one can be *that* perfect in real life. It was a fantasy night in a fantasy place. Just like in one of your books."

"Not unless he's a zombie," she laughs. "God, Dusty,

I'm just so *happy* for you. Are you okay? I mean…was it good for you?"

I almost feel emotional at the question. "Yeah. It was." *So much more than good.* "I'm glad I waited for him."

"Oh, hell, honey. He must have really been something special."

"He was."

"Are you sure you didn't pick up any details we can use to find him?"

"I've tried. There's nothing. It's fine. I'm okay with that."

I have to be okay with that.

"I still think it's worth a shot," Emma insists. "We need to have a pow-wow when you get here and go through everything."

"We can try. It's unlikely though, Em."

She sighs. "Well, in that case, there are plenty more fish in the sea, girlfriend. We'll hit New York. We have thousands of loaded hedge fund guys here for you to live out your billionaire fantasies with."

"Yeah. Sure." But I feel sort of devastated at the thought. And I know that "hitting" New York isn't going to get Ace out of my head, any more than hitting Austin would. Our entire night together plays in a near-constant loop in my brain. So much so that it's making me wonder if there's any coming back from this particular brand of intoxication.

It was the searing intimacy of the whole thing that's

freaking me out. It wasn't only physical. It was emotional. We got each other so high it felt almost spiritual. I'm not going to bother trying to explain to Emma that I felt closer to Ace—a man I literally know nothing about and who I spent a total of twelve hours with from beginning to end—than I've ever felt to *anyone* before. Ever.

And that feels dangerous.

"Sweetie, I have to go," Emma says, "but I want to hear a *lot* more about your night with the hot billionaire. I'll call you later. In the meantime, let me know if I can help with any of your planning. And don't get distracted from your dream job by daydreaming constantly about some guy with a perfect dick—not that it probably *is* perfect, you realize. You need a few more to compare it to first."

"Nope. No more dick, thank you very much. No dating. Business as usual. Laser focus."

"Got it out of your system for now?" She giggles lightly.

"Exactly."

If only that were true.

10

CASH

THE OFFICE IS BUSY, even though it's almost seven p.m. by the time I get in from the airport. People are talking, researching, discussing. Everyone clearly knows about the fiasco now. And in the middle of it all is a stressed-looking Noah, who looks like he hasn't slept since I left.

He sees me and tilts his head toward the elevator. I nod in reply and watch as he gently extricates himself from the people who surround him.

I should never have gone away. The whole place is in a fucking frenzy.

Even so, I'm very glad I did.

Once we're in the haven of my office, Noah closes the door and leans his back against it, letting out a deep, exhausted groan. "Thank fuck you're back." He sits wearily on the leather couch.

"I take it everyone knows?" I head straight to the

bar, which is concealed in one of the cabinets that line one wall. It's a clever design. There's even an ice machine. I pour us both a whiskey on ice. We both fucking need it.

"Yes," he confirms. "There was a press leak, but we threatened to sue since an investigation hasn't been confirmed yet and they pulled it. Colton and I held an employee meeting this morning to try to reassure everyone that we're on top of things. We're offering overtime and a generous bonus to anyone who finds anything we might be able to use. We wanted to wait for you but in the end decided to go ahead without you. We thought you'd be back yesterday. You weren't answering your phone."

Noah is the best person I know. He's loyal. He's a genius at what he does. And he's a genuinely good guy, with a cut-throat edge, especially when it comes to business.

He also knows me very well. Through his exhaustion, he smirks. "She must have been something special."

I can't help but relent at his expression. I sit in one of the leather chairs, clinking my glass against his. Despite everything, I feel like celebrating. "She fucking was."

"You definitely seem more relaxed, brother."

It's true. And it's a point of difference. I don't want to compare Tex to Rylee in any way because there's no comparison. But it's glaringly obvious—not just to me, but to my brother—that Rylee had the opposite effect and so have most of the other women I've been with in the past.

Not that there have been hundreds. I'm not a player.

Not because I've got holier-than-thou scruples, but more because I've been too busy and too distracted. Women always seem to fucking complicate things and cause more stress than they're worth. I have never in my life fallen blissfully into any kind of relationship without immediately feeling trapped by it.

Until now.

Sex with Tex was—I'd never say this out loud— miraculous. I feel so fucking *good*. Almost *happy*, which isn't something that shows up on my radar all that often.

But where the fuck is she?

Who the fuck is she?

I'm a Type A billionaire CEO. And I can't find the girl of my dreams—who's *real* and who walked out on me —to save my goddamn life.

I've spent every possible opportunity over the past eight hours googling like a maniac, following every possible lead I can think of.

There were four companies from Dallas represented at the Emerging Into Investments conference. But none of them put photos of their employees online. So I wrote down the name of every female employee at each of the companies I could find and started stalking them.

So far, no luck.

I remembered overhearing Tex talking to someone

named Sky when I sat down next to her at the bar. So I spent another hour googling people named Sky in Dallas. Basically, a ridiculous thing to do.

I found nothing.

I'm starting to get the feeling Tex doesn't live and work in Dallas.

But I'm hardly going to lay all of this out to Noah. He's got enough on his plate. "Let's just say Hawaii is more beautiful than I remember it."

Noah smiles. "Good to hear."

He looks so exhausted. "I want you to go home and get some sleep," I tell him. "I just have a few more questions first."

"Fire away."

"Is there any chance we've got some idiot working for us who didn't know what they were doing was illegal?"

"It's a possibility. But I'd say an unlikely one."

"Have we lost any clients?"

"No. Only the Gleeson group has contacted us. But Colton and I decided to send an email. We want the information coming from us, instead of through hearsay. I cc'd you."

"Thank you."

Noah swirls the whiskey round in his glass before taking a long sip. "We have an email."

"An email?"

"We're trying to figure out whether it's as incriminating as it looks. Some of the leaked information can be traced back to one of our company addresses."

My brain spins and I sit forward. "If we know it's from one of our email addresses, surely that's everything we need? Whose email was it?"

"It's been sent from one of our no-reply addresses rather than a specific person's."

"So whoever it was used our servers. It's definitive."

"Yes. If someone had done it from a personal work account, it would be easy to track. But it wasn't. We know it was sent from within the building. It has one of our IP addresses, it's from our network…but the IT guys can't trace it to a specific computer."

"Fuck." I tip back the rest of my drink. "Can we at least tell who the information was sent to?"

"Someone at Sanderson Fitzpatrick."

I blink at my brother, flicking through the Rolodex of clients in my brain. "We don't deal with them."

"No, we don't."

"Have they ever expressed an interest in working with us?"

"Not to my knowledge, no. I spoke to the CEO directly. They're looking into it. They're in the middle of a merger but he agreed to meet with me as soon as he has time. He said he'd make it a priority."

"What a fucking mess. Do you have any gut feelings, Noah? What's your hunch?"

My brother is one of those people who's eerily intuitive. "Between you and me? Probably the same as your hunch."

I run a hand over my jaw. "There's only one person here that hates me enough to do something like this intentionally and out of spite. And believe me, the thought crossed my mind." We both know I'm referring to Rylee. "But I don't think she'd risk her career like this."

"I don't either. Either way, we have nothing yet that could pin it on her."

I sigh deeply. "Go get some sleep. Thanks for handling this shitshow, Noah. I appreciate it."

"Of course." Noah drains his whiskey and runs his thumb along the cut-glass pattern. "So, are you going to see her again?"

I hesitate, but this is Noah. The brother who's not only my most trustworthy ally, but also the one who knows more about me than a therapist would, if I had one. "No."

"You should. It's been a long time since you've looked this…" He waves a hand at me.

"This what?"

"Normal."

"What do you mean, 'normal'?"

"Like you just got laid really, really well and you're finally thinking about something other than your job."

Is it that obvious? I guess it is. "Yeah. It was a good night. We met at the bar and one thing led to another. The only problem is, when I woke up, the little minx was gone. And I don't even know her fucking name. *Or* the name of her company. All I know is she's originally from somewhere in Texas."

Noah almost smiles, but it's sympathetic. "Shit. How can you not know her name?"

"She had a Texan accent. I started calling her Tex and she never corrected me."

My brother is highly entertained by my anguish. "What did she call you?"

I shake my head. "I'm not telling you that. Go home."

"No way. You have to tell me. I'm your favorite brother. And you owe me one."

I owe him a lot more than one. "Ace," I admit.

Noah laughs. A real laugh, and it's almost worth the humiliation. And the regret, that I was such a fucking idiot that I let her slip through my fingers.

At least I've lightened his mood. "Go home," I tell him. "I don't want to see you again until you've had at least eight hours."

Still laughing, Noah gets up to leave. "You should sleep too. She obviously wore you out. You look exhausted. Sweet dreams, Ace."

"Fuck off."

More laughter as he shuts the door behind him.

With Noah gone, I pour myself another whiskey.

Alone in my office, I check a few emails, looking through the ones Noah cc'd me on. He and Colton have handled everything as well as they possibly could have. I'm grateful. And we still have time.

I've made a point of *not* being the kind of boss my father was. He was king of his kingdom, with total control. When I set up Invested Enterprises, I knew that delegating would be a major part of my strategy.

And it's worked. It's why IE has grown so quickly.

My father kept people in line through fear and manipulation and by scrutinizing their work so thoroughly that presenting new ideas to him was enough to send employees home sick with PTSD. There wasn't much that was ever good enough for him. If it was, he gave his minions—and his four sons—a pat on the back before taking all the credit.

I'm glad to say I am not my father. I go out of my way to recruit people who are at least as smart as I am. The company can only continue to thrive if the people around me are at the top of their game. I want experts and industry-leading pioneers working with me, helping make the vision I have for the company a reality. It's their vision too. They all bust their asses. And they're rewarded for it. We value loyalty. We compensate innovation. Honesty and integrity are things we seek out in the people we hire.

Which is why the thought of one of them going behind my back is so fucking infuriating.

Even so, I feel surprisingly calm. I'll be methodical and I'll deal with whatever I need to deal with.

Tomorrow.

For now, I allow myself to drift back to my obsession with the goddess I spent the night with. Did I dream her?

I pull her little note out of my wallet. *Ace, Thanks for an amazing night xx Tex*

Damn it, Tex.

I scour once again through the list of women who work for the companies in Dallas that were at the conference, diving deeper into my research.

I finally exhaust every single possibility.

Okay, then: Houston.

Her Texan twang was real. And strong. Which makes me think she still lives in Texas.

So, I start going through the four companies from Houston who had representatives at the conference.

I glance at the clock and it's one a.m.

Fuck. I've been poring over this shit for hours.

It must be…8 p.m. in Hawaii. And midnight in Texas.

Where are you, baby girl?

She's like a drug that was so damned good it turned me into an addict from my very first taste.

My head is swimming with flashbacks.

Of the way she looked when she kissed the head of my cock. Licking.

How she gasped when I pushed inside her for the first time— and fuck, it was her *very* first time.

I wish she'd told me that.

I hope you're okay, wherever you are.

I could've taken care of you if you'd let me.

I could take care of you now.

My cock swells as I picture her, naked and gorgeous, spread out right here on my desk. *Fuck, she tasted so fucking sweet.* It takes all my effort not to loosen my belt and fist my cock.

I scroll through the employee names of the first company in Houston. I'm encouraged to see they have photos of their people on the website.

Eleanor Beatty, Vice President

Veronica Stratton, Financial Strategist

Janet Eames, Customer Relations

They look like they're each pushing sixty.

Anyway, they're not her. Not even close.

The next name on the list doesn't have a photo. *Jasmine Flaherty, Finance Intern.*

Maybe that's the job title they give they're new graduates. So I start googling her name. There's an Instagram page. The girl is round-faced with short red hair.

Fuck.

I'm losing my mind.

I have more important things to think about right now than a nubile virgin—or at least she was yesterday, and how is it possible that was last night?—who had me wrapped around her pretty little finger at first glance.

I try to imagine her life outside work and my head fills with a hypothetical Instagram feed with pictures of her in Daisy Dukes and cowboy boots, looking fucking adorable.

Pull it together, Maddox.

Usually I'd get my driver to take me home, but I gave him the night off, knowing I'd probably be working late.

I grab a cab, staring out the windows into the dark streets. I hate that all I can think about is the dreamy little stranger who fucking ghosted me.

She was beautiful in a way I've never seen before, or felt. Her *thoughts* were beautiful. Kind-hearted and aspirational, like she'd never had a mean-spirited emotion in her life. Her green eyes glimmered when she talked about something she was excited about.

Every single thing about her was beautiful. Sexy and beguiling. Her face. Her voice. Her laughter. Her *body*—holy hell.

She made me smile. She made me realize I don't smile very often, because I spent the whole time I was with her grinning like a lovestruck fool.

My Texan girl was beautiful all the way down to her soul.

And now she's gone.

I take the elevator up to my two-story seventeenth-floor Park Avenue penthouse. I don't bother turning the lights on. The city lights outside the wall of windows and the low lights that sense my presence are enough.

Everything about the space is clean lines. Shiny black marble surfaces. Dark wood. Expansive windows to take in the New York skyline.

This place is my sanctuary and it's luxurious as fuck. No expense has been spared. There's a large outdoor patio with a jacuzzi. Five bedrooms. A home office I hardly ever use. A state of the art gym. An Olympic-sized pool on the fifth floor.

Usually, as soon as I enter this space, it calms me. But tonight all I can do is compare it to the penthouse suite in Hawaii.

The apartment feels empty.

My brain is being hijacked by thoughts of tongue-fucking Tex on my deluxe couch. Taking her to bed and sliding my cock deep inside her tight, perfect pussy until she's spasming around me.

Having no idea where she is or how I'm ever going to track her down is making me crazy. I want her more desperately than I'd like to admit.

I think about the conversations we'd have, the ordinary things we'd do, like drinking coffee together or getting dressed up to go out for dinner. I'd take her to my favorite restaurant. Dancing, if she wanted to. Then I'd take her to bed and feast on her luscious body. *And this time, I wouldn't let her go.*

Most men would be losing sleep over their company tanking, not a random stranger they slept with on a work trip.

Except she feels nothing like a stranger.

I've never been in love before.

Not once.

Lust, sure, but it always fades out almost before it begins. Before morning, I'm always cured.

No one has ever gotten under my skin like Tex has. I've never fucking *pined* for a woman like a goddamn puppy.

There has to be some way to find her.

It's true that not all the Houston companies list their newer employees. Fuck it, I'll hire a private investigator if I have to. It can't be *that* hard.

Maybe if I track her down and spend another night with her—or a week—I'll get her out of my system. Nothing is ever as good in reality as it is in your head.

Except with her, it would be.

I took something from her, something she'd been saving. Hell, no girl who looks like *that* gets to the age of 23 and is still a virgin unless she's made a conscious decision to hold out. She would have had guys throwing themselves at her since puberty.

But she waited. For what? Why?

Why me?

I mean, yes, our chemistry was off the charts, but was she really okay with losing her virginity to a complete stranger and then never seeing me again?

For some reason, I really can't handle that.

I need to know she's okay.

And if I don't find out soon, I'll end up losing my fucking mind as well as my company.

11

Dusty

I WALK down Bleeker Street and see the sign for the bar where I'm meeting Emma. Stepping inside, excitement swells in my chest.

I'm in freaking New York. I made it.

Okay, I haven't *made it* made it yet but I'm here and I can feel it in my bones that I'm one step closer.

The bar is swanky, with big gleaming windows embossed with the bar's logo, wooden beams, walls of exposed brick and lots of shiny chrome. I see Emma at a table by the window and she waves.

"I ordered us two Pinot Grigios," she says as I slide into the plush leather booth. "I hope that's okay."

"Perfect." It was my drink of choice in Hawaii, in fact, that gave me the exact amount of liquid courage I needed to flirt with McDreamy Dirty-Talking Big Dick Armani.

God, I miss him.

It's been over a month now since I enjoyed my dirty deeds done dirt cheap with the hot stranger.

Of course I've regretted, late at night, our decision—my decision, more accurately—to give each other fake names. And lie to him about where I was from.

But mostly I'm glad I did. Of course I am. I don't have time for anything more than a perfect one-night stand, which will remain preserved in my memory as a shining pillar of sunsets and pleasure. The worst thing I could do would be to drag it out into the harsh light of reality. I'll remember him as he was that one tropical night.

"So, how'd the interview go?" Emma asks, her brown eyes bright. Emma has curly brown hair that frames her face in shiny ringlets. She's curvy and wears little round glasses and upmarket vintage clothes that give her a retro edge. Her look is sort of fifties pin-up girl meets New York Gen Z.

"It went well, I think. I was nervous but they were nice enough. Very no nonsense and straight to the point. Em, their office is insane. It has a rooftop pool with a swim-up bar, if you can believe that. And one week out of every month is 'creative,' which means they encourage their employees to travel and meet people and explore. They say it helps people come up with innovative ideas they might not have thought of in the same, day-in-day-out setting."

"Wow. That sounds amazing. Who interviewed you? The CEO?"

"No, it was the HR Director, the CFO and the leader of the team I'd be joining. *If* I get the job, that is."

"When will you find out?"

The waitress appears and I wait as she sets down our glasses of wine and two menus before heading to the next table. "They said I was the last person to interview and that they'll be meeting tomorrow to make a final decision. They'll notify the successful applicant as soon as Monday."

"There's no second round of interviews?"

"No, they said they only do one round. That's why the interview was two hours long. They interviewed me, then they gave me a tour of the offices."

"When does the job start?"

"They'd want me to start as soon as possible. So I told them I could give my two weeks' notice and start immediately after that."

"Maybe we should look for an apartment together, Dust. Just the two of us."

"I'd love that. But you're not going to believe this. They have staff accommodation. The company owns an entire building and they offer apartments to a lot of the employees. The job I just applied for includes a one-bedroom apartment as part of the employment package. Can you believe that?"

"Holy shit."

"They also offer a signing bonus that's literally more than I'd make in six months at Stellar Investments, plus they'll pay for all my moving costs."

"Wow, Dust."

"I know. I was sold anyway by the job and the offices. But this company is next level. It's literally more than I could ever have thought to hope for."

"That manifesting shit you talk about all the time is really paying off." Emma seems impressed. "Don't tell me, the icing on the cake is that your boss is a total smoke show. I've heard that about Invested Enterprises. Apparently the owners are brothers and all of them are insanely hot."

I shrug. "I guess the CFO was an objectively handsome guy, now that you mention it. But I was too distracted to notice much beyond that. I was totally focused on trying to come across as the perfect junior analyst." There was something almost familiar about Noah Maddox that I couldn't quite put my finger on.

Emma holds up her glass of wine. "Well, let's toast to my bestie getting her dream job in New York City."

I clink my glass against hers. "And to *my* bestie. Thank you for putting me up this week. I couldn't have done it without you, Em."

"We both know that's not true," she laughs, "but I'll take the credit anyway."

I take a sip of the cool, crisp wine. "Anyway, I can't get my hopes up too soon. They told me they had four hundred applications and narrowed it down to twelve interviews. So the competition is fierce."

"I've got a good feeling about it, Dust. Of course they'll want you. You're beautiful. And hot. And smart. You're a power chick. Even if you don't get this one—and I know you will—you can stay with me for as long as you want to, whenever you want. I mean that."

"Thank you, Em. You're the best."

"Although, I really *do* hope you get the job because I don't want to have to abstain from sex for months on end just because I've got my best friend sharing my minuscule bed."

"I can always crash on the couch if you need me to." I happen to know she's taken a break lately from the dating apps because she secretly has a crush on her new work colleague, who told her his current relationship is on the rocks. So she's been patiently waiting to see how it plays out.

"I'm not an animal," Emma laughs. "A paper-thin wall is all that exists between my bed and the very lumpy couch. I mean, I love you, Dust, but we have to have boundaries." Her eyes flash mischievously at me. "But I guess there's always the fire escape if I get desperate—if Joshua happens to have a break-up and needs a shoulder to cry on."

"I hope you're not hinging all your hopes on a guy who may or may not ever break up with his girlfriend."

She sighs. "I know. It's pathetic. I seem to have a thing for nerds, don't judge."

"No judgement here." I smile at her, taking another sip of my wine. Pre-Hawaii, I'd always try to gently avoid talking to Emma about her sex life. It's hard to find much to say when you have no point of reference. But now? *I'm remembering how I rode Ace's huge cock like I was a sex-crazed rodeo hero instead of an inexperienced virgin.* Since then, everything she describes sounds sort of…not nearly as romantic as my Hawaiian fairy tale.

I've told Emma most of what happened. She knows that Ace and I met at the beach bar and had one very hot night in his penthouse suite. She even somehow got it out of me that I lost count of how many orgasms I had—*and* that Ace was a beast between the sheets. But I've also downplayed exactly *how* hot and beautiful the whole thing was and how much I'm still thinking about Ace. I know she'd think I'd lost my mind if she had any idea how hung up on him I still am.

"If you get the job," she says, "our next mission is to find you another scorching Wall Street suit. Since that seems to be your new type."

I dodge her suggestion gracefully. "If I get the job I'll be too busy to date."

"You don't have to *date*," Emma insists. "Just do what you did last time."

I don't bother telling her I'm not interested in another one-night stand. It's a little depressing to realize that Ace has completely ruined me for one-night stands. How could anything top *that*?

But I'm determined to be optimistic about my future relationships, even if I can't bring myself to think about anything but him. Not yet, at least. He's too fresh in my mind.

Emma's internet stalking—and mine, secretly—didn't come to much because I really don't have a lot to go on.

I'm sure he's moved on. There's no way a man like Ace, with all his money, ambition and experience, would think twice about me. Even if I *could* track him down, what then? Subtly slide into his DMs?

Hi Ace, remember me?

That would be more than a little humiliating, especially if he ignored me or deleted my message. I really don't need that kind of reality check when I'm on the verge of having everything I've ever wanted.

Dreaming about our time in Hawaii…*how Ace's mouth felt when he sucked on me and the way his cock throbbed and surged inside me…*is giving me plenty to fantasize about.

For now, that's enough.

Because it has to be.

12

———

Dusty

I WALK ALONG THE RIVER, drinking my super-sized travel mug full of coffee. It's Monday morning and I'm on my way to work. I got back from New York late last night after a delayed flight and a mishap with the luggage carousel that meant I didn't get back to my apartment until after midnight.

Now that I'm back in Austin, sleep-deprived and very close to broke, the dream job feels a lot more aspirational than it did when I was in New York. I'm exhausted. And my bank account is not thanking me for the small amount of shopping I couldn't say no to, or my nights out in Manhattan with Emma.

How am I even going to afford New York? is the question that's bouncing around inside my brain.

Maybe my fantasy of living and working in New York City is exactly that: a fantasy. Maybe I should be content with the job I have now and stick to my original plan of seeing it out for at least a year. At least that way I could save some money. Then again, I haven't managed to save much yet even though I've been working at Stellar Investments for a while now.

I'm almost at work when my phone buzzes in my bag. I pull it out.

It's an unknown caller. "Hello?"

"Dusty, it's Penelope Callahan here, HR Director at Invested Enterprises. How are you this morning?"

"I'm…fantastic, thank you." *Aside from the fact that my heart feels like it's about to thump right out of my chest because there's really only one reason you'd be calling me.* "So nice to hear from you."

"I have good news. Noah and Evan and I met with the CEO and COO. We were very impressed not only with your resumé, but also how you came across in the interview. We like your drive and your vision. You really stood out from the crowd."

"I did?"

"Yes. We think you'll be a perfect fit for the team."

"Really?" *Holy shit.* "I got the job?"

"We'd love for you to start at the beginning of next month. Will that work for you?"

Today is the fifteenth. "Yes. I'll…I'll give my notice today."

"Wonderful. I'll send you an email with your contract and all the information you'll need about your move. As discussed, we'll cover all your travel expenses, and we have a travel agent who will reach out to you within the next day or so about flights. There's a ten thousand dollar stipend for shipping any belongings you'd like to move, which will be deposited into your account as soon as you've signed the contract. If you need more than that for your move, that can also be discussed."

"N-no," I stutter. "That will be more than enough."

All I have is one suitcase. Maybe two at a stretch.

"You'll also receive a signing bonus of twenty thousand dollars."

I can't even respond to that. *Did she just say twenty thousand dollars?*

"For housing, we've been able to accommodate you in the East Building. You'll have a furnished one-bedroom apartment on the twelfth floor. The building itself is newly renovated and it's connected to the main office building by a glass Sky Walk. You won't even need to go outside for your commute."

"Wow," I gasp.

"You'll also have a company credit card, a clothing allowance and an entertainment allowance. The building has a heated pool, gym and spa, as well as a rooftop garden, and these amenities are all included for employees. We have an extremely comprehensive health insurance package, also included. And our retirement and investment plans are award-winning. We were written up in Forbes last month for our innovative approach," she says proudly. "My email will contain information about all of the above, but please let me know if you have any questions as you read through the job description. I'm here to help."

"Thank you." I realize my face is wet. From my own tears.

"Does that mean you'd like to accept the job?"

"Yes. Absolutely yes." This is literally more than a dream come true. With everything Invested Enterprises is offering me, I'll be able to help my mom and sister out even more and, since I'll have next to no expenses other than food, I'll really be able to save money for the first time in my life.

"Thank you so much, Ms. Callahan."

"Please, call me Penelope. Your email is on its way. We're hoping to receive your signed contract as soon as you've had a chance to read through everything. How's Wednesday?"

"Wednesday is perfect."

"Fantastic, Dusty. Welcome to Invested Enterprises."

13

Dusty

THE NEXT TWO weeks pass in a blur of quitting my job, packing, moving out of my apartment, saying my goodbyes to almost everyone I've ever known, and reassuring my mom I'll still come home for the big holidays.

When I told my boss at Stellar Investments I was leaving, she was more in awe than disappointed. If Invested Enterprises offered her a job, she'd jump ship too, she said.

"At least I'll have someplace to crash when I start touring," Skylar tells me, helping me lug my two oversized suitcases to the front hallway. My ride to the airport is on its way. I said goodbye to my mom before she left for work and my eyes are still red from crying. It's surprisingly hard to leave them.

When I told Penelope I wouldn't be shipping anything to New York because everything I owned fit into two suitcases, she insisted the relocation stipend would still be included as part of my signing bonus. It's company policy. So, until an hour ago, I had thirty thousand dollars sitting there innocently in my bank account like it belonged there. Which means that I had thirty times more cash in my bank account than I've ever had in my life. What does a person even *do* with that much money?

Helping out the people I love felt like the best use of it. So, around an hour ago, I deposited ten grand each into my mom's and Sky's accounts. Which Sky hasn't noticed yet.

I open the front door and Sky and I just stand there for a few seconds. My sister tucks a strand of my hair behind my ear. "I'm really going to miss having you around. Even if you are a pain in the ass," she smiles sort of sadly.

"I put some more money into your account," I tell her. "I want you to be able to concentrate exclusively on your music for a while."

"Dusty, you don't have to do that. Save your money for New York."

"I had some extra."

"Are you sure? I'll pay you back. For everything. I really mean that."

"You can pay me back when you're a superstar. I put some into mom's account too. So she doesn't have to work so hard."

My sister gives me a heartfelt hug. "You really are the

best sister. Thank you for believing in me. I won't let you down."

"You never have, sis. Good luck with the gigs."

The car drives up. It's more like a limo, paid for by my new job. "Now go and slay New York, Dusty Rose. They won't know what's hit them up there in the Big Apple. Make all your dreams come true."

"I will if you will."

"Deal," she laughs.

The driver arrives at the door to take my bags for me.

I give Sky one more hug.

"Those dreams, by the way," Sky calls after me, "include balance. I'll look forward to hearing all about the dating scene in New York City."

"Sure thing." I never ended up telling Sky about Ace. Everything has been so busy, I haven't had the chance. And there was really no point. Ace is gone.

But she's right, of course. My love life—aside from that one crazy, beautiful night where I totally lost my sanity and self-control and loved every minute of it— might as well have tumbleweeds rolling through it.

Once I get to New York I'll forget all about Ace.

No, you won't.

I'll meet someone even more perfect.

Impossible.

And I'll get on with the rest of my life without him in it.

14

Dusty

EVEN THOUGH I told Emma I was being picked up from the airport by a company driver, the first thing I see when I walk through the arrivals gate is her bright, beaming face. In one hand she's holding a gigantic bunch of flowers and, in the other, a glittery sign with *WELCOME TO NEW YORK, DUSTY ROSE!!!* emblazoned across it.

It's actually exactly what I need. It helps tone down the nerves fluttering through my stomach. I haven't been able to eat much in days. I'm too nervous and too excited. Turns out that moving away from the one city you've ever known is, in every way, a big deal.

She gives me a huge hug and then I notice another, much more subdued *DUSTY ROSE* sign, being held by a man in a black suit who's standing next to Emma.

"This is Joe," Emma tells me. "We've bonded over our Dusty Rose signs. Joe said I can ride with you guys to make sure you get settled into your new apartment without a hint of loneliness or overwhelm that goes along with leaving your entire life behind and moving to one of the most bustling metropolises in the world."

"Hi, Joe." I can't help but smile at my best friend's enthusiasm. "You really shouldn't have," I tell her. "But I'm glad you did."

"Ms. Rose," says Joe. "I'm here to help you retrieve your bags. And your limo is parked right outside."

"Limo?" Emma squeals. "Joe, you didn't tell me *that*!"

"Invested Enterprises likes to welcome their new employees in style," Joe says.

There's even champagne chilling in the back of the limo, which Emma insists on popping.

On the ride in from the airport, New York looks different than in did only a few weeks ago. It's mine now. My new home. It looks better, somehow. More shiny and exciting and impressive.

It's not long before we're pulling up outside the doors of my new apartment building, slightly tipsy.

"You have a *doorman*," Emma whisper-shrieks as a man in a red jacket opens the door for us. "And a concierge!"

And then there's the apartment itself. I open the door with my new key card and Emma walks in with me. She's still clutching the bottle of champagne in one hand. We're sort of leaning our shoulders against each other for support and in anticipation. We both gasp when we see the sun-drenched space.

The apartment is a one-bedroom, so I'd sort of imagined something like Emma's, but smaller. The similarities begin and end with the fact the apartment is located on the island of Manhattan.

"You get *sun*," Emma exclaims, and by now I know that this is a lucky score in New York apartments. "God, there's so much natural *light*. Holy shit, look at your *view*, Dusty."

It's not a huge space, but the entire wall of windows makes it look much larger. The view over the surrounding buildings is expansive. I can even see a sliver of the river in the distance.

The apartment is open plan and very modern. There's a small kitchen made of granite and blond wood, a compact living area with two comfortable-looking cream couches and a large flat-screen TV mounted on one wall. It's sparsely furnished but all the furnishings are stylish and high end.

Down a hallway, there's a walk-in closet, a small but luxurious bathroom and a roomy bedroom with a king-sized bed and that same wall of windows and floor-to-ceiling cream velvet curtains. Emma pulls on one, marveling at the lush fabric, and it completely blocks the light. Which might come in handy for sleeping in and for privacy from the next building's windows.

"Plenty of room here for your bestie to bunk with you on a regular basis," Emma says.

"I can't believe this is where I get to *live*."

"The place suits you, Dust."

"Sure it does," I scoff.

"It does," she insists. "You've worked your ass off for this for a long time. You deserve this. Don't forget that."

"Thanks, Em."

Before I can get too emotional about it all, she pulls me by the hand. "Come on. We've got a bottle of champagne to finish."

15

Dusty

I'M FLOATING on a bed of clouds, more comfortable than I've ever been. There's a light ocean breeze and a view of the waves. Ace is wrapped around me. His lips are soft but demanding, his body deliciously hard, just like I remember it.

But he's fading, like a ghost.

I cling to him, trying to keep him here but he's disappearing, slipping through my fingers like mist.

No, Ace, don't go! I'm not from Dallas!

He's gone and I miss him so much. My heart aches unbearably. Where is he?

My eyes blink open.

God, it was dream.

I'm not at home. Or in my apartment in Austin.

Am I in…Hawaii?

It's dark in here. Just a sliver of blue light from the small opening between the drawn curtains.

It all comes rushing back to me.

I'm in New York.

My sheets are twisted around me in my new, extremely-plush bed.

I reach for my phone.

It's 6:59 a.m. My alarm is set for 7 so I turn it off before it rings.

Emma went home around eight last night, to give me some time to start to unpack and to get ready for my first day at my new job.

The only thing I unpacked was my toothbrush, a small make-up bag and the outfit I laid out for my first day. It's a cute black dress that's one of my favorites, both professional but also fashionable, somehow in an Austin-meets-New York kind of way.

Showered, dressed and as ready as I can possibly be, I recite Emma's pep talk in my head as I take the elevator down to the sixth floor, where the Sky Walk is located. I stop to admire the view, looking out through the windows of the glass closed-in bridge, down to the traffic jam below me.

I worked very hard for a very long time and I deserve this. I'm good at what I do. I'm not an imposter. They liked my drive and my vision. I belong here.

The streets and sidewalks are packed with morning walkers and commuters. Standing here in my cocooned, sun-drenched vantage point, I feel separate.

I feel lucky.

I think of my surfing lesson. The wave I caught and the things Lucas said to me that day. *Now you can watch your life explode with good energy.*

It did explode.

It's exploding right now.

Your life is never the same again after you catch a wave. It changes everything: your Karma, the way you manifest the rest of your future, your entire path. This has been the day everything started to change for you. You'll see.

Weirdly, Lucas was right. First Ace and now this. Even though it feels sort of frivolous in this sophisticated setting, I do it anyway: I send a silent message to Lucas, wherever he is. Probably giving a surfing lesson in that same spot.

Thank you.

And by the time I reach the Invested Enterprises offices, dressed in my little black power dress, my black heels, my hair in a high ponytail, a simple gold chain around my neck and matching gold hoop earrings, I feel almost ready to face my day.

I stare up at the shiny embossed letters above the large office doors.

INVESTED ENTERPRISES

You can do this.

I square my shoulders and show my ID to the security guard, who waves me through.

The offices are sleek and modern, nothing like the crowded, stuck-in-the-50s offices that I was based in, back in Austin.

There are leather chairs, neon sign accents and a dark-wood reception desk, with a full-wall print of the Empire State Building behind it. The office is stylish and very New York, with a young, hip edge.

It's not surprising that there would be a youthful energy to the place. Invested Enterprises is owned by three twenty-something brothers who are known not only for their business savvy but also for their good looks, as Emma loves to point out. She said they're often listed on social media sites as the "most eligible bachelors in New York."

I've never seen a picture of the brother who started the business, whose name is Cash Maddox. Rumors are he's a workaholic.

The youngest of the three, Colton, often shows up on online. He serial dates New York heiresses, socialites and models. I follow a few of them on Instagram. I've seen the occasional picture of him at some party or event.

And I've met Noah, at my interview, the CFO and the oldest of the three. I read somewhere there's a fourth brother who runs the family business, the oldest, whose name is Alexander. He's in charge of the empire they inherited from their father.

"Dusty." Penelope is walking down a hallway toward

the front desk, a huge smile on her face. "Welcome to New York!"

"Hi, Penelope. Thank you so much."

She gives me a brief hug. "How was your trip?"

"Very smooth."

"And the apartment?"

"Absolutely amazing."

"I live on the fifteenth floor," she tells me. "We could meet on the rooftop for a drink after work sometime." Penelope's probably only a few years older than I am and as I look around the office I notice most of the staff are probably in their mid to late twenties.

"I'd love that."

She shows me around the spacious office, which has the feel of a giant, airy, up-market Soho loft. "Here's the main office space. Everything's been designed to ensure that there's a flow, but there are plenty of quiet work-spaces too."

The desks are grouped together into zones and there are plants and casual seating zones liberally dotted around. The break areas have glass-fronted fridges stocked with drinks and there are baskets on countertops overflowing with healthy-option snacks.

There's a noticeboard on one wall with a schedule of "Need A Break?" sessions, listing massages, meditation, yoga, Pilates and Reiki.

"I know you had a brief tour during your interview,

but I want to make sure you know exactly where every-thing is, now that you're here full time," Penelope says. "On the next floor up we have the gym, the spa and the restaurant. The gym is open 24/7, the spa from 9 to 5, and the fully-catered kitchen from 7 a.m. to 10 p.m. The top floor is where the executive offices are located and the roof has the heated pool, the jacuzzi and the bar, which also has an after-hours restaurant. I'll show you all those after you meet with Evan and get settled. Here's your desk right here."

My desk is in the middle of a row of three, facing a mirror image of the same layout. It's empty except for a large Mac desktop computer, a MacBook and an Invested Enterprises mug full of pens.

"You've met Evan, your team leader. He sits over here," she gestures to the desk directly opposite mine. "And these desks are the other people on your team. Lacey and Patel."

Lacey and Patel are the only ones at their desks. Lacey is next to me and Patel is opposite her, next to Evan. Patel nods my way, barely glancing up from his screen.

"I'll leave you to settle in," says Penelope, handing me a Post-It. "Here are your login details. I'll be back in ten to take you up to meet the CEO. He likes to meet all new employees face-to-face as soon as they arrive. We'll do the rest of the introductions after that."

"Sounds good," I smile, trying to relax. "Thanks."

As soon as Penelope's gone, Lacey beams and swivels on her chair so she's facing me. "I'll fill you in on every-thing you *really* need to know about Invested Enterprises," she winks conspiratorially. It's not hard to read that she's the office gossip. She blinks long silk eyelashes at me. "So, have you heard about the insider trading fiasco?"

16

———

Dusty

"Insider trading?"

Please don't let my too-good-too-be-true new job be over before it's even started. Please don't let my too-good-too-be-true new job be over before it's even started.

Lacey glances around, like she doesn't want to be overheard. "They're doing major damage control right now. Rumors are that someone leaked some info illegally, but no one knows who it was."

"Is it true?" If it is, it's a huge deal. Insider trading can be disastrous for any company and especially for an investment company.

"The SEC is still considering an investigation." Lacey's voice is low. So far, Patel hasn't joined in as we chat, but now he puts his ear pods in his ears and lightly scowls in Lacey's direction. But Lacey is undeterred. "I'm surprised they hired you, to be honest, with all the heat that's on the company right now."

Lacey seems nice but she clearly thrives on drama. So much so that it's hard to tell if her revelations are something I should worry about or not.

I've just moved across the country for this job. If the company is in trouble, I'll be homeless and jobless. And possibly penniless. Is it possible they could ask for their sign-on bonus back because they're in financial difficulty?

I've already given half of it away.

Within less than a minute of talking to Lacey, I know two things. One, she's fun and will tell me all her deepest secrets. Two, she can't be trusted with anything confidential.

"Cash, Noah and Colton are desperately trying to reassure everyone," she continues. "I guess we'll see soon enough if it's just some kind of error or if someone really did leak the info."

If it's common gossip in the office, then there's probably some basis to it. What the hell have I walked into?

"Nobody's sure if it's even true or not," Lacey continues. "I mean, no one has come out and admitted it, which makes me think someone either is so totally clueless they don't realize what *counts* as insider trading, or they did it with complete knowledge on the sly for some quick cash and are trying not to get caught."

"That's crazy."

"Right? I mean, to be honest, I thought Cash would

have a handle on things by now. This company is his baby. He's usually all over any shit that goes down. But he wasn't even the one to tell us. He was out of town when the news broke. And now we've got the visit from the SEC hanging over our heads while Cash is meanwhile walking around here with a spaced-out look on his face, like he's mentally on a beach somewhere. I haven't seen him so much as smile in weeks."

"He keeps a low profile," I comment. When I researched the company before my application and interview, it almost seemed strange that a CEO would be so discreet. I couldn't find a single picture of him, and there were only a handful of interviews. It's unusual. Most of the time when hotshot entrepreneurs make it big like this, they're hungry for adoration.

"He likes privacy," Lacey confirms. "Being a Maddox, he doesn't need visibility to make money. He already has the name, the legacy and the money-making genes. I heard he knows someone at Google and they wipe his online profile whenever anything comes up. It's a new thing, apparently. To make yourself invisible on the internet. It's supposed to give you a mysterious, powerful aura, like a professional superpower or something." She almost scoffs, like wanting to be invisible is a foreign concept to her.

I kind of like the idea.

Lacey takes a sip of coffee. "Cash is a good boss— well, boss's boss, more accurately. But whatever's going on at the moment seems to have totally thrown him. I get it, but now's not the time for him to lose concentration." She lowers her voice. "It wouldn't surprise me if it's his ex that's distracting him. She still works here but he broke it off with her a few months ago and now he won't even give her the time of day."

"Oh."

"She wasn't an employee when they started seeing each other, but still. Apparently Noah hired her and didn't know they were fuck buddies at the time."

It's interesting information, I guess, but I sort of wish she'd stop telling me all this. It feels personal. "Yikes."

"All the Maddox brothers are ridiculously gorgeous, of course, and single, which is seriously unfair considering we have to look at them all day. Plus of course they're smart *and* loaded. Which is why Rylee didn't want to let Cash go."

"Rylee?"

"Yeah. Rylee Winters. She was seriously in love with him, but he dumped her after only a few weeks and now it's really awkward because she's obviously still pining for him. And she's got claws, that one. Trust me, you'll definitely want to steer clear."

I make a mental note to avoid Rylee Winters wherever possible. The last thing I need is to make enemies before I've even logged in.

"So none of the brothers are in relationships?"

"If you count out being married to their jobs, no.

Cash has sworn off women after Rylee, as far as I know. I don't know this for sure but I've heard he'd like to have her fired. But the company has a two-month trial period, and after that, it's hard to fire someone without a legal reason for it. Anyway, Noah seems too busy to date. And Colton…well, he's Colton. A total fuck-boy. But he never dips his quill in the company ink, if you get my meaning. Even though everyone in the office spends every Friday afternoon trying to change his mind."

She pauses and there's something loaded about it. I feel my eyebrows rise. "Everyone?"

Her face gets pink. "Okay, I'm *mildly* besotted. He's always crystal clear about the fact that it'll never happen, but fool that I am, I can't resist trying anyway. I mean, he flirts outrageously when we're both at the bar but then ignores all my emails and DMs."

"You email him? At work?"

"Sure," she shrugs. "It hardly matters. Cash is the discreet brother. Colton is anything but."

I smile but feel a knot clench in my stomach for Lacey. With what's going on with the insider trading rumors, the company will surely keep a tab on every email and message being sent. It sounds humiliating.

"Looks like I've arrived at a crazy time."

"Oh, for sure," she sounds wildly pleased about this. "But it'll all calm down once the SEC figures it out. Assuming we haven't lost all our clients by then."

"Dusty!" I hear Penelope calling me from across the

office and swivel around to see where she's standing. She beckons me over and I'm relieved to have the excuse to get out of the pressure-cooker that is Lacey's compulsion to over-share.

When I reach her, Penelope's standing with Noah and Evan. They're both looking at the iPad Noah's holding but they look up as I walk over to them.

"Dusty, you'll remember Noah and Evan from your interview," Penelope says.

"Nice to see you both again."

Evan nods and Noah shakes my hand. "Fantastic to have you on the team, Dusty." He's as business-like as he was during my interview, and with that same almost-familiarity I can't quite place, but I like him instantly. He's got a calm, in-control vibe. Even if the company is on the verge of imploding, you get the feeling that everything will be fine if Noah's in charge.

"I'm excited to be here." Which is true, but it's a tiny bit easier to keep it in check after Lacey's gush. It's my dream company but there are obviously cracks, just like with everything in life. Nothing is ever as perfect as it seems.

"Who's this?"

I look up to see a tall, good-looking man who resembles Noah—and damn, really reminds me...crazily... *of Ace.*

I must really be losing it if I'm hallucinating this badly. My dream made his memory feel so fresh again.

Get a grip!

"Colton, meet Dusty Rose, the newest member of the Invested Enterprises team."

"Dusty. A pleasure. Colton Maddox." His voice has the same deep huskiness as Noah's, but where Noah's tone is warm, Colton's comes out as mischievous and walk-the-line playful. Colton's large hand finds its way into mine, holding on for a fraction of a second too long. His eye contact is so direct it makes me blush. "I'm Cash and Noah's younger, much better-looking brother."

Penelope smiles at him almost giddily, her slick HR professionalism slipping as she giggles like a schoolgirl. "I do my best to keep our new recruits away from you as long as possible, Colton." Does he have this effect on everyone?

"Nice to meet you, Colton."

"Dusty will be part of Evan's team," Penelope tells him. "She's joining us from Stellar Investments in Austin, Texas."

"Well, yeehaw," Colton laughs and, as much as the comment might be borderline obnoxious, he has the easy charm to pull it off.

"Is Cash in his office?" Penelope asks.

"Yeah, he's in," Colton says. "And in a bitch of a mood. Almost bit my head off five minutes ago."

Penelope glances at her iWatch. "Cash always wants to meet the new starters. I'm sure he won't mind a quick meeting. I told him I was bringing Dusty up to meet him."

"Good luck," Colton laughs.

I follow Penelope to the elevator and once we're inside, she shakes her head almost sheepishly. "Just ignore Colton." Like she takes Colton's playfulness as her own personal responsibility. "He's just way too cocky for his own good."

Which makes me wonder what Cash will be like. I hope we're not catching him at a bad time.

The elevator doors slide open and I follow Penelope into a foyer with three desks and three large wooden doors. The offices of Cash, Noah and Colton, I'm assuming. There's also a hallway that looks like it leads to several glass-walled meeting rooms.

A petite woman with a dark brown bob and black-framed glasses looks up from one of the desks.

"Hayley, this is Dusty Rose, our newest employee."

"Hi, Dusty. Mr. Maddox is expecting you." Hayley presses an intercom and says, "Dusty Rose is here to see you." She's no-nonsense and seems like the perfect gate-keeper a CEO needs in charge of his door and his diary. One of the doors makes the clicking sound of a lock unlocking. "Penelope, Noah wanted you to look through this list with me before lunch. Do you mind?"

"Not at all, I'll do it now," Penelope says. "Dusty, go on through. It's the door on the left. I'll be right with you."

I'm not sure why my heart is beating fast. Some sixth sense feels like it's tuning in to a cosmic wavelength. I have no idea what that means, except that I'm an intuitive person and my intuition is currently being slow-zapped by a high-wattage electric current.

As I open the door and cross the threshold into Cash Maddox's office, my eyes are immediately drawn to the view through the floor-to-ceiling walls of windows. You can see the entire city from here. And on such a bright day, the office is flooded with light, casting the man sitting at the desk into relative shadow. I can't make out his face at first, but there's something *very* familiar about his outline, his frame and the way his suit clings to his muscles.

It takes a moment for my eyes to adjust to the brightness, but when they do, my heart leaps into my throat.

It can't be.

But it is.

Holy shit. You've got to be kidding me.

He's the fucking CEO?

Cash Maddox, my new boss…is *Ace.*

17

Dusty

IN A MOMENT OF SHEER DISBELIEF, I find myself face to face with Cash Maddox.

The CEO of Invested Enterprises.

Multibillionaire and investment guru.

Fiercely private third son of Benjamin Maddox, one of those old school New York moguls whose family gets mentioned in the same sentences as the Rockefellers or the Vanderbilts.

A beast in bed.

One of the most "eligible bachelors" in Manhattan, along with his brothers, according to Emma.

Ace.

As he stands from his chair, he looks just as devastatingly handsome as he did that night in Hawaii—no, scratch that. He looks better. He looks dark and powerful and freaking dazzling in his suit, with the city view as his backdrop. He radiates alpha male power and unimaginable success.

I've manifested a lot of shit lately, but there is no way on the planet this can actually be happening. My brain is short-circuiting.

But then it slowly revs up again. And it occurs to me that, if I do want to keep this job—which I desperately do because it's not only my dream but also my life raft at this point—then I absolutely *cannot* do…what I want to do.

Which is to walk over to where Ace is sitting and climb onto his lap.

And kiss him.

And unzip his pants.

And take that enormous, hot, thick manhood he's packing in my hands, just like I did in Hawaii. Like I was ready to do in my dream before he disappeared.

God. He guided—no, forced but I was so willing—me into positions I'd never even heard of. His cock was so big and so deep as he growled dirty words.

"That's it, Texas. Fucking ride me. Fuck yeah, baby girl. Look how damn gorgeous you are. Your pussy's so wet and tight around my big cock. You feel so fucking good."

But I don't.

I can't.

I won't.

Because he's now my boss.

"It's you," I manage to gasp.

He walks closer.

God, he's beautiful. Those freaking muscles under that to-die-for suit. The broad shoulders. The hint of shadow across his square jaw. Just…all man.

"You said you were from Dallas." The accusation has a grumpy edge and the bass notes of his deep voice bring back a rush of filthy, delicious flashbacks that make me instantly wet. *Damn it!*

"Austin, actually," I admit. I'd almost forgotten how ridiculously handsome he is.

"Why the fuck would you—" he starts, but the door opens with a flourish of *here-I-am!* energy.

Penelope walks in, chattering brightly. "I am *so* sorry about that little hold-up. Mr. Maddox, have you met Dusty Rose, our newest junior analyst? She's going to be working on Evan's team. Dusty, this is Mr. Cash Maddox, our CEO."

Ace walks over and reaches for my hand, to shake it. His strong grip sends a thrilling little jolt up my arm and a flurry of butterflies to erupt in my stomach. Even blindfolded I would recognize his electrifying touch. And that scent. *God, he smells good.* Leather and mint and that pure, uncut man-spice that's all Ace's.

He's just completely, totally intoxicating. *Especially since I know what it feels like when he unleashes that gigantic orgasm-wand he's got stuffed down his pants.*

What I really want to do is to cling to his broad chest and breathe him in.

I found him!

I don't, obviously.

Ace's gaze holds mine. An entire silent conversation passes between us before I pull my hand from his. The loss of contact feels like an ice bath after a blazing sauna. But I have to be realistic. This is my entire career on the line.

"Dusty Rose," he says, slowly, his eyes burning me with their intensity. "It's a pleasure." I can hear in those husky tones of the word "pleasure" all the intimate things he did to me. *Biting. Licking. Pinning me under his weight. Groaning as he came.*

"And you, Mr. Maddox." My voice sounds steady enough, despite the chaos thumping through my heart. I need to keep this professional. I need to remember why I'm here.

"We're glad to have you on board," Ace says, and there's a hint of steel behind his tone.

Fine. Good. I can play it that way. He's right. We'll pretend like nothing ever happened. I'm glad we can agree on that. "Thank you. I'm excited to be here."

But then, as soon as Penelope's back is turned, his gaze turns darker. He's challenging me, daring me to react to him.

Penelope seems oblivious to the insane sexual tension in the air—I can only hope.

Can she tell my panties are saturated at the thought of fucking my boss right here on his mahogany desk?

Penelope clasps her hands together. "We've got some

final contractual things to go over so we'll leave you to it, Mr. Maddox." I'm wondering if his tone has caused her to cut this meeting short.

Thank God. I need to get out of here before I melt into a puddle on the floor.

As we leave Ace's office, I make a point of not glancing back at him. Which is borderline impossible. Somehow I manage to do it but I can feel his eyes on my back like laser beams.

I exhale with relief when the door closes behind us and Penelope rambles on about the office perks as we take the elevator to the upper level. I nod and smile and try to give the right responses.

We spent one night together months ago. It's over. He's not Ace anymore. He's Cash Maddox.

For the sake of my career and my sanity, Cash Maddox needs to remain absolutely, totally, completely— without even considering any relapses whatsoever, at all, under any circumstances—off-limits.

18

CASH

Fifteen minutes earlier…

"Fuck."

I pore over yet another spreadsheet. We're still no closer to zeroing in on the culprit of this disaster and it's starting to seriously piss me off.

And I'm distracted.

I refuse to admit I'm still obsessed with a certain virgin-turned-sex-goddess who refuses to budge from my dreams and my thoughts. It's like she's lodged herself there, all sultry and gorgeous, torturing me, just like she did that night in Hawaii when I couldn't get enough of how fucking perfect she was.

Right before she vanished into thin air.

The intercom on my desk buzzes. I almost ignore it.

It's Hayley, letting me know that my next appointment is here. A new employee, Penelope mentioned. It's my policy to meet every new arrival. I like to be able to match names to faces and let people know up front what we expect from them.

"Dusty Rose is here to see you," Hayley says through the small intercom.

Dusty Rose.

Something about the name gets my attention.

I'm really not in the mood to meet a new recruit this morning. I'm up to my eyeballs in irate phone calls and paperwork from hell. I consider telling Hayley I'm too busy.

I vaguely remember Noah telling me about a recent interview. He was impressed by some new junior analyst who'd applied. He thought she'd be a good fit. We'd discussed whether it was the right time to be hiring, considering what we're dealing with, but I wasn't about to admit defeat and put our plans on hold because some fucking moron is trying to make a quick buck.

Still, the thought of meeting this woman who may not have a job by the end of the month if everything turns to shit puts me on edge. If she hasn't already heard about the leak, she will soon enough, and then she'll have questions. Which at this stage I'm not sure I'll be able to answer.

I could leave it to Penelope to fill her in on all the details she'll need.

But it's important to at least keep up appearances. Avoidance might do me more damage than good. People might talk. Or speculate. Whoever this new hire is doesn't need to know that we're on the verge of hemorrhaging some serious money. Those particular concerns are way above her pay grade. And I intend to get a handle on things so it stays that way.

Dusty Rose.

Is it me or does the name sound almost…*Texan?*

I click the button that unlocks my door.

It opens.

A young woman walks into the room and…*holy fuck.*

Am I so stressed out I'm hallucinating?

The door closes behind her.

Tex.

My Tex.

She's here.

Have I fantasized about her so much that my brain is playing tricks on me?

She was gorgeous in Hawaii but now, standing here in the middle of reality, she looks a thousand times more beautiful. Her long hair is pulled up, revealing her stunning face. Her eyes are bright, that light dusting of freckles across her nose faded now. Flags of pink warm her cheeks. She's wearing a little black dress that shows off her mind-numbing curves. Gold earrings catch the sunlight. Her full lips branded me in a way I still haven't recovered from. Now, they're painted a shade of lipstick that's somewhere between pink and red. My cock thickens.

"It's you," she says.

I stand up from my desk, still half in shock. I'm wild with relief but also rage. This girl has put me through hell, thinking I might have lost her for good. "You said you were from Dallas."

"Austin, actually."

"Why the fuck would you——?"

I almost jump when the door opens and Penelope swans in. "I am *so* sorry about that little hold-up, Mr. Maddox. Have you met Dusty Rose, our newest junior analyst? She's going to be working on Evan's team."

Oh, I've met her. I've also feasted on her delectable pussy until she came on my tongue. And then I fucked her like there was no tomorrow.

Willing my dick not to get a raging fucking hard-on, I walk over to her, playing along with the formalities.

The last thing I want is for Penelope to pick up on the electricity sparking between us. Dusty is staring at me, shocked, but she's keeping it in check. Even so, her skin is flushed. I wonder if she's wet for me.

I want to run my hand up her thigh and find out, fingering her little clit until she moans.

"Dusty, this is Mr. Cash Maddox. Our CEO."

Slowly——because I get to touch her again and I need to keep my cool——I hold out my hand.

She places her hand in mine, gripping lightly. I'm remembering what it felt like when she gripped my cock.

"Dusty Rose." I can't help the edge to my voice when I say her name. *You little minx.* Our eyes are locked. "It's a pleasure."

"And you…Mr. Maddox."

Call me Ace, baby girl, like you did when you rode my big, bursting dick as we both came hard.

She keeps the handshake brief, pulling back.

I channel my inner aloof CEO, which is easy enough to do. I know how to play it, so Penelope doesn't pick up on the sparking tension between us. After all, my father was the perfect role model for the distant, asshole boss. "We're glad to have you on board."

"Thank you. I'm really excited to be here." Dusty is saying all the right things too, but her voice sounds almost breathless. Even so, there's a resolve to her tone I don't like. A barrier between us.

I have to restrain myself from reaching out to her and pulling her into my arms. Breathing her in, kissing that luscious mouth. She's really fucking *here*. I'm not dreaming her.

It takes all the willpower I possess to turn away from her.

Penelope takes this as her cue. "Right, we've got final contractual things to go over, so we'll leave you to it, Mr. Maddox."

My fingers grip the back of my leather office chair so hard they leave dents.

I watch Tex follow Penelope out the door without so much as a backwards glance.

She's mine.

Tonight.

If I can wait that long to get her alone.

19

—————

CASH

ONCE TEX LEAVES MY OFFICE, the tension in my fists loosens, but my cock hasn't gotten the memo. The fucker is painfully hard and hot. I can only hope my suit jacket hid the worst of it.

I open my desktop and find her company files.

Dusty Rose.

My Texan girl. I *love* this. Her name suits her.

The files are extensive. We're thorough about our research. 4.0 grade point average at her local high school in Austin. Graduated near the top of her class at UT. Employed by Stellar Investments immediately after graduation.

The name Stellar Investments rings a bell.

I looked them up during my search and I do another quick search now. They have branches in both Houston and Austin. They don't list their junior employees on their website.

I would never have found her.

Her body language was hard to read. She was obviously shocked. Flustered. And conflicted.

Is she regretting taking the job?

She didn't give me her name in Hawaii for a reason.

She lied to me about where she was from.

She left without saying goodbye.

Maybe she never wanted to see me again and now her dream job has turned into a nightmare because of me.

Fuck.

This girl has literally haunted my dreams every night since she left me.

We need to have a conversation. I need to tell her about the insider trading bullshit myself so she has all the facts. Normally I wouldn't care about new employees overhearing rumors, but I want her to hear the truth from me directly. This feels important.

I also need to tell her that from the moment I woke up in an empty hotel bed and realized she was gone, I've been obsessed with finding her.

I start typing an email.

to: drose@investedenterprises.com
from: ceo@investedenterprises.com
subject: tex

Dusty,

You are required in my office as soon as you receive this. There have been some recent developments in the company and I want to make sure you have all the facts before you begin your job.

Hayley will show you in.

Cash Maddox
CEO Invested Enterprises

I let the automatic signature remain in place, resisting the urge to sign off as Ace, only because the IT people currently have fucking temporary free rein over all inter-office emails.

I consider changing the subject line but fuck it.

Twenty minutes later—and yes, I've spent nineteen of them pacing and waiting for the ping of my inbox because I'm completely losing my goddamn mind—I get a reply.

to: ceo@investedenterprises.com
from: drose@investedenterprises.com
subject: tex

Mr. Maddox,

Thank you for your message. I've had a briefing

from a few of my new colleagues, so it'll be ace to talk it all through. I'll be able to get to your office by 11.

See you then,
Dusty

It could almost be mistaken for a typo. *Little minx.* My cock throbs hotly.

The time now is 10:27.

Only 33 minutes to go.

Jesus, I'm in big fucking trouble.

20

Dusty

P ENELOPE GIVES me a tour of the rooftop pool, the Sky Bar, the work pods and "chill zones," which are unbelievably luxurious. Clearly no expense has been spared at Invested Enterprises.

Another reason I *really* want to keep this job.

Which means Mr. Best Night of My Life needs to remain firmly in his executive office and far away from my bed.

I could read it in his eyes that he remembers me. Very well.

Which means nothing, of course. He was abrupt, almost cold. As he should be. Whatever we shared in Hawaii is in the past. Where it will firmly remain.

"I'll email you the rest of the online forms you'll need to fill in, Dusty," Penelope says, as we get back to the offices on the lower floor. "I'll send them now."

"Great. And thanks for the tour."

"My pleasure."

Penelope heads back to her office.

I sit at my desk and wait for her email. Lacey is over at the coffee machine, so I take my opportunity.

Pulling out my phone, I google him.

Cash Maddox.

Of course I've wondered what kind of life he went back to after our night in Hawaii. I knew it was possible he was in a relationship with someone else. Or that he was a player on the prowl. I pushed visions of him in bed with other women out of my mind too many nights to count.

Cash Benjamin Maddox, 27, is a New York businessman, investor and philanthropist. He's the third son of A.J. Benjamin Maddox III, who inherited the helm of Maddox Enterprises from A.J. Benjamin Maddox II, currently run by Alexander J.B. Maddox IV. Cash Maddox remains on the Board of Maddox Enterprises but left his role as Vice President three years ago to form Invested Enterprises, where he is CEO and primary equity holder. Invested Enterprises is currently valued at upwards of $10B. Cash Maddox was ranked this year as #13 on the Forbes list of the richest Americans under 30.

Wow.

I continue scrolling.

Cash Maddox avoids the spotlight and is known for his elusiveness when it comes to publicity. He attended last year's Financiers' Fundraiser with supermodel Adora Flynn and last season's Met Gala with influencer Ashlynn Chamberlain. He briefly dated former model and heiress Rylee Winters, daughter of financier James Winters II; Rylee is currently employed as an investment analyst at Invested Enterprises, but the relationship is rumored to have ended after only a few weeks. Cash Maddox has had no known long-term personal relationships and appears to currently be single.

Rylee Winters is a former model and heiress? Why's she even working here in that case? And more importantly, how do I compete with someone like that?

You're not competing, I remind myself. It doesn't matter to me who Cash Maddox has or hasn't dated.

He's single.

Not my concern.

My inner sex goddess is screaming with glee over my chance encounter on the executive floor. But I mentally discipline the little psycho.

He's my boss.

So?

I will not jeopardize my career for an orgasm.

How about five?

I can't help myself. I google *Adora Flynn.* Of course she's breath-takingly beautiful.

I type in *Ashlynn Chamberlain.* Also stunning.

And finally: *Rylee Winters.* Okay, not on the same level as the other two, but she's pretty in a severe, corporate kind of way, with platinum blond hair and bright red lipstick. Three photos of her pop up and she's not smiling in any of them.

Lacey sets a coffee down on my desk, making me jump. "I was making a skinny latte so I made two."

"Oh. Thanks." I slip my phone into my bag.

Lacey slides into her chair. "Did you get to meet the famous and elusive CEO on your tour?"

"Yes," I say, smoothing my hair off-handedly. "He was in."

"Was he a grouchy prick like usual?"

"Uh, no…not really." *Grumpy in a sexy AF kind of way, maybe.*

Lacey takes a sip of her coffee. "Dusty is such a cool name. Is it common in Texas?"

"Not at all. Where are you from?" I'm learning to steer all conversations back to Lacey, so she talks mainly about herself. I've already decided to give her only the most necessary information about myself. I really don't want to be the subject of her next juicy water cooler conversation.

"A small town in Ohio not far from Toledo," she says. "Boring as hell but I miss my brothers to the point of craziness. I went to NYU, so I've been in New York for almost five years now. I love it, of course. *So* much better than Ohio, obviously. The only things I really miss are my brothers, even if they are monster-truck-driving rednecks with no interest in culture whatsoever."

An email alert pops up on my screen.

It's from Penelope. Links to the online forms she wants me to fill in.

I start working through them when another email pops up.

The first thing I see is the subject line: *tex.*

Oh shit.

It's from him.

"What's wrong?" Lacey asks. "Why are you blushing?"

"Oh, it's nothing." I quickly minimize my email screen, bringing back up the online forms. I work on them until Lacey is distracted. She's called over to Evan's desk.

Making sure no one's watching, I bring up the *tex* email again.

to: <u>drose@investedenterprises.com</u>
from: <u>ceo@investedenterprises.com</u>
subject: tex

Dusty,

You are required in my office as soon as you receive this. There have been some recent developments in the company and I want to make sure you have all the facts.

Hayley will show you in.

Cash Maddox

CEO Invested Enterprises

Jeez. Bossy much?

But his stern message is having an effect on me, like everything about him insists on doing. I feel a pulse in a *very* intimate place.

I guess he's referring to the scandal, and it's true it would be good to get the facts straight from the horse's mouth, so to speak.

to: ceo@investedenterprises.com
from: drose@investedenterprises.com

Ace,

I bite my lip, immediately deleting *Ace* and replacing it with *Mr. Maddox*. It's probably safe to assume that internal emails are visible to the tech crew. So I keep it mostly professional.

Thank you for your message. I've had a briefing
from a few of my new colleagues, so it'll be nice to
talk it all through. I'll be able to get to your office
by 11.

See you then,
Dusty

By the time I finish typing my message, I squirm in my chair because the light pulse between my legs is warmer now.

Yikes.

He wants to see me in his office.

Alone.

I delete *nice* and replace it with *ace*, because I can't resist. Then I hit send.

Why am I playing with fire?

I close out my email window and finish filling out the forms. Lacey returns and as I'm getting ready to submit the forms to Penelope, my phone vibrates with an incoming message. I pull it out to take a quick look. I'm always hoping Sky might have some good news.

I said you're required in my office. Now.

Oh my god.

He's texting me now? My heart is racing.

I text him back.

I'm sorry, I'm not sure who this is

You know who it is

How did you get my number?

It's in your file. And texts aren't traced.
Emails are. I need to see you now

Fine. I'll play along with this. But only so I can tell him face to face that we're keeping things strictly professional.

Okay, boss. See you in 5

I wait for the three little dots of his reply but there's nothing.

"Who are you texting?" Lacey asks.

It's a good thing I've decided I am one hundred percent *not* sleeping with the CEO, because nothing would slip past my attentive work colleague. "My sister." A little white lie won't hurt. I stand up from my desk. "I'll be back in a few minutes."

"Where are you going?"

What to say? "I think I left something upstairs when Penelope was introducing me to Hayley. I better go check."

It's a slightly lame excuse and she gives me a curious look but I'm saved when Evan calls her over to his desk again.

I stop by the bathroom on my way to the elevator. I look flushed, but in good way. In a I'm-fully-alive-and-I-get-to-see-him-again way.

Stop it.

You will remain completely professional.

You will not under any circumstances get carried away by how hot he is.

You will absolutely not spend the entire meeting thinking about how well hung he is. Or how good it felt when his big cock throbbed inside you as you came together.

I reapply my lipstick and smooth my hair.

Lacey is chatting with some colleagues over their partitions.

I straighten the skirt of my dress as I walk past them to the elevator, channeling the cool, confident, ambitious Dusty that got the job in the first place. All I'm doing is talking to the CEO about an important issue. It's completely innocent.

As I step from the elevator into the lobby of the executive floor, Hayley looks up from her monitor and waves me through.

I like the fact that this is uninteresting to her, that she hasn't stopped to look me up and down and wonder why I'm already being summoned to the CEO's office—unless this is a regular thing and she's so used to it that, by this point, it's unexciting. Is that a possibility?

I knock on Ace's—Cash's—Mr. Maddox's—door.

21

Dusty

ALMOST INSTANTLY, he opens it. He holds the door open and I walk through, feeling suddenly like I'm entering his lair. I hear the click of the automatic lock as he closes the door behind me.

His gaze roves hotly over my body. "Tex."

"Ace." And my gaze roves—okay, hotly—over his. Now that I'm over my shock, I can fully appreciate the ridiculous specimen of A-list manhood that's standing in front of me. He's tall, and big. His dark hair is thick and slightly more unruly than you might expect from a CEO. He's wearing an extremely well-cut suit but doesn't seem entirely at ease in it, as though it constricts a barely-controlled wildness that's a definite part of his vibe.

The wildness that was like crack to me that night in Hawaii.
And he's doing it again.

"Take a seat on the couch," he commands.

I have the urge to *not* obey his grumpy command but resist it. I don't want to rile him, or myself. That could be disastrous.

So I walk over to the plush seating area by the wall of windows with its killer view out over the Manhattan skyline. The cluster of leather furniture, the swanky built-in bar and this entire scenario reminds me of a scene from *Mad Men*. How many women has he invited into his office, sitting too close to them on his fancy couch?

Maybe he does this all the time.

"I don't," he growls.

I slide him a look as I sit, taking up as little room as possible on the luxurious couch. "Don't what?"

"Invite women into my office. Ever."

"Unless they happen to be an employee." I'm almost surprised I've said it.

He can hear the light petulance in my voice. He can probably guess that I've googled him. And that his little tryst with Rylee Winters is still one of the office gossip club's favorite topics. "That ended months before I met you."

I shrug a little. "It hardly matters."

"Of course it matters."

Ace stands in front of the windows, his hands shoved into his pockets. His big frame is outlined by sunlight, like his silhouette has been forged from molten dreams. He's the epitome of suit porn. I let myself drink in the sight of him.

His height.

The cut of his clothes.

The thickness of his hair.

Everything about him is just…completely, wildly impressive.

As I watch him all I can see is…*my Ace.*

How the hell are we ever going to work together after…that night?

"I thought I was going to lose my mind when I couldn't find you," he tells me gruffly. "Why did you walk out on me like that?"

"That was our deal."

"That was *your* deal."

"You went along with it willingly enough."

"I went *along* with spending the night with you because you were the most beautiful woman I'd ever fucking seen. What I *didn't* go along with was having the best sex of my life and then waking up in an empty bed with no leads, no trail, no nothing."

Okay, I guess we're not going to skirt the issue.

"I even searched the fucking airport to see if I could catch you before you flew out," he says sulkily.

He did? "You're a lot grumpier in New York than you were in Hawaii." Just an observation.

"I'm *grumpy* because you *lied* to me. About more than one thing." I know what he's referring to, of course. Dallas. And the virgin thing.

"That one was more of an omission than a lie."

"You should have told me."

In all honesty, I didn't want him to hold back. I thought that detail might have made him more…careful. "I guess I wanted…the untamed beast."

"Well, Texas, that's exactly what you got."

"I know." I can't help almost smiling as I remember the things he did to me. *I really did get his beastly side. And I loved every minute of it.*

"Did I hurt you?" There's a sincerity to his question that catches me off guard. And angst in his voice at the thought.

"No, Ace. You didn't hurt me." I realize my slip too late, calling him Ace. But he is. *He's my Ace.* "It was perfect."

The dark heat in his eyes tells me he's remembering. "It really was."

Was. Not is. Not will be.

"I'm going to tell you everything you want to know," he says.

I feel my smile fade and my professional persona slide back into place. Enough about Hawaii. I'm here to do my job and begin the next phase of my career. "You mean about your relationship with your employee? That's none of my concern."

"You can stop with the fucking attitude."

I glare at him. He's *so* cocky. And downright rude. *A grouchy prick,* just like Lacey described him.

I absolutely don't want it to and I'm making a point

of not letting it, but his damn aggression is setting little fires along my bloodstream.

Can't fight biology, girlfriend. You love him cocky and rude. You're dying for him to dominate you right over the edge, just like he did in Waikiki.

No.

That can't happen.

I stand up, ready to leave, standing close to the windows.

His smoldering blue eyes pin me in place. "Rylee and I lasted a few weeks, if that. It was hell then and it's hell now. I'm working on getting her fired but I need a reason or she'll sue for wrongful dismissal."

I look out at the floor-to-ceiling view, not convinced. "She seems like your type. Rich. Beautiful—"

"She's not my fucking *type*, Tex," he seethes. "*You're* my type."

I can't look at him. I stare out at the Empire State Building, ignoring that last line of his little rant. It's too much to absorb, here in this wonderland of beauty and success. So I focus on the first half. I mean, what do I expect? He's a hot billionaire. Of course he has a past. It shouldn't shock me that he's slept with at least one of his employees. "Anyway, you were smart to end it. Mixing business and pleasure is never a good idea."

"There was nothing pleasurable about it. The whole thing made me feel like jumping off the nearest skyscraper. I thought I'd never find what I was looking for."

At this, I do glance at him. His fists are clenched and he looks…just…unfairly handsome. He's weakening my resolve with his honesty and all those big muscles that are threatening to bust out of his Hugo Boss. And there's a hanging insinuation on the end of that sentence.

But there's no point in wishing that his insinuation will somehow overlap with the dreams I've had of him every single night. He's my boss now. It can't—and won't —happen again.

He walks closer to me and, just as I'm about to take a step back, he stops walking. "As for the insider trading accusation, someone leaked incriminating information from one of our internal servers. We don't know who it was but we're working on it. Noah and Colton were as shocked by it as I was and we're working around the clock to resolve the situation. I'm not guilty of a crime." He pauses, his gaze intense. "I wanted you to hear that from me."

I guess it's nice of him to clarify that. "Okay."

He's frowning at me like he's waiting for me to doubt him.

"I believe you. Was there anything else you wanted to talk to me about?" I brace myself before I ask the question, but I need to know. "Are you going to fire me?"

His eyebrows furrow, making him look even sexier, if that's possible. "Of course I'm not going to fire you."

"I really want to work here. This is my dream job. It's why I moved to New York and it's what I've been working toward my whole life. I'll make sure that…what happened between us won't affect my work."

He's quiet for a few seconds but his expression is stormy. "Under usual circumstances I'd agree with you. Unfortunately things are different this time."

What the hell does *that* mean? "They are?"

"Yes. They are."

"How?"

"Let me take you out to dinner tonight. We can talk about it then."

It's not a good idea. "No."

He eyes me, almost curiously. Like he's never been rejected before. "Why not?"

"Because you're my *boss*, Ace—uh, Mr. Maddox."

"I don't give a fuck about that."

"Well, *I* do. I can't risk my job."

"You don't have to risk your job. It's just dinner."

I roll my eyes without meaning to. As if we'd be able to keep our hands off each other. "What if I…"

"Fuck your CEO?" he offers helpfully.

I glare at him. "Don't say that."

His eyes are so dark, so full of emotion. I know him well enough after our night of passion that I can read him surprisingly well. He's angry with me. He's conflicted about the decision he's already made. He's as powerless to resist the chemistry exploding between us as I am. And there's that mischief in him entwined with his rage and his lust that's as addictive as a drug.

A low anticipation settles deep in my belly. I don't know how this man does what he does but I have never in my life experienced such a desperate pull of white-hot lust. *Except for the last time, when you surrendered to it.* I'm well aware that my panties are already saturated.

Ace takes another step forward. Reflexively, I take a step back, until I'm half-sitting against the edge of his desk.

He leans in. His big body is so close to mine I can feel the heat radiating off him.

His voice is a low growl close to my ear. "What if I tell you I'll fire you immediately if you don't take your panties off right now and show me how wet that sweet pussy is for me? You know you're remembering how good it felt when you rode my big cock, baby girl."

"*Ace*," I whisper. "*Stop.* We can't do this."

"We can't *not* do this. I've missed you too much." His voice is so low, so deep. "I've been losing my fucking mind, Tex."

Damn it! He's too close. Everything about me is leaning in, drinking in those top-shelf pheromones he's radiating. My breasts rise and fall. My nipples have beaded into taut little wildly sensitive peaks. When Ace brushes his thumb lightly against one, I'm lost. Even my sane mind, which is my only hope, allows me to tease him. "This is wildly inappropriate, Mr. Maddox. I might have to report you to HR."

Sexy little crinkles appear around his midnight-dark eyes. "How about this?" He places his warm palm on my thigh, slowly sliding it higher. "Is *this* inappropriate?"

"*Ace*," I gasp. *Tell him to stop! Walk away from him right now!*

"How about this?" His fingers slowly, slowly rub my clit over the damp, clingy lace of my panties as he watches my eyes.

"Yes," I manage to breathe. *Pull your skirt down and leave this office immediately!*

"And this?" His fingers push the lace to the side, delving, teasing my clit in slippery little circles.

I'm already very, *very* close to coming. But I absolutely *need* to stop this before we take it too far. I've worked too hard to throw it all away for one exceptionally sexy CEO. "*Please*," I breathe. "You can't."

"But you're so wet for me, angel girl. And I'm just getting to the best part." His hungry eyes penetrate my soul. "Do you know how crazy I've been going since you left me? I can't concentrate on the meltdown of my business because all I can think about is you. I've spent all my time googling like a fucking maniac. And now you're *here*." A flicker of emotion touches his expression. "Did you think of trying to find me?"

I almost lie. Instead, I say, "Yes. But I didn't have much to go on."

"I didn't either," he scolds.

"If you'd found me, we both know you never would have agreed to let Noah hire me. This is a complication neither of us need." The whiskey-and-cinnamon scent of him reminds me of the beach bar, the warm breeze at sunset and the gentle roar of the ocean behind us. It felt so damn good to be near him. Then, and even more right now.

His mouth skims the delicate shell of my ear.

Code Five Alert!! my sanity is screaming.

But my inner sex goddess knows she's already won. I don't pull away when he slides his strong, warm hand around the nape of my neck. Or when the fingers of his other hand continue to play me in the most intimate, devastating way, lightly skating and pinching, until the pleasure rushes tease me.

"I can't do it, Tex," he murmurs. "I can't see you and not be able to touch you. Not when I've been going mad with desperation. I've lost too many nights thinking about what I'd do if I ever saw you again to let you walk out of here now."

Of course I should push him away. I know I should fight this. It's pure carnal desire and it's every bit as dangerous as I knew it would be.

"*Ace.*" His fingers are so slick from my own lust, they slide deeper inside me and the curl of them rubs against an insanely sensitive trigger. "*Oh god.*"

"Why are you so fucking wet for me if you want me to

stop, baby girl? Say the word and I will." His thumb slides over my clit, flicking gently, and I'm so close to coming I see stars.

"*Oh.*"

"Oh? Or no?"

My inner muscles quiver around his fingers. The swelling rush of my orgasm is waiting there, ready to crash over me like a tidal wave. But he's not letting it.

"Let me hear you say it."

"*Ooh.*"

"Give me a yes, Texas." Another slow, teasing caress.

Oh, fuck it all. I can't resist this man. "Yes. Yes."

"That's my good girl." His mouth devours mine, our tongues tangling and sliding. My brain is being overridden by the crazy need of my body. I'm confused and disoriented by the rush of heat that's burning between us. I place my hand on his chest and feel his heart pounding.

Ace's fingers slide from my body. He grips me, ripping my panties, lifting me so I'm perched on the edge of his desk as he unfastens his pants. His gigantic cock springs free and—*oh my god, I've missed him so much. I want it. He's mine.*

I reach for his huge shaft, taking it in my hand, fascinated by the velvety heat, the long, hard steel of it and the rigid thickness. I run my fingers along the underside, tracing the veins, smoothing my fingertips over the silky head, swirling the moisture there.

"*Fuck, Tex.* Wrap your legs around me."

I do, and his strong hands clamp onto my hips. His huge cock slides against my pussy and we both moan.

This is so wrong but so freaking hot I couldn't slow it down even if I wanted to. He feels too damn good.

And there's something even more primal about the way he's fisting his cock and rubbing it over my pussy, parting me with it, letting the head *almost* slide inside me. He's already crossed a very definite line and the worst thing is: I want him to.

"I'm on the pill," I gasp. "I thought I might…you know…New York and everything." I want him to know, though: "There hasn't been anyone else, Ace. Only you."

Ace's eyes lock with mine and he stares deeply into my eyes. "There hasn't been anyone else for me either. I haven't been able to even look at another woman after that night in Hawaii. I don't know what you did to me but you fucking branded me with your sweet perfection. I fucking need you. Right now."

Is he for real? But again, just like in Hawaii, I have no idea why, but I believe every word he says to me.

"I've never done it bareback before," he tells me, *as* he's sliding his cock inside me in a way that's very much bareback. "Ever. I take that stuff seriously."

If there was a moment when I could have stopped this, it's now over. We've made the decision to trust each other. And we're too damn hot for each other to overthink it.

I know I'll only have myself to blame if this blows my

whole world up, but everything about me is centered in the place where his heavy cock is pressing *into me.*

He feels so unbearably good.

Ace isn't conflicted either. "I've thought about you every night. All day, every day. Dreaming of fucking you just like this."

With no barrier between us, the slick, skewering pleasure is unendurably good. My orgasm starts slowly. I'm riding the wave. It's a sure thing, taunting me with the magnitude it's promising.

Ace thrusts and his big cock slides deeper. The stretching burn of his impossible thickness makes me dizzy.

"*Fuck.* You're so damn *tight*, baby. So fucking *beautiful.* I want to fuck you on my desk. I want you to sit on my face and I want to eat your pussy every morning for breakfast. I want to bury my cock so deep and come inside you until you're full of my cum, baby girl. You're mine." He grips my ass, thrusting deep, until I'm fully impaled.

I can feel every vein on his thick cock as he fucks me like his life depends on it.

"*Ace*," I moan and he takes my cry in a kiss, thrusting his tongue into me, kissing me as lustily as he's fucking me.

"Come for me, Tex," he hisses, like he's losing control. "Let me feel you."

"*I am, Ace. I am.*"

The pleasure explodes in a rich, feral rush. Each

ripple of my orgasm grips the huge, thick length of him and he groans like his heart is breaking. I feel the hot throb of him and the flooding wetness, deep inside me. My pussy milks him tightly as he comes and comes.

It lasts a long time.

"Holy fuck, Texas."

We're both panting. Ace kisses my closed eyelids, then my dewy cheekbone. He licks his tongue across my bottom lip as I slowly return to myself.

The chirp of his email inbox tries to bring us back to reality, but we're still locked in this pulsing, secret, pleasure-heavy bond.

Holy fuck is right. "I just did it with my CEO. On his desk."

"You dirty girl. You just got a promotion."

"Very funny." It occurs to me then that there's an office full of people outside that door. Or at the very least, a highly attentive assistant. "I hope that door is soundproof."

I can feel his soft chuckle *inside* me and it almost brings tears to my eyes. I should be mortified. I've very possibly just thrown my career away in a moment of total abandon. And I'm emotional because he feels so good all I can think about is how much I want to stay here and do it all over again. "It is," he says.

The comment jars me a little. Why does it need to be soundproof? Does he do this all the time? *Did he fuck Rylee on this very same desk?* I hate myself for even thinking it right now.

"Hey," he murmurs, looking down at me almost sternly, like he's reading my mind. "Kiss me."

I don't, because all my doubts and fears and questions are swirling through my head, but he tilts my chin up to him and kisses me anyway. Teasing my mouth open with coaxing licks and nips that make my pussy clench around his barely-softening cock, which slides deeper inside me.

Damn him.

"We need one more orgasm each and then we'll go back to work."

"No. I should go." I push at his chest—and it seems amazing to me that we're still fully clothed. My skirt is bunched around my waist, my arms and legs are wrapped around him and my panties are long gone, but other than that we're barely ruffled. It makes our spilling, throbbing connection seem even more erotic, somehow.

And I'm starting to come again.

"One more," he purrs, gripping my ass with both hands, lifting my hips higher so he can slide even deeper.

"Someone's been eating their Wheaties," I breathe.

"That's not all I'm going to be eating, every fucking chance I get."

Oh god, I'm really close to coming again.

"You deserve this after leaving me," he growls. "Hanging me out to dry, *lying* to me, walking out on me."

He thrusts with each accusation, like he's making a point, until I can feel that he's fully hard again.

"Are you Superman or something?" I breathe. "Clark Kent-ing around in your executive office?"

"You could have at least left me your number."

"I didn't know if you'd call."

"Of course I would have called." Another deep thrust *and I am very, very close.*

"You really looked for me at the airport?"

"I had them make an announcement over the loud-speaker. But your flight must have already taken off."

I weave my fingers into his thick hair. I need an anchor. And I want to mess him up. I want to claim him. *He's mine.*

He's reading every squirm and every whimper. His drives are measured and relentless. He coaxes a rising surge. "Come for me, gorgeous girl. That's it. Can you feel me?"

"I feel you, Ace. I feel everything."

"That's my good girl."

His thick bulk pushes the pleasure to an impossible peak, shattering me *again.* I cling to him as my inner muscles work his own orgasm with long, tight, silky pulls. He groans like his heart's being ripped from his chest.

After the waves calm, Ace strokes my hair sort of absent-mindedly. "Tex?"

"Yeah?"

"I think I'm addicted to you."

I laugh a little. "Or maybe you just like sex."

"I especially like sex with you. With no barriers. That right there is the best thing that's ever happened to me." His inbox chimes again. "Fuck," he growls.

He kisses my face. Then he gently pulls himself from my body with a gush of liquid.

Wow.

He stands above me, all hulking and outrageous. His mussed-up hair frames his heart-breaking face. Even though I might lose everything for what I just did, I *love* this. The cool, unapproachable top-floor CEO turned untamed sex god.

You've lost your mind.

Yes. And it's almost worth whatever happens because nothing has ever felt so good as he feels.

Ace pulls some tissues from a box on his desk and cleans me. "I've made a mess of you."

It's incredibly intimate, and the thread of tenderness almost overwhelms me. There's a closeness between us that the reality of this situation shouldn't really allow.

He helps me up and smooths my skirt back into place. Then he picks up my ruined panties from his chair and holds them to his face, taking a deep breath. "These are mine. I'll know you're at your desk without them, your wet little pussy overflowing with my hot seed."

I bite my lip. *Yikes. It's true.*

"What are you doing to me, Texas?"

I almost say, *working for you?* But it sounds wrong. "Leaving you."

He frowns at me. "Until tonight."

"No. Ace—"

"Tonight," he says again, in his CEO's voice.

"I don't think it's a good idea."

"It's the only idea I can live with."

"So…I'm going to be your dirty little secret? Is that how this works?"

"We're going to be each other's dirty little secrets. No one has to know. The last thing the company needs is another scandal right now."

"Am I a scandal?"

"Since the second I saw you."

I shake my head. This is crazy. "Maybe…we just needed to get it out of our systems. It was a shock to see each other again and—"

"We both know that's not true. Nothing is out of my system. In fact you've just made my problem a hundred times worse." He steps up behind me, his hand gripping my hair and pulling lightly. He leans in and presses his mouth to my neck, biting gently, licking. "I'll see you tonight. We need to have an actual conversation. Without you jumping my bones before we can talk."

I give him a look and he grins.

Damn, he's beautiful.

"My driver will pick you up after work."

"I'm really not sure if—"

"If you're serious about working here then I'm afraid I have to insist."

I hate that he's putting me in this position. He's using his power over me to get what he wants. He's not inviting me for coffee, somewhere impartial where there's no chance our conversation will turn into anything more. He's bringing me to his home, straight into the lion's den.

I know if I agree to go, I'll end up in bed with him again. But if I don't, then what? We'll just prowl around each other, totally distracted until we end up fucking in the stationery closet and getting caught by an intern on an innocent Post-It run.

At least if we talk, there might be a way to salvage my job. A way to make it work. An arrangement.

And if not? Well, the damage was done from the moment I let Ace summon me to his office and fuck me on his desk.

"Okay."

He raises one eyebrow.

"You're right," I admit. "We do need to talk."

"Good. A car will be waiting for you at five o'clock. The security guard will make sure you find it."

"Fine." I straighten my clothes one last time, wishing I had a mirror to see just how disheveled I look.

Will they know?

I try to smooth my hair. "Do I look…"

"Like you just banged your CEO on his desk?"

"This isn't funny, Ace."

"It's a little bit funny." He grins almost guiltily, tucking a loose strand behind my ear. "You look like the sexiest, most stunningly beautiful girl in New York, that's how you look."

It's hard to know if this is two people who might be on the verge of something real. Or if it's just me literally *dripping with the ultra-hot CEO's cum* on my first day of my new job.

Is this how love stories start? Or is it how people—me, specifically—crash, burn and lose their jobs? "I, um, I guess I'll see you later, then."

"You'll see me when my driver brings you to the back door of my apartment building."

"Back door? Oh. Right."

"We'll be discreet until I can get a ring on your finger."

What? I stare up at him but he smirks and opens the door for me, knowing I can't reply to that now that we have an audience. "Y-yes, Mr. Maddox."

As I go, I try to catch Hayley's eye. I'm desperate for a read on whether she thinks anything is up, but she's buried in paperwork and doesn't seem to notice me leave. Either that or she can't bear to look me in the face after she just heard me begging the CEO to fuck me.

22

Dusty

SOMEHOW, my legs carry me back to my desk like nothing has happened, like I'm not still overflowing because *the freaking CEO just came inside me and it's now dripping down my legs.*

If anyone looks at me closely, I'm sure it's obvious. I can feel the burn from my still-flushed cheeks and the light bruises he made with his gripping fingers.

I'm on the pill.

Please go right ahead and have unprotected sex with me.

Twice.

I really am losing it. I stop in the bathroom to tone down any evidence.

"How'd it go?" Lacey glances up at me as I return to my desk. "You look sort of…wild-eyed."

"Wild-eyed?" I'll take it.

"He's so intimidating, isn't he?"

"Oh…yeah. Totally."

"But a total smoke show, am I right? I mean, all the brothers are. Personally, Colton's more my type. I like the fun bad boys, not the grumpy power players." She studies me more closely and I can only hope and pray there aren't tell-tale signs of what just happened written all over my face. "I take you more as a CEO type of girl."

"No way," I laugh. *Help.*

She looks up as someone approaches. "Oh, hey, Rylee."

"Hi, Lacey." A model-thin woman in sky-high heels is standing there, assessing me with something that's one level closer to disdain than curiosity. She looks exactly like her online photos. Long platinum hair. Red lipstick. A cold, severe expression. "This must be the new intern."

"Not quite," corrects Lacey. "This is Dusty Rose, our newest junior analyst. Lacey, meet Rylee Winters."

So this is Ace's ex.

"Oh, hi," she says, dismissively. "Is Evan around?"

"He's in a meeting with Noah but they should be finished any minute."

"Thanks." To me, she gives an off-hand, "Nice to meet you," but she's already walking toward the open area where several glass-walled meeting rooms are located.

It's interesting to see the differences between us. There are a lot more of them than any similarities we might have. She's willowy and blond, with a steely expression and an haute-couture-meets-Wall-Street style. As I watch her, I can see why it didn't work out between her and Ace. She glides through the office like a shark, swimming slowly, looking for someone to bite.

Or maybe it's just jealousy rearing its ugly head. "She's beautiful," I comment. Stunning, in fact.

"On the outside, maybe," says Lacey.

Evan returns a short time later and we go through some of my work assignments. He's professional and extremely smart but also laid-back and easy to work with. I spend the rest of the day going through the spreadsheets he's given me, and the tasks are a welcome distraction from the constant movie-replay of my morning double whammy of hot sex on the executive floor.

I'm determined to make sure Evan sees me as an asset and doesn't question my capabilities. This office is buzzing with good ideas and brilliant minds. It's fun and challenging and everything I could ever have hoped for in a work environment.

I *did* it. I'm in New York and I have a job that can take me all the way into the stratosphere. *This* is what I need to concentrate on.

I know I'm good at what I do, now I just need to prove it.

And not give anyone in this company any—or at least another —reason to fire me.

I want to make sure my success has everything to do

with how good I am at my job…*and absolutely nothing to do with who I'm sleeping with.*

Slept with.

I feel the resolve that Ace obliterated this morning settling back into place. It's imperative that I draw a line. What happened between me and Ace really, *really* can't happen again. I look around at the scene of my dream job and I renew my decision. This is the way it has to be.

I don't care how hot he is or how good he feels. This is a close-knit, extremely savvy group of people, including two of Ace's brothers. It would be naïve of me to think that Ace and I can sneak around and not have someone find out about it.

I can just imagine Lacey figuring out that I met Ace on a work trip, had a one-night stand with him, then somehow conveniently got hired by Invested Enterprises. I'd never be taken seriously in my job again.

Yes, I relapsed. But I'm determined to keep things between myself and the CEO strictly professional from now on. Even tonight, when I'm alone with him in his apartment.

I'll have one drink and one drink only, we'll talk about what we need to talk about, we'll dissect this whole mess and we'll come to an agreement.

Then I'll politely be on my way.

There will be no touching, no lingering looks, nothing.

We will absolutely not be having sex again.

23

CASH

"WHY IS YOUR HAIR MESSED UP?" Colton ruffles it even more before I can dodge him.

I try to fucking smooth it. "It isn't."

Noah and Colton have just arrived in my office with news. But they seem far more interested in the state of my hair and—*goddamn it*—the fact that my shirt is partly untucked. I shove it back into place.

Both of them are scrutinizing me with curious smirks on their faces. And Colton has much less of a filter. "Are you screwing Rylee again?"

"What? *No.* Fuck no."

"Then why do you look like you just got laid right here in this office?" Colton grins.

"I have no idea what you're talking about."

My brothers are way too observant for their—or my—own good. I slide my hand into my pocket to make sure Tex's panties aren't sticking out. I clutch them in my fist.

She's real. My Hawaiian dream girl exists and I get to see her again tonight.

Noah's hardly more subtle. "Who is she?"

I abruptly change the subject. "There is no 'she'."

I'm acutely aware that I confessed to Noah about the girl I met in Hawaii. I told him she was Texan. I'm half panicking that he'll make the connection.

"Can we please get to the reason you're here? What did you find out?"

I'm grateful when Noah's concentration returns to business. "I just got back from a meeting with the CEO of Sanderson Fitzpatrick," Noah says. "His name is Eliot Bentley. He seems like a decent enough guy. He was as shocked by all this as we were. And he confirmed that the email that contained the insider trading info was sent from our office and was addressed to a person at Sanderson Fitzpatrick who doesn't exist."

"Doesn't exist?"

"We know the email was sent <u>fucm@sandersonfitzpatrick.com</u>," Noah says. "What we didn't know is that there's no one at the company with those initials or a name that's even remotely similar to whatever that means. There never has been."

My brain still isn't functioning as well as it should be after the most intense two orgasms I've ever had in my goddamn life. Sex without condoms is a game-changer.

Sex without condoms with my sweet Texan goddess is fucking mind-blowing. "So the email was sent to their server from ours, addressed to no one and for no apparent reason."

"For one reason," Colton points out.

It's dawning on me.

FUCM.

Fuck you, Cash Maddox. "To bring down Invested Enterprises," I murmur. *It has to be her. It was* Rylee.

Colton is pacing. "So we have an enemy inside our own walls."

Noah sits on the arm of one of the leather couches. "It would appear that away."

I'd suspected it, sure, but I never thought she'd go that far. She hates me so much she's willing to bring down the company and potentially risk jail time. This is serious shit.

I think we're all making the same assumption. "The woman I'm no longer fucking."

"Is she really *that* pissed off about the break-up? That she'd ruin us over it?" Noah is incredulous. Knowing my brother as well as I do, all his break-ups are amicable and his exes still end up adoring him and calling him for advice even months later.

You deserve whatever's coming to you. That's what she'd said to me.

"It sure looks that way," I confirm. "Now all we have to do is prove it."

24

———

Dusty

As PROMISED, the doorman is waiting for me in the lobby of the building. I'm later than I'm supposed to be. Lacey and Evan invited me for a drink in the Sky Bar and I didn't want to turn them down on my first day on the job. Now, glancing at my phone, it's just after six.

"Miss Rose," the doorman greets me, opening the door for me. "Your car is waiting for you right outside. It's the black one with tinted windows."

Of course it is. "Thank you."

The driver sees me coming and opens the rear passenger door for me. "A bottle of champagne on ice is chilling for you, Miss Rose."

"Oh."

"The drive will take around twenty minutes in this traffic."

I slide into the back seat, and the driver closes it

behind me, sealing me into the luxurious interior. It's obviously a wildly expensive car, but also understated. It's the kind of car a super-rich person who wants to remain inconspicuous would drive. I feel like a superstar, but one who's committing some kind of heist.

We pull into the rush hour traffic.

I shouldn't have any champagne, of course. I've already had a glass of wine with Lacey and Evan. But my nerves are on overdrive. Plus, how often do I get to ride in the back of an incognito limo with a bottle of bubbles on ice? YOLO and all that. So I pour myself a glass, sipping as I watch the fashionable people walking along Fifth Avenue.

This is it, the life I've always dreamed of.

Except for the part where I now have to resist my hot billionaire boss, because the last thing I want to do is sabotage my entire career by sleeping with him—again.

I'm determined to have iron-strong self-restraint this time. So I steel myself for what's coming and fortify my courage with another sip of Moët.

Exactly twenty minutes later, the car pulls up to the curb and the driver gets out to open the door for me.

No sooner have I thanked him when another doorman opens another door. "Miss Rose. Please take the elevator up to the top floor. Mr. Maddox is expecting you."

I'm still getting my bearings in New York, but I'm pretty sure we're on Madison Avenue, somewhere around

57th Street. If this is the back entrance then his apartment must be on Park Avenue.

It's not just the silent speed of the elevator that makes my stomach do a funny little swoop. It's the thought of seeing him again. Being alone with him. And I shouldn't have finished that second glass of champagne. I need every single inhibition I possess to resist him. I'll definitely make a point of drinking water from here on in.

As I step out of the elevator into the spacious penthouse lobby—which only has one door leading off of it—it dawns on me just *how* rich my new boss is, and how different our lives really are.

The foyer to the penthouse is outrageously swanky, with huge windows, black marble walls and a marble table with a vase that looks like it could be Ming Dynasty or something equally ridiculous.

The door of the apartment opens. Ace is standing there. He leans one burly shoulder against the doorjamb.

I know right then that I am in deep, deep trouble.

"Hey, Tex," he drawls.

"Hey, Ace."

He's wearing a pair of worn jeans that hang low on his hips and fit his big, lean body like he just stepped off the set of Yellowstone. Which he shouldn't. It's unfair for him to be this gorgeous and this…*hot*. And when I say hot I mean *scorching*. His masculine beauty hits you like a freight train.

His white cotton button-down shirt is open to the

middle of his chest. I've never seen Ace dressed this casually before, probably because I've only met him twice, both in semi-business settings. I try not to think about how, both times, I was having sex with him practically within the hour.

No wonder.

That is not, however, going to be happening tonight.

Yeah right. Would you look at this guy? He's a freaking god.

Not happening.

I am a very restrained and highly professional woman, taking New York by storm. I've worked my ass off to get here and I'm determined, no matter what curveballs life throws at me, to keep my dream job. Even if it means resisting this dream man. I'm not naïve enough to think I can have both. Life has proven to me that things never work out like you hope they will.

Except for meeting Ace at the beach bar, just like Earl and Lucas and the whole Karma thing seemed to promise.

But I'm not in Hawaii anymore.

Ace steps away from the door to make space for me to enter. "Come on in, Texas."

I step inside the most insanely luxurious apartment I've ever seen in my life. It's absolutely palatial. Floor-to-ceiling windows frame the entire apartment. One thing I'm learning about New York is that windows equal money. Windows with outstanding views equal lots of money. And windows with views like *this* when paired with vast amounts of floor space and decorated with this much stylish furniture equals *insane* amounts of money. It boggles the mind to think about how much something like this would cost.

Large arched doorways offer tantalizing views into a formal dining room and a gleaming, immaculate chef's kitchen. Rustic wooden beams, leather furniture, inlaid bookshelves and lamps casting golden light soften the masculinity of the place, giving it a surprisingly romantic feel. Gorgeous wood floors are overlaid with thick, plush-looking Persian rugs.

A sliding door opens out onto a low-lit patio area that's as big as the interior. There's an outdoor seating area with couches, opulent outdoor lighting and leafy plants. There's even a hot tub with steam rising off of it, overlooking the view of Manhattan.

Wow.

In Hawaii, we were on a more even playing field. Yes, he was in the penthouse, but I only found that out after we'd talked for a while. For all I knew, his company could have been paying for him to be there. We met at the bar like two vaguely normal, everyday people.

But nothing about Cash Maddox is ordinary.

"I like what you've done with the place," I comment off-handedly, trying not to be too stunned by my awe.

"Thanks," he smiles, walking over to the bar. "What'll it be? Pinot Grigio? Dom Perignon? Whiskey on ice?"

"Just water for me, thank you."

His grin widens and he pops the bottle of Dom

Perignon, pouring two flutes. "Oh no you don't, gorgeous. You promised me one drink together."

"I said we needed to talk, that's what we agreed to."

"Just one. Then I'll take you home."

Ace is going to YOLO me right over the edge if I'm not careful, but what the hell. I feel like I'm living inside in a dream right now. "All right, just one."

He hands me a flute and I take it. Then he clinks his glass against mine. His blue gaze is playful. "To stars aligning." His shirt sleeves are rolled up, revealing the arm porn of his hair-dusted, muscular forearms.

The same ones I clung to as he was fucking me with that ginormous cock.

Stop it.

His scent is clean and woodsy, his hair still barely damp from a shower.

Which reminds me that I'm still in my work clothes after a very busy day—*which happened to include getting laid with no protection by my boss on his mahogany desk.*

I'm still not wearing any panties.

I ignore the fact that Ace is clearly also remembering our morning relapse. His eyes rove over every inch of my body as I take in the luxurious surroundings.

"Take a seat," he offers.

I do, and he sits next to me on the leather couch. Our knees aren't quite touching and I make a point to keep my thigh from rubbing against his. "Your apartment is very nice." It's so much of an understatement it's laughable.

"I bought it a few years ago, right after we started really getting some traction. Unfortunately my father never got to see it. He died before things got going for us."

"I'm sorry."

He shrugs it off but I get the feeling there were layers to his relationship with his father. "Tell me about your family. Are your parents still in Austin?"

"My mother is. My father walked out on us a long time ago."

"I'm sorry to hear that. That's tough."

"We were better off without him."

"How old were you when he left?"

"Four. My mother tried to track him down and eventually she did. He'd changed his name and was living a different life."

"Fuck." He seems sort of shocked by this information and I'm reminded again that it *is* shocking, that your own father would run out on his family like that.

"And then he died in a drunk driving accident."

"I'm sorry."

I shrug a little. "I'm mostly over it."

He contemplates me for a few seconds. "I imagine it would be very hard for you to trust men after that."

He's perceptive. "I imagine you might be right."

It occurs to me that Ace and I actually know very little

about each other. I'm sure he's googled me, like I googled him, as soon as we found out each other's real names. But I don't have much of an online presence. I was always too busy working for social media.

"Sounds like your father was a real asshole." He's watching me thoughtfully, like he's picked up on my most deeply-buried and tangled emotional issue. Which is true enough. "Something we have in common."

As sexy and astute as he may be, I remember why I'm here and what I'm supposed to be doing. "We don't know each other very well."

"That depends on how you define 'know'." His eyes glimmer in the golden lamplight. "That's why we're here. To get to know each other a little better. Besides, what I do know about you so far I really fucking like."

I can't help a small smile from escaping. "In a professional capacity, I'm sure you mean."

"Yes. But also in an I'm-addicted-to-you capacity."

That's my cue. "Which leads us nicely into the reason we're here tonight, Ace." I say it gently, trying to stay strong. "To set some boundaries. You're my boss, which means that…what happened between us can't happen again. This job means everything to me. I've spent my entire life trying to get here." I almost feel emotional about how true that statement is. "And, as…"—I wave a hand over the spectacle of him— "…gorgeous and perfect and hot and successful as you are, and as crazy as the chemistry between us seems to be, I can't go there again."

"Go where?" His blue eyes are dancing. He's not taking this seriously at all.

"You know where. I mean it, Ace. We can be friends. Business acquaintances. I'm your employee and you're my CEO. We'll still see each other all the time. But that's all this can be."

He tops up my glass of champagne, which I've only taken a few sips of, that's sitting on the chunky wooden coffee table in front of us. I'm resolved not to finish it. Then again, I might have just one more sip because this is harder than I thought it would be and he's so beautiful and built and has those blue eyes, not to mention that this space is romantic and basically like living in a fantasy world.

But I can't be lulled into an erotic haze again.

The stakes are too high.

"So," I continue, "I just wanted to make myself clear, since we're here to talk this through. We got…well, we got it out of our systems and from now on we need to keep our relationship purely professional. You'll call me Dusty and I'll call you Mr. Maddox and that will be that. No more Tex. No more Ace. Okay? Are we on the same page?"

Ace takes a long sip of his champagne. "Actually, no. We're not on the same page at all. How about we discuss it in the hot tub?"

"What? No."

"Come on."

"No. I'm not going in the hot tub with you."

"Why not?"

I say it patiently. "Because of what I just *told* you, of course."

Mischief lightens his sapphire eyes in that way that makes him the most irresistible man I've ever, ever seen. "Unfortunately, I haven't gotten anything out of my system, Tex. Quite the opposite. And there are a few things I need to say to you. But I'm not sure you're ready to hear them."

"What things?"

"As I said, I don't think you're ready yet."

"I'm ready. Just tell me." I get a sinking feeling in the middle of my chest. Is this the part where he fires me, even though he promised me he wouldn't?

I force myself to remain strong. Whatever he's about to tell me, I'll figure it out. I can live with Emma for a while. I can hit the mean streets of New York again and resume my job search. Nothing could ever compare to this job, but…actions have consequences.

And there were actions.

Lots of them. Extremely hot ones that I can't entirely bring myself to regret but *damn it! Why did I fuck up my entire life?*

"First of all, all your student loans have been paid in full."

I blink, stunned. "What?" I can't have heard that correctly. My student loans are massive.

"Your mother's house in Austin has been purchased in a cash sale with her name on it."

I blink again. "I don't—"

"Your sister has a new manager. Her name is Roxie Tucker. She's one of the best managers in the business and she sees huge potential in Skyler's talent. I had her check out Sky's Spotify."

More blinking. "What?" I must be drunk. Am I hallucinating?

"And that brings us to you." He clinks his glass against mine. "You'll keep your job but I'll be considering you for a promotion—*if* you continue to perform as well as you did at Stellar Investments. You were underutilized there."

I shake my head a little, trying to clear it.

"You'll keep your apartment, of course, but you'll spend the weekends with me, starting now."

"I—"

"It's non-negotiable."

I stare at Ace, my brain a jumble of shock, disbelief... and anger. "You can't do that."

"Do what?"

"Any of it. Why would you do all that?"

"Because I want to make all your dreams come true. It's what I do now."

I can't get my head around this. "You really paid off my student loans?"

"Yes."

"But…why?"

"Because."

"Because why? Ace, you can't just…*do* that. Out of the blue."

"Actually, I can. And I have."

I'm still processing what he's just told me. The sheer overload doesn't want to sink in. "You bought my mother's *house*?"

"Everything's in her name. There's also an account set up that'll drip-feed her tax payments for the next five years."

"Ace. You shouldn't have done all that without asking me."

"I knew you'd say no, and it wasn't really a yes-no sort of a situation."

"Ace, I'm not…a charity case."

"Of course you're not. You're the opposite. That's not why I did it."

"Then why did you?"

"Because I want to make your life as easy and happy and stress-free as I possibly can. I don't want you to have to worry anymore. About anything. I want you to be able to live your life as the very best version of yourself. Which means I'm going to make sure, from now on, that all the things that have dragged you down in the past don't drag you down anymore."

My eyes suddenly pool with tears. I don't want them

to but he's hit some kind of reservoir inside me. That is without a doubt the nicest thing anyone has ever said to me. Ever.

He wipes a tear with his thumb, even though I don't want him to do that either. More tears well and fall until I'm sobbing against his chest as he strokes my hair.

I don't want him to feel so comforting and warm. I don't want him to smell so damn good.

I have no idea where this gush of emotion is coming from but it wants *out*. It's the *relief,* maybe, that's indescribable.

"That's my girl. I've got you."

I cry out what feels like years' worth of angst, worry and fear until Ace's white shirt is wet with my tears.

When I finally regain at least some of my composure, my common sense breaks through the rest of this wild torrent of emotion.

"Honestly, though. I can't accept any of this, obviously," I tell him. "You'll have to take it all back. All of it. I mean it. I appreciate the thought. Really, I do. But it doesn't make any sense for you to do all that."

"It's just money, baby. I have shitloads of it. And I mean shitloads."

"You don't need to...*buy* me, Ace."

He laughs. "I'm not *buying* you, Texas. I'm *freeing* you. Because you've freed me. It's only fair. No strings attached, just the way you like it. I just felt like I owed you one."

"But…what do you mean? Why do you owe me one? How have I freed you?"

Ace sighs, sort of soulfully. "I'm twenty-seven years old, Tex. And you know what? I don't know if I've ever been happy for a single fucking day of it. Sure, there have been plenty of times with my brothers, when we've had fun and felt close. But all the rest of it—" He waves a hand at the space around us, or the universe itself, maybe. "*None* of it. Not the silver spoon upbringing. Not the huge hole my mother left in the middle of our family when she died. Definitely not the strict father or the boarding schools. Not the family legacy or the money. Not even the building of my company—which is now in some deep shit and I can't even bring myself to *care*, because I'm too fucking obsessed with *you*. Not the apartment. The houses. The cars. The fucking portfolio. *None* of it, Tex, actually made me *happy*."

I don't even know where he's going with this. "It… didn't?"

"No. It didn't."

"Well…that's sad."

He throws up his hand, in a *right?* gesture. "It *is* sad. And I'm not even sure I fully realized how sad it was until *you* showed up. Because you know what *does* make me happy?"

"What?"

He gets a sort of dreamy, nostalgic look. "That sweet memory of seeing you walking along the beach that day in your little leopard print bikini with your sassy little attitude. Fuck, you looked beautiful. Catching that wave. Falling off but climbing back onto your surfboard with the biggest smile on your face. Feeling like I could wring that little surfer punk's neck if he so much as laid a finger on you. That surge—for the very first time in my life—of jealousy. Of pure, uncut *happiness*. It was fucking *intense*, Tex. And you know what was even more intense?"

"What?" I'm sure I look like a hot mess but I don't even mind.

"Thinking you'd left the next morning and wondering why the fuck I didn't run after you that very first night. I was sitting there getting ready to change my flight, to leave the next morning. But I changed my mind. You know why?"

"Why?"

"Because I was hoping to run into you again. And then, there you were, sitting at the beach bar in your little green dress that basically made all my dreams come true while also giving me an instant fucking hard-on that hasn't gone down since. And I don't *have* dreams like that, Tex. I'm not a fucking *dreamer*. Never have been. I'm an investor. I'm a hard-ass numbers guy without a romantic bone in my body—until that moment. You turned me into someone who wanted to fall in love. Like, *hard*. Deep. For *real*. As soon as I saw you, I wanted you more than I've ever wanted—*needed*—anyone or anything in my goddamn *life*." He's staring into my eyes with a blazing intensity. "You want to know what was even more intense than that?"

I'm so riveted and sort of deeply, raptly in love with this man and the way he looks and the things he's saying, I can't move. "What?"

"*Tasting* you for the first time. Fucking hell, baby, you're heaven on earth. You fucking *slayed* me. I was instantly, totally addicted. And it only got worse—*exponentially* worse, Texas. Tasting you, holding you, being *inside* you as you came around my spilling cock. I couldn't believe how fucking *beautiful* you were and how good you felt. Nothing in my life compared to that. And you want to know what's even more intense than *that*?"

My breath hitches as I continue to recover from my crying jag while at the same time try to deal with all the things he's telling me. "What?"

"Thinking I'd *lost* you. Discovering it was your first time after you walked *out* on me. Chasing after you but it was like you disappeared into thin fucking air. Do you know how *crazy* that made me?"

I shake my head a little.

"Very. Fucking. Crazy. And *then*, you walk into my office this morning in your little black dress, looking like you'd just materialized out of my wildest, manic fantasies. I *found* you. I thought—no, I *knew*—that I'm fucking in *love* with you. I don't care if we just met each other. I've been able to think of literally nothing but you since you left me. Nothing. I don't care if you work at my company,

Tex. I don't fucking care! That's not a stumbling block because I won't let it be."

Wow. He just pulled out the L word.

I mean, these are without a doubt the sweetest things anyone's ever said to me. But the realist in me pokes her head through the fog of wanting to believe him *so badly*—because he's perfect, it's the only way to describe him. "But...you hardly know me, Ace. We've met...twice." Okay, both times were extremely orgasmic and downright magical, but still. This is the little girl with major abandonment issues he's dealing with. The one who's never known a man that's stuck around. "What if you end up changing your mind?"

"That's not going to happen."

"What if it does?"

"Then you'll still have a job and no student debt."

I don't say it. I can't say it, after all the things he just told me.

"Tell me what you're thinking right now," he demands.

"It's nothing. Never mind."

"Say what you were going to say." With our history, I guess it's understandable: he gets agitated now, I've noticed, if I'm not completely honest with him.

"It doesn't matter."

Sternly: "Tell me."

I say it softly. "Because...I could sue for wrongful dismissal?"

His lightness instantly fades at the reference to Rylee and his eyes flash. His voice is gruff when he continues. "You think I say what I've just said to you to every woman who comes along?"

"No, Ace, that's not what I—"

He lifts me into his arms. "All right. You doubt me, that's fine. I need to prove myself, I can do that. All this has happened at the speed of light and there's a lot to lose, I get that. I have no problem proving myself to you. I'll fucking prove myself right now."

"Ace. I don't *doubt* you. Where are we going?"

"To start phase one of proving that I'm not making this shit up."

He sets me down on my feet next to the hot tub. There's a sort of tropical-leaf privacy screen around part of it, and we're higher up than all the buildings around us. With the open air around us and the view, it feels like we're looking out over the entire world.

Slowly, watching my eyes with a dark fire in his, like he's challenging me, he pulls on the tie of my dress. Despite all my earlier resolve, I don't stop him. I don't know why. I'm too far gone. He's not the only one with the L word etching itself into his heart, even though it's the very last thing I expected or even wanted.

Ace eases my dress over my shoulders and it falls away. It has a built-in bra, my panties disappeared early this morning and I left my shoes at the door. So I'm standing here completely naked.

"Fuck, you're beautiful," he murmurs. "It's a crime for you to wear clothes, angel girl. Now get in."

Of course I could refuse. I could storm out of here—tipsy, horny and half in love—and stick to my original game plan.

He just obliterated the money problems that have plagued my family our entire life, set my mother up and is giving Sky a real chance.

Because I made him happy.

None of this feels real. Maybe I'm dreaming.

And that hot tub really does look inviting…

Damn it!

So I climb into the warm water as Ace goes to get the champagne and our glasses. The warm, bubbling water feels like heaven.

Ace returns and pulls his shirt over his head, revealing his sculpted shoulders, broad chest and those killer abs I've been dreaming about since our night in Hawaii. He takes off his jeans.

Oh. My. God.

His giant cock is fully hard, taut against his stomach, veined and hot-looking.

I am done for.

Who was I kidding coming here, thinking we'd actually sit there chatting over canapés and champagne and keeping a respectable distance from each other? I swore I would draw the line yet here I am, naked with him in his hot tub. We're like magnets who can't resist each other's pull.

Girl, you can't argue with physics. Or biology. Or scorching hot chemistry. Especially when it's this well hung. And especially *when it gushes heartfelt soliloquies about how it thinks it might be in love with you.*

He sits back against a few of the jets, which make the bubbles fizz up around his shoulders.

It's overwhelming, the magnitude of the shifts my life keeps taking.

He hands me my glass of champagne. "Drink it."

"Or what, boss?" I sass him. "You'll fire me?"

"Or I'll stuff my cock into that dirty little mouth."

I glare at him, ignoring how my body responds to him. I'm mad at him for taking liberties with my life. Who does he think he is? It's crossing a line. I want to take out my emotional overload on him. "Go ahead. I dare you."

"My turn first, Texas. I didn't even get to taste you this morning. You were too desperate for me to fuck you."

More glaring. *He's not wrong.*

But he meets my glare with a sexy sneer. "I need to feast on that sweet pussy. Come here, baby girl. Give me my fix."

I'm feeling insolent. And so turned on I can't think. How dare he turn my life upside down…with more hopefulness than I can handle? My nipples are insanely sensitive and my pussy feels like it's been dipped in warm honey.

How does he do that? It's so freaking easy for him to reduce me to a pile of primordial ooze.

"Be a good girl and offer your wet, candy-pink pussy to your big bad CEO."

I watch him, twirling a finger through a loose strand of my hair. But I don't obey him. I'm clinging to my very last shred of wondering if he's going to be my downfall. *Or something very different. Like quite possibly the love of my life.*

Ace smiles, easing closer, replacing the finger that's twirling my hair with his own, gently tugging. "You want to know something?"

"What?" I'm surly because I'm so hot for him I feel like I'm going mad. Plus I'm still floating on a cloud of unfamiliar relief. For now, at least. Until I convince him he can't do all that for us. It's too much.

"When I first saw you, I couldn't believe you were real, baby girl. I didn't know anyone could *be* so stunning. You're so damn pretty it hurts."

His mouth is so close to mine. He's so big and sexy. So mind-numbingly masculine.

His lips touch mine in a light, sensual brush. At first I don't respond. But he sinks his tongue into my mouth and groans. When he slides his tongue against mine, I draw him deeper, teasing him because my body and soul are full of more emotion than I know what to do with.

The soft sound he makes is low and savage. Slowly, deeply, he kisses me, as though the taste of me is over-whelming to him. Like he can't get enough.

"Fuck, you're so fucking sweet. I want to fuck your mouth, but first I need to feast on your pussy until you're coming on my tongue," he's murmuring, positioning me, caressing my breasts, twirling my nipples until I moan. "That's my girl. Give me everything. I'll take care of you."

Ace pushes my legs apart, wrapping them loosely around his shoulders as I lean up against one of the raised seats and the jets. He's kissing my thigh and the scratchy burn of his stubble against the tender skin of my thigh is deliciously painful.

So much for refusing him.

I simply can't resist how good he feels. Not just physically, but emotionally. Spiritually. Freaking existentially. He's like a religious experience. I can see the city lights of New York City down below me and the stars up above.

And then Ace kisses my pussy. Gently at first. Then he starts licking and sucking with open-mouthed gusto. Little starry jolts of pleasure vibrate through my body.

I'm already close to coming and he can feel this. He's teasing me, tasting me, driving me crazy with lust. I'm in a trance of hyper-arousal so intense that nothing exists beyond this blooming tide of feeling that's radiating from Ace's mouth to my belly to my goddamn soul.

The pleasure is crazy. He slides his tongue into me, in and out, in and out, stroking the wave higher. And higher. He replaces this movement with his fingers as he draws my clit into his mouth, milking me in greedy pulls.

The waves rise then crash through my body in mind-blowing clenches that send zinging jolts through my entire being. My pussy clenches tightly around Ace's fingers, over and over. I cry out as my body spasms and quivers with the overload of pleasure.

It lasts a long time. Ace licks me gently, spinning the ripples further, feasting devoutly on my pleasure like he's worshipping me.

"Ace."

"Right here, angel." He kisses my clit so slowly and lewdly that if he keeps doing that I'm going to come again.

But then he lifts me from the hot tub, wrapping a towel around me. He carries me to his bed. He dries us both off and lays me down. The lighting is dim and I'm too focused on Ace to take in much of the surroundings, but I vaguely notice that his bedroom is just as luxurious as the rest of his apartment.

He lays next to me. "You all right, baby girl?"

He stares deeply into my eyes and know in that moment, that I could: I could fall in love with this man. Maybe I already have.

You have.

No one ever tells you orgasms forge a bond with the person who gives them to you. You don't just run away from people who can make you feel this much pleasure. Even though it's the only thing I know how to do.

I'm still sort of mad at him. For so easily turning my

world upside down. For waving a magic wand at every single thing about me and somehow claiming it. I'm mad and I'm hot and I want to take it out on him. His cock is warm and rock-hard against my leg. "You promised," I whisper.

"Promised what?"

"That you'd stuff your cock in my mouth. I want to taste you."

His pupils almost entirely swallow up his blue irises, making him look dangerous.

But I feel dangerous too. Dangerously sexy for this big hunk of male perfection. Slowly, I climb down his body. I take his huge cock in my hands.

"Tex," he groans. "Fuck."

"The big CEO thinks he can control everything. But now he's at my mercy." His cock is heavy and outrageously hard. It's silky and hot. A pearl of moisture beads at the tip. I lean closer and touch my tongue to the wetness. I suck gently, licking him with my tongue.

"*Oh, fuck.*"

There's a feminine power to this I wasn't expecting. The bossy, all-powerful CEO is *mine*. He doesn't hold *all* the cards in this equation. The feeling makes me greedier and I suck on him more strongly, taking him deeper.

I want him to lose control. I want to overwhelm him with pleasure, like he's so good at doing to me. My fingers explore as I take him even deeper.

"Get up here and ride me, Texas, or I'm going to come in your mouth."

"Do it," I murmur. "Give it to me." Then I take him even deeper. I explore him with my fists and my fingers, cupping him as I suck on him.

It doesn't take long.

His cock surges and the pumping gush floods my mouth as he comes. I really must be losing my mind because I'm *thirsty* for him. I swallow, but there's way too much. It spills and wets my face.

I lick and kiss his wet, still-pulsing length. It's softer now but not completely. I caress the weighted bulk of it in my hands.

"Tex," he growls. "Come here, baby."

I climb up and he takes me in his arms, staring at me like I'm a vision he can't believe. He smooths my hair. He takes my face in his warm hands and kisses my lips.

"Tonight didn't play out at all like I was planning," I confess.

"Move in with me."

I stare at him in the dark room, lit by the stars outside the windows and the lights of the New York night. "Ace—"

"Stop protesting everything. So what if it's fast. Who cares. I want you with me."

"But I'm still mad at you," I whisper.

"Well, I'm in *love* with you, so there. I win."

I'm stunned. *Can we really fall in love this fast?* "You can't be."

"I can and I am and there's not a damn thing you can do to change my mind. You can't even run from me because now I know your name."

"You're crazy," I whisper.

"Crazy hot for you, Texas. I'm going to make you so happy you'll never want to leave me. And I'm only just getting started."

My eyes sting like I might start crying again but I hold them back. Ace has a way of hitting deeply buried veins of emotion with his off-hand, monumental promises.

I've spent my life digging in, worrying that it'll never be enough, fighting with everything I've got to give myself a buffer against the fear. I don't know if even Ace can cure me of all that, but there's something life-changing about hearing him say he wants to.

"You have to take it all back," I tell him.

"I can't." Ace plumps my breast to his mouth, circling his tongue lazily around my nipple. "All of it's already signed off."

"I'll pay you back."

"You already have, angel, I told you that. Now get up here and ride me. Then I'm going to fuck you from behind when you're all warmed up." His cock is already getting hard again.

Warmed up? And the pulls of his mouth at my nipple are making me moan.

Maybe he's right: it's going to take a few more tries to get this out of our systems.

25

———

Dusty

It's after midnight when we finally come up for air. Even after the shower we took together to cool off (where we ended up doing it against the Italian marble), we're now wrapped around each other, slick with sweat, still coming down from our last orgasm. We're lying on our sides, staring into each other's eyes.

This is all…so unlikely.

So intense.

So absurdly…perfect.

It *shouldn't* be this perfect. In so many ways he's still a stranger to me. In so many others, I know him better than I've ever known any other person in my life.

"I'll be surprised if I can walk tomorrow," I murmur.

"Then I'll carry you." His voice is low when he asks the question. "Why did you wait?"

"Wait for what?"

"There must have been a million guys chasing after you in college. And high school. Why did you wait for me?"

Oh. That. "I guess I never met anyone I really connected with, enough to…give myself to them in that way. I always felt like I was just an object. A way for some jock to relieve some tension or put another notch on his bedpost. Not one of them seemed to actually *see* me. For me."

"And you think…I did?" His eyes are denim-blue in the low light.

"Yeah. You did. Being with you in Hawaii was the least *like me* thing I've ever done. Second only to what happened today at the office. Okay, and third to being here tonight. I'm not usually impulsive. I don't break rules. I don't do anything *casually*, Ace. But meeting you… I guess it just felt right. I didn't want to hold back with you. And I knew it was only for that one night—or so I thought—but it didn't matter. I'd never felt so…"

"So…?" He's eager for me to continue, and it's cute that this hairy, burly he-man billionaire is waiting to hear what I have to say to him so expectantly.

"Like my whole body was lighting up just from one look. And I thought, if I'm going to do this, why not do it with someone who makes me feel that way? I'd always kind of hoped that would happen to me some day. That it would light me up with a real connection."

His fingers weave through the long strands of my hair.

"It did feel real, didn't it? It *does* feel real. It did then and it does now. And I can tell you, Tex, it doesn't usually feel like this."

"It doesn't?"

"No. Not even close."

"I kind of figured it didn't."

He licks my lower lip lightly. "It never, ever does. Until now."

"What are we going to do about it?" I whisper.

He traces his thumb along my cheekbone softly. It's a gesture that makes my stomach do a little swoop. Because he doesn't need to do it. It's extra. He's feeling this very intensely. "Well, first, you're going to spend the weekend with me. I'm going order some food for us. I'll probably shower you with extravagant gifts because I feel like it. And I'm going to make love to you a *lot*. Because I'm addicted. And then we're going to take it from there. Since my obsession with you is on overdrive, that's the only thing that will work for me."

"Okay," I finally say. "I'll stay. For the weekend." It's too soon to think any further than that. I repeat his words. "And then we'll take it from there."

His voice is so deep, his words brushing against my ear as he nuzzles into me, it almost feels more intimate than any of the other things we've done in the past few hours. "I honestly have no fucking clue how I'm ever going to be normal around you." The hard length of his erection presses against my stomach. "With everything going on at work, I know I don't need a distraction. But I can literally think of nothing but how good it feels to be inside you."

He rolls me onto my back, his teeth grazing my neck. He pushes my knees high and the broad head of his cock presses barely inside me. "Do you want me, baby?"

My body's sore and aching but I'm still slippery from the last time he came inside me. "*Yes, Ace.*" Almost before I gasp the words, his cock plunges thickly into me.

The pain is pleasure-heavy. I want more of it. It never feels like enough.

Ace thrusts deep, his cock grinding against my clit as he slowly fucks me.

I see stars. I *feel* stars. Maybe because we've done this four or five times today and I've eaten nothing since breakfast, I'm light-headed, like the world around me is sparkling and spinning.

As he pumps into me from this intense angle, I know he's fully, thickly inside me. I gasp his name with each heavy thrust.

"Look at me, baby girl."

I'm getting better at holding myself back, at not surrendering to the pleasure the minute his cock fills me. But I can feel it starting.

The sweet heat is rising and he knows this. He won't relent. He can tell I'm starting to come. All I can do is moan for him. I can feel the zinging jolt all the way to my fingers and toes. The center of me is pulsing with ecstasy.

I'm writhing and squirming. I think I might be telling him I love him. Because maybe I do.

He thrusts again and it tips me over yet another cascade of rapture. His big cock jerks inside me as his fingers grip me. Ace groans and I feel the warm, thick jets of his cum, filling me. I come again. Even harder. *How can he feel so good?* The pulsing beauty is too much. The swell is excruciating. I can only ride it and wonder if I'll ever recover from this.

I'm grasping his hair in silky handfuls. I'm crying his name.

My lover is some sort of sensual genius. A magician and a work of art, all rolled into one.

In time, I come down. Reality starts to ease its way in. But then I remember that reality doesn't bite quite so hard as it did before this weekend. "I still need to talk to you about all that stuff you did. It's way too generous and we need to talk about that. I'm sure you'll end up coming to your senses."

His tongue plays my nipple, circling it. He takes the taut nub lightly between his teeth until I squirm. "There's nothing more to talk about, except that you'll probably find you have a lot of messages from your family that you'll eventually need to reply to. After I taste you some more and tell you how fucking perfect you are a few more times."

Ace kisses me, answering all my deepest desires,

making all my dreams feel real and true and so, so beautiful.

"*Ace.*"

"Right here, baby."

It's all I'm capable of, so I say, "Mine."

He's smiling that smug smile again and this time I'll admit it's just a little bit warranted. "All yours, Texas. All yours."

26

Dusty

AND so I stay with him the entire weekend.

We shower together, he feeds me, we make love, we talk, we laugh and, occasionally, we sleep.

I wake up with his arm slung around me. We're in his California king-sized bed and I hear my phone chirp from my bag on the chair.

Ace is asleep, so I crawl out from under the relaxed weight of his arm to go and check my messages, which is way overdue. I pull an oversized t-shirt of Ace's on, fish my phone out of my bag and tiptoe out into the great room so I don't wake him, sitting on a forest-green velvet chair by the window, curling my feet under me.

There are a flurry of texts and missed calls from my mom.

Sweet Dusty. It's too much!! Ten thousand dollars? How are you earning so much money already?

Dusty! The bank manager came yesterday and gave me the fully-paid deed to the house!! I can't believe you did this honey! Call me!!

Honey I love you so much. Are you sure about this? Are you sure you can afford it? Please call me xx

Call me sweetheart. Your sister is so over the moon. Roxie Tucker??? How did you manage that??

I guess the new job is going well? I hope you're loving New York. How's Emma?

I still can't believe the house is paid off honey. How did you do this?? Call me sweetie xx

And now our taxes are being paid every month for five years??? Dusty Rose, you are the biggest sweetheart in the world. Are you sure you can afford this?

DUSTY CALL ME

I love you honey. Pls call me xx

So I text her back.

Hi mama. All is well. I'll call you soon. I've been swamped with work but everything is really amazing here in NY and I'm loving the new job!

What to say about the paid-off house? I still want to convince Ace it's way too much and he needs to take it all back, but every time I bring up the subject he shuts it down and tells me it's already a done deal. So I do my best to act like this is all normal and not some seismic shift in my space-time continuum.

> I'm glad you like your surprise. I hope it makes things easier. You've always worked so hard and I appreciate you so much. I'll call you as soon as I get a chance, I promise. I love you mama xx

And then I read the messages from Sky.

> WHAT THE HELL DUSTY ROSE ARE YOU SERIOUS ROXIE TUCKER JUST CALLED ME OUT OF THE BLUE AND WANTED TO TALK ABOUT HOW MUCH SHE LOVES MY MUSIC!!!!!!

> SHE SAID MY SISTER'S CONTACT WHO HAPPENS TO BE EXTREMELY WELL CONNECTED CONVINCED HER TO LISTEN TO MY SPOTIFY AND SHE LOVED IT AND NOW SHE'S OFFERED TO BE MY FREAKING MANAGER!!!!!!!!!!!!!

> And this is incredible timing because Billy the asshole broke up with me yesterday and told me he wasn't going to give me any gigs at the Blue Lounge and I didn't want to tell you but I've kind of been at the end of my rope, Dust

Thank you soooooo soooooo soooooooooooooooooooo much you are the best sister in the history of the freaking world

ROXIE IS SOOOO NICE AND SHE'S SENDING ME A TICKET TO NASHVILLE AND HAS A SPARE ROOM FOR ME TO STAY IN AND SHE'S PUTTING TOGETHER A CONTRACT!!!!!!!

ROXIE'S BROTHER KADE TUCKER (OF THE FREAKING TUCKER BROTHERS!!!!!!!!!!!) LISTENED TO ONE OF MY SONGS AND SAID HE LOVED IT!!!!!!!!!!!!!!!!!!!!!!!!!!!

CALL ME YOU CRAZY BEAUTIFUL WOMAN HOW DID YOU DO THIS????

I'M LEAVING TOMORROW MORNING TO GO TO NASHVILLE CALL ME

ROXIE WANTS ME TO RECORD AN ALBUM ON THE SAME LABEL AS THE TUCKER BROTHERS!!!!!!!!!!!!

I LOVE YOU DUSTY ROSE THANK YOU SO MUCH!!!!!!!!!!!!!

WHERE ARE YOU CALL ME I'M IN NASHVILLE!!!!!!!!!!!!!!

I laugh and text her back.

Hey sis, wow them with your genius and HAVE FUN. I'm sorry I haven't called, been busy with work but I will call you later in the weekend or on Monday. You deserve this. Remember: you're wildly talented and beautiful and amazing!!! I love you Sky Rose. Good luck!!!!! xxx

My phone's battery is on 3% so I go back into the bedroom, fish my charger out of my bag and plug it in.

Ace's eyes are open. The sheet barely covers the low, muscle-quilted, hair-dusted plane of his abs and he looks warm and sleepy and delicious. "Hey," he purrs. "Everything okay?"

"I think it's safe to say that you've made my mom and my sister very, very happy. I still feel like we need to talk about that."

He pats the bed next to him. "Come here."

So I do, crawling back in with him.

"The question is," he drawls, "is Dusty Rose happy?"

"Of course I'm happy, Ace. But I'm still mad that you did that without asking me. It feels so uneven. I don't know if I'll ever be able to pay you back for all that."

"I told you, I owed you one. To me, it feels uneven the other way. There's still more I want to give you to repay you for converting me into a romantic and making me believe I'm actually capable of falling in love."

Despite the fact that his big, rock-hard body wrapped around mine feels more comforting than anything ever has, the die-hard cynic in me has to challenge him. "Stop throwing around the L word. It's too soon for that. And we still have to address the whole you're-my-boss dilemma."

"I've already addressed it."

"How?"

"By coming in your mouth. Once you drink the magic elixir, you own me. You've already transcended my power. You're the queen of my kingdom."

I laugh, rolling back on the pillow. "I'm trying to be serious here."

He presses his tongue to his plump bottom lip, watching my face as though enchanted in a hot, manly way. But his tone is more measured when he continues. "You want serious? Okay, here's some serious. I want to hear about that day when you were four years old and you realized your father had left."

I blink at him and my smile fades. I wasn't expecting that. "Oh. You mean *really* serious." It's the most serious of all my damages. In fact, it's the cause of them too.

Ace seems to get this. "Tell me about it."

And so I somehow end up confessing things to Ace I've never really talked about with anyone else. "Well, he went out for the proverbial pack of cigarettes on a sunny Saturday morning and he never came back. I was on our porch playing with the little horses Sky and I used to love. We had this stable we'd made for them out of shoeboxes.

And my mother came out and sat on the porch and watched us play. It's one of my earliest memories. She sat there until after the sun went down, crying silent tears. She already knew."

Ace's arms and legs are languidly wrapped around me and he holds me close. "That's hard."

"Yeah. It's so cliché. But that's exactly what happened. He disappeared off the face of the earth, as far as we could tell. Later my mom heard from her hairdresser that someone had seen him and that he was working in Tulsa, Oklahoma. So she went over there to confront him and he'd changed his name and was living with his new wife, even though they'd never divorced, not legally."

"What a coward."

"Yeah. He hid from us so he didn't have to take responsibility for us or pay for us. He wanted to wash his hands of us so much, he created an entirely new identity for himself just so he could avoid us. I mean, who does that?"

"Someone who has no integrity, or self-respect." His fingers play with mine absent-mindedly. "I'm sorry you had to go through that. And that your family did."

I sigh, more heavily than I mean to. "You know, I honestly don't care anymore. Once he left, there was nothing left to salvage anyway. I always felt like we were better off without him."

"I'd say you were. And look how far you've come, without his help or anyone else's. It's all you."

"I guess so." And I guess I'm accepting that he's not going to take back his way-too-generous offers. "And now you."

"That's still you," he insists. "Because of the way you smiled at me that night in Waikiki. I was like the Grinch. My heart grew three sizes and busted out of its mean little cage. I felt, for the first time in a long time, like I was capable of real happiness."

This makes me smile. "Well, I'm glad." And I ask the question carefully. "What about your father? He must have been very successful."

Ace is quiet for a long moment. "We had a complicated relationship." I get the feeling he's putting that diplomatically. "We never really saw eye to eye on much. I'd just told him I was leaving the family company to go out on my own. And to top it all off, I was poaching two of my brothers. Needless to say, he wasn't happy about any of it. He was determined that I would fail. We had a big blow-out over it and we both said some things we—or at least I—regretted. Three hours later he died of a massive heart attack."

I look up him. "I'm so sorry. You must have felt like it was somehow partly your fault."

He leans his head back against the plush pillows. The twisted regret is easy to read. "Good guess."

"It's not your fault, though. It's okay for you to want to live your own life and not his."

"He didn't see things that way. Anyway, it turns out he might have been right."

I brush the backs of my fingers against the stubble of his jaw gently. "Don't say that. It's not your fault that someone leaked some info they shouldn't have leaked. You can't control everything all the time."

"I'm the CEO. It's my job to control everything all the time."

I ease him onto his back and climb up his body. My breasts press against the warm surface of his broad chest. "I'm sure the whole thing will blow over. Maybe they've already tracked the person down and isolated the incident."

With one hand wound into my hair, he angles my head, contemplating me, assessing every detail of my face. "It's possible. And it's something I'll need to deal with. On Monday. Right now I'm going to devour the most beautiful girl I've ever seen because I really don't know how to handle how hard and fast I'm fucking falling for her. Now I know why they call it falling."

This is what he does. He convinces me.

I kiss him. His warm lips open mine and the kiss turns slippery and greedy. "Texas, I'm losing my goddamn mind over you."

"Good," I murmur against his mouth.

His fingers stroke me, finding the wetness he knew

was there. He swirls it all over my pussy, painting me with my own arousal, sliding his fingers into my slick, fluttering core. "My girl is always so fucking wet for me." He cups me, playing me with his fingers until I'm whimpering with need. "You're ready for my big cock, aren't you, Texas. You're sore because you can't get enough of me. But still, you want more."

He lays me back, replacing his fingers with his hot, engorged length and I can feel every vein as he slowly, slowly drives in, and in. Gripping me, leaving marks as he sucks and bites on my neck.

Ace makes love to me with a passion he can't quite contain.

I'll admit it's a strange feeling, to feel so incredibly *treasured*. He makes love to me with a kind of unrelenting joy that reaches deep into my body and soul. He doesn't hold back. He's gentle but commanding. He fucks me with a quiet desperation, like he wants to consume me, whispering words to me about how he's never felt like this, how I'm the only thing he can see.

I can tell you this much: when a man like Cash Maddox growls very dirty sweet nothings into your ear *as* you're having simultaneous crazy-intense orgasms, it creates a powerful, life-changing bond. His grip and his groans are *real*. They're full of heartfelt lust that makes you *believe* him. And not just believe him, but to lean in and *feel* him.

I'm falling for him and I'm doing it willingly.

In fact I've fallen so hard for Cash Maddox over the course of one weekend—plus one hell of a one-night stand—the whole thing is kind of giving me vertigo.

For now, he gives in to his obsession and I give in to mine, because we seem to be incapable—at least tonight—of anything else.

27

Dusty

BEFORE I EVEN OPEN MY eyes, I can feel the emptiness on his half of the bed.

My eyes blink open.

"Ace?" He's gone but the duvet is wrapped snugly around me.

No answer.

So I get up and wrap the sheet around myself and wander into the living room. It must be Sunday morning. The slant of the golden rays of sunlight onto the rustic earth-tones of the art and the furniture and the wood make the apartment look like even more of a dream world. The opulent interior, framed by the insane view, gives the space a grand but also cozy atmosphere. Basically I never want to leave.

Ace isn't on the patio so I keep wandering. I find him

in the kitchen. It's as over-the-top as I've now come to expect.

He glances up at me from the feast he's setting out on the marble kitchen island. There are a dozen or more bags and boxes full of food.

"Hey, gorgeous." There's a huge fruit plate with mangoes, pineapple and papaya, bagels with cream cheese and lox, gourmet-looking donuts, an antipasto platter with olives and cheese, French bread, omelets, rashers of bacon, hash browns, maple syrup, fresh-squeezed orange juice and a bottle of champagne on ice. "I had some stuff delivered," he says.

"Wow."

"I hope you're hungry."

"I'm starving."

"No wonder. You really worked up an appetite." That crooked grin. His eyes are a light sky-blue this morning.

I smile, biting my lip. "Guilty as charged."

All he's wearing is a pair of gray sweatpants—Lord, help me—that hang low on his hips. He's shirtless, barefoot, he needs a shave and his too-long hair is still a mess from bed. His chest hair and his muscles and the way his sweatpants hang low on his hips is just so…*the kind of thing you fall in love with. On a second date. Or maybe we can count this as our third.* "There's enough food here to feed an army."

"We need energy. For later."

"What's happening later?"

"We're going to go back to bed. I'm going to give you

a massage then you're going to ride me into a gilded sunset after I fuck you from behind like an animal."

I smile. *God, this man.* "Oh. Again?"

"Yes. Champagne?" I notice he's already poured two glasses. One of them is only half full. He hands me the other one.

"What time is it?"

He checks his phone, which is sitting on the counter. "Two fifteen."

This weekend feels like a fever dream. It's gone so quickly.

And tonight's our last night. Tomorrow morning we both have to be back at work. "Isn't it a little early for champagne?"

"No. We're on vacation for the weekend. Which I've never done before. And which I definitely shouldn't be doing now, but I'm doing it anyway. So we're going to make the most of it."

He's never taken a weekend off. Until me. It's a heady thought, that *I* have this kind of power over him, to make him drop his billionaire lifestyle and his company/investigation/portfolio to hide me away in his apartment and keep me all to himself.

But we can't keep the rest of the world at bay forever. Even now, his phone keeps vibrating on silent mode.

"Do you need to get that?"

"I'll call them back."

I'm really in over my head here. Maybe we both are.

Because what is this? What are we actually doing? I'm staring at my CEO with heart-shaped eyes while he pretends that there's nothing happening outside our little lust bubble.

On the kitchen table, there are two wrapped packages, a big one and a small one. "Those are for you. Open them."

"I don't want you buying me anything, Ace. You've already done too much. This is too—"

"Fast, yes. Inappropriate, possibly. Too good to deny, definitely. Open them anyway."

He lifts me and sets me so I'm sitting near the corner of the huge kitchen island. He lowers the sheet I wrapped around myself to my waist. My exposed nipples tighten in the relative coolness of the open air. But by now, I'm so used to him licking, sucking and feasting on every inch of me that I barely even blush. "No gifts," I tell him.

But Ace goes over and takes the smaller one and brings it to me, opening the sheet and pushing my knees apart so he can stand between them. Those gray sweatpants are doing nothing to conceal a *very* gigantic hard-on. "Please?"

It's almost…adorable—if an alpha billionaire hunk can be described like that. He's excited for me to open his presents.

So I unwrap the present, carefully removing the fancy wrapping paper—so he can save the wrapping paper if he wants to reuse it—to reveal a robin's-egg-blue box. I open it.

Inside is a bracelet. "Ace." Three rows of pink diamonds are held together by inter-locked gold nests, all the way around. "This is…not real, I hope."

"Of course it's real." Like he's insulted.

My huff of laughter is incredulous. "I can't accept this. This must've cost—"

"Tex. Jesus. You don't analyze the cost of something when someone gives you a gift. You just say thank you." He takes the bracelet and lays it over my wrist, doing up the clasp.

It really is the most stunning thing I've ever seen. I hold out my wrist to admire the sparkle of the diamonds, which catch the light, turning it up, then down. "It's so, so beautiful…but I *really* can't—"

"Stop protesting. Here." He sets the bigger box next to me. "This one's more practical."

Practical? Okay, I'm curious. I open the box. And pull out the most gorgeous suede coat I've ever seen in my life. "Whoa." How did he know I love suede? Especially in my favorite fawny brown color.

"I thought, since you're from Texas and not used to New York winters, that it might keep you warm." Here he goes with the adorable thing again. The sincerity in him is killing me. Combining it with his sculpted muscles and that colossal beast inside his sweatpants is almost more than I can handle right now.

I run my fingers over the velvet-soft coat. It's Ralph Lauren. "It even has a little bit of fringe along the back." How did he know I love fringe?

"It kind of looked Texan. I thought it looked like you." He drapes it gently around my shoulders, sliding my hips forward so my bare pussy is almost touching his cock, which is so hard the head has escaped the waistband of his sweatpants. It's hot-looking and there's a slick of wetness.

"It's absolutely beautiful, Ace. But you have to stop—"

He licks his tongue into my mouth, kissing me slowly. I take the offering, sucking gently on his tongue. He groans, pushing his sweatpants lower, positioning his cock so the broad head pushes barely inside me. "You're going to take everything I give you. Whenever I want to give it to you. Say thank you, Ace." He grips my ass and his cock drives deeper.

He's so big but I'm so wet. The thick friction is already starting to make me come. "Thank you, Ace," I gasp, as his heavy, skewering cock slides all the way to the hilt.

Once again, Ace gets his way.

28

Dusty

I'm on the orange couch in the quiet corner of the top floor of the UT library. The place where I spent a good portion of my teenage years, studying like hell to get to where I need to go.

I don't really want to be here. Sometimes I wish I could hang out at the mall with my friends from school. Anyway, I glance at my watch and it's time to go do my paper run. Then pick up some things at the store with the money that's left, which might buy us a loaf of bread and some canned spaghetti. I'm hungry.

Mom will be working. Sky will be hanging out with her friends, boys who are never as nice to her as she deserves.

I'll make us some spaghetti, then I'll keep studying. I have to get straight A's so I can get into UT. I have to try harder. I have to help mom pay the rent and still pass my test, I just have to…

I wake, surfacing slowly from a very deep sleep.

My dreams were vivid and still seep through the edges of my awareness, slowly filtering away.

It occurs to me now, in the darkness of these extremely luxurious surroundings, that I'm *here*.

I made it.

I'm in New York.

I'm where I always hoped and worked and strived to get to.

I'm also in my boss's bed.

Sore and aching from our weekend sex-a-thon, overflowing with his cum, still wearing the diamond bracelet that catches light even in the darkness of his room.

Way to throw it all away, Dusty, some little voice scolds. *Way to fuck up your entire career for that giant orgasm-wand and the CEO attached to it.*

No. That's not what happened here. That's not what this is. It was much more than just sex.

You think he's your knight in shining armor? You think he's different than all the others? You think he'll stick around and never leave you?

I don't know. That one's a little harder to answer.

You're willing to throw away your dream job because you think you're falling for him?

No.

Well, you can't have it both ways! Someone will find out! You'll be the talk of the office. Lacey will have a freaking field day with this.

Fuck.

I know I didn't sleep my way into this job. But if one single person in the office gets the tiniest whiff of what happened here this weekend, I might as well kiss my career goodbye.

Every contribution, every achievement, every promotion or opportunity will all be assumed to be mine because I gave the CEO an awesome blow job. I'll be hated for it—and I could hardly blame anyone for that.

Ace and Tex might be made for each other. But Cash Maddox and Dusty Rose can't be together, it's as simple as that.

That's not necessarily true.

He's your boss! You're his employee! Stop dreaming of a happily ever after when you know they don't exist! Have you ever seen one in real life?

No. But that doesn't mean—

Dusty, be practical. It was a beautiful weekend. But now it's Monday morning.

I wish the little voice in my head would shut up.

Unfortunately, she has a point.

Today's the day reality will sink its teeth back into our lives.

Ace can't run from it any longer. And neither can I.

Either you walk away from your dream job, or you walk away from your dream man. That's your choice.

How can I abandon my lifelong New York dream, the only thing that's ever kept me anchored, just because I finally experienced a serious case of nymphomaniacal lust? My cock-drunk endorphins are trying to ruin my entire life's plans.

They always leave, you know that.

I know.

My dad left. All the losers my mom felt a glimmer of hope about: every single one of them left. All the scumbags and jackasses who have made one promise after another to Sky: gone. I've never known a single man who actually stuck around. It's sad, yes, but it's one hundred percent true.

But Ace might be different. He *is* different. He promised me that and I believed him.

It's too risky! You're playing Russian roulette with your whole life, which you simply can't afford to do.

As much as I'd love to stay in his warm, comforting embrace, my common sense is having its way with me. I'm the only one I've ever really been able to rely on and I have to choose myself and my future, no matter how hard it is.

And it *is* fucking hard.

I watch him sleep. His face is peaceful, his perfect mouth relaxed. The strong nose, the lightly curved eyelashes, the dark stubble of his beard. His features look enchanting in the dawn light. *I love his face so much.*

If I wake him, he'll convince me to stay. He'll look at me with his bedroom blue eyes and he'll wrap his iron-strong arms around me. He'll make me feel like I could ask for the universe and he'll get it for me. And I'll believe every word he says.

Do I love him?

Probably.

And now my inner sex goddess is having her say. *You do. You really do.*

Do I know how to love?

Probably not. It's too fast, anyway. It can't be love. It's just lust.

It's fire. It's the most beautiful thing that's ever happened to you.

Am I willing to throw everything away to find out?

I'm annoyed by the conversation going on in my head. But it's convinced me that I really do need to be realistic. What started with cock-drunk will most likely quickly devolve into career-destroying total humiliation.

And I need to think about Ace too. He has so much to worry about right now. He even said I'm a distraction. What he needs to be doing is concentrating on his business. I don't want to be the iceberg to his own personal Titanic.

We have to put some distance between us.

He can't keep ignoring his company. And I can't throw away an opportunity of a lifetime because there's a handsome man with an impressive (and amazingly perfect and also enormous) dick who wants to keep fucking me.

Very carefully, I ease myself out from under his arm. Exactly like I did once before, all those months ago in Waikiki.

I tiptoe around, finding my clothes and my bag. I check my phone. The time is 4:17 a.m.

Searching for a pen and a piece of paper, I find one.

It's the little pad from his hotel room in Hawaii. I'm touched by this. He kept it, just like I did.

> *Ace,*
>
> *I wish I could stay here with you, I really do. But we need to be honest with ourselves. I work for you. As much as we both don't want that to matter, it does. I loved our weekend together. A lot. But I need some time to figure out how to deal with all this. Please don't make this any harder than it already is. I'm so sorry.*
>
> *xx,*
> *Tex*

On top of the pad of paper, I leave the bracelet. The suede coat is still in the kitchen. I won't be taking that either.

Very quietly, I let myself out of his apartment.

29

———

Dusty

Back on the street, a cab pulls over and I climb in. Tears blur my vision. I fumble around in my bag to find my compact and the key card to my apartment and realize…shit. It's not here. All I can find is the key card for work. My brain does a rewind to where I might have left my apartment key and my stomach sinks. It's still on my desk at the office.

"Excuse me," I say to the driver, "can we take a detour?"

It's 4:42 a.m. when I get to the office. I have my pass around my neck, and with the staff gym and pool being open 24/7, I know I'll be able to get into the building, but I have no idea about the office itself.

The thought of running into any of my new colleagues is somehow worse than the thought of the office being locked. They could probably guess, just by looking at me, what I've been doing all weekend. I need to go home, take a long shower and get into some clothes that aren't the same outfit I was wearing on Friday.

Thankfully, my key card works.

The office is quiet. Only a few lights are on, and the neon signs of motivational quotes that are dotted around the large space.

It always seems impossible until it's done. I think that one was Nelson Mandela. Thanks, Nelson. I needed that right now.

If everyone is moving forward together, then success takes care of itself. That one was Henry Ford, if I'm not mistaken.

A diamond is a piece of coal that stuck to the job. I can't place that one. But it reminds me of a certain diamond bracelet I left behind.

It reminds me of how hard things have been in my life. And how much I want to be able to buy my *own* diamonds. And rely on *myself* to get where I need to go. Like I always have. It reinforces my resolve: I can't throw away my career, I just can't.

I'm relieved to find that the place is empty.

I get to my desk and there, next to my abandoned coffee mug, is my key.

Thank fuck for that.

I grab it and quickly make my way back toward the foyer, when something catches my eye. Movement. In one of the communal work zone spaces. They're glass offices where people can work alone or in small groups. They're soundproof and are designed to allow people to remove the noise distractions of the busy office while still being a part of it.

Someone is in there. The lights are off, but the desktop computer is on, glowing brightly in the early morning light.

Which seems weird. Who would be working at 4:30 a.m.? I mean, we're all on the Type A spectrum around here but this is ridiculous.

Her back is to me but I recognize her hair. Of course I do. There's only one woman with blond hair so long and straight it's like a trademark.

It's Rylee Winters.

So they were right about her. Something is off about this.

She turns, sensing my gaze.

As soon as she sees me, she abruptly closes out the screen she's working on and logs out.

Shit.

She grabs her bag and closes the door of the room behind her. "Hi, Dusty."

"Hi, Rylee."

"What are you doing here so early?" Her tone is light but she gives me a steely—and very attentive—once-over. I have no doubt she can tell I've had a sexual free-for-all of a weekend.

I did my best in the cab to make myself presentable

but I'm not sure I've pulled it off. My hair was untamable and my cheeks are still flushed. "I was, uh, staying with a friend this weekend and realized I forgot the key to my apartment. How about you? You're here early."

"I wanted to finish up a project I'm working on. Couldn't sleep so I thought I might as well get some work done."

"Oh." I laugh a little, trying to lighten the tension. "Those motivational quotes must be doing their job."

She slings her bag over her shoulder and her silky hair swings. "And by the way, I have a guy that watches Cash's 'back door' on the weekends. Because I'm the jealous ex type, what can I say? It's a weakness."

I feel my face pale. *Fuck fuck fuck. She saw me.*

"I used to go in that way too, did you know that?" Her question is scathing, and hurtful.

"I, uh…no." My life—all that work, the studies, the internships, the trying so hard for so long—literally flashes before my eyes. So does Ace. *He must have told her to come to his less-conspicuous entrance too. Did he also tell her all those beautiful things he told me? Did he tell her, in the heat of a moment, that he was falling in love with her?*

Rylee walks past me toward the door. "I highly recommend you *not* mention you saw me here this morning. To anyone. Not Cash. Not Noah. Not Penelope. Definitely not Lacey. No one. If you can manage that, I'll keep your little secret from the team. I'm sure they'd all be very interested to find out that you're sleeping with the boss.

How long has it been going on? Since before you got hired, by any chance? I'm impressed, honestly. You *really* wanted this job."

"It wasn't like that." Wow, she's cold-hearted. And I react to it. I can't stop myself. "They know it was you."

She blinks, shaken. But then she regains that ice-queen composure. "They might suspect it was me. But they can't prove it. And neither can you. So do yourself a favor and keep our secret to yourself."

Rylee doesn't know me very well. She doesn't know that I'm not a pushover. Or that I'm tough because I've had to be. But I'm also kind, because I've always found that grit and kindness are the best ways to get what you want. For me, it's the only combination that's ever worked. "Just saying, this is the worst, most obvious heist in the world. Everyone in this office suspects you. And you were never going to win him back this way."

At the mention of Cash, a vulnerability softens her expression. I can see there that she's not purely evil, she's just really hurt. She loved him. She still loves him. So much, maybe, she's blind to how crazy her actions are.

I can relate. I happen to know how easy he is to fall for.

"It's not late to fix this, Rylee."

She wavers. She takes a few seconds to consider that.

"I'll help you," I say. But she notices again the look of me. The obviousness of what happened after I was ushered through the back door of the CEO's building.

I watch her jealousy slide back into place. Her disdain. "Fix what? As I said, I came in early to work. If you insist on discussing that with anyone, I'll take you down with me."

With that, she walks out.

30

—————

CASH

I ROLL OVER, reaching for her. Finding her half of the bed empty.

My eyes open and I can *feel* the emptiness she's left behind. The energy of the place is cold, without that warm beauty she infuses into everything. "Tex?"

No answer. Her bag is gone, and her clothes.

Fuck.

I throw the covers off and get up. It's like Hawaii all over again, but this time I'm furious. How could she just leave without saying goodbye, after everything that's happened?

If she'd kissed me and told me she needed to go back to her apartment before work, I would have understood. I'd have had my driver take her home.

After I made love to her again, feasting on her lush perfection.

Twice.

As much as I would have liked to have escorted her, obviously it's probably best if we keep this whole thing under wraps for now.

But walking out? What the fuck?

So it's fucking Groundhog Day. I search for a note and find one. Sitting under the diamond bracelet she left behind. *Damn it, Tex.*

> *Ace,*
> *I wish I could stay here with you, I really do. But we need to be honest with ourselves. I work for you. As much as we both don't want that to matter, it does. I loved our weekend together. A lot. But I need some time to figure out how to deal with all this. Please don't make this any harder than it already is. I'm so sorry.*
> *xx,*
> *Tex*

I crumple the note in my fist.

But then I uncrumple it, smoothing it. Because it's hers. I want to keep it and I'm going to go through each fucking bullet point with her and convince her she's wrong about everything.

Be *honest* with ourselves?

I grab my phone and hit the call button for her number. It goes straight to voicemail.

"Now you listen here, Texas. You want honesty? Well, here's some fucking honesty: I'm coming into the office now and I'm going to tell the whole company we're together. Because we are. We're *together*. I'll shout it from the fucking rooftops if you want me to. I'm addicted to you and I'm in *love* with you. Do you hear me? I told you that! And I don't give a damn who knows about it. I don't care that it's happened like a runaway freight train on fucking steroids. The only thing I care about is making sure I can see you again tonight. If I have to sling you over my shoulder like a goddamn caveman and carry you through the office kicking and screaming, then I will. Is *that* honest enough for you?"

I refer to the note, still pacing, butt naked—with a fucking hard-on—and absolutely furious that she would walk out on me again.

"Yes, you work for me. So the fuck what? Lots of people work for me! That doesn't mean we can't be together. The two things don't have to be mutually exclusive. I'm the fucking CEO! I own the majority shareholding of the company! *I* get to make the decisions. And here's my decision: I want you. For the first time in my life, I don't want to be half-assed about it. I'm *all in*, Texas. Now stop running from me."

I check the list.

I loved our weekend together. A lot. This calms me down by a single degree. "Yeah. Our weekend was pretty damn spectacular, wasn't it, baby girl? I loved it too. And I'm not making things harder. I'm making them easier. I don't care if my empire crumbles around me. That just won't matter to me if you're not *in* my empire. Or at least near it. I can build more empires. I've done it before, I can do whatever it takes. And as for being sorry, Tex, you fucking *should* be! But you can make it up to me tonight. You're going to be *very* sorry when I spank your sweet little ass for leaving without even so much as a goodbye kiss." *Fuck, I'm rock-hard again.* "So I'm going to hang up now and I'm going to come into the office and we're going to meet and talk things through. No more running. I *need* you, baby."

Goddamn it. I end the call, pissed off that I sound like a crazed stalker.

But I don't seem to be able to tone it down. I'm already jonesing for her like an addict who's gone too long without my fix. My heart feels like someone—*her,* obviously—has reached inside my chest and now she's squeezing it tightly in her fist.

She has abandonment issues, I get that. She told me all about it. She doesn't trust that I'll stick around. She's young and inexperienced and she doesn't understand yet that this is next level shit. This kind of chemistry doesn't just crackle, it *burns.* It leaves a scar. Our pheromones are so electrically charged, she's branded me with her goddamn imprint.

I don't fucking know.

All I know is that she's all I can see.

Over the course of this weekend, my obsession for her

has morphed into a beast that won't take no for an answer. And so has my dick. I can't get the damn thing to *deflate.*

Yes, the sex was incredible. Passionate. Tender. Wild. Just the right amount of twisted. Gentle. And all in equal measure, meshed into a carnal frenzy that's so sweet and hot you just never want it to end. It felt like our souls weren't just colliding but melting into one. I looked into her eyes and I could see there that she was falling just as hard for me as I was for her.

Her reluctance to give in to the feelings that are so clearly simmering between us is pissing me off. But it's also making me more determined than ever.

I'm used to getting what I want. And I want my Texan girl.

It's that horny, pissed-off-as-hell energy that leaves me fisting my cock in the shower.

But I don't have time. And I want it to be *her* hand on my cock. I want her on top of me, riding my face, grinding her perfect pussy against my tongue as she moans my name. I want to thrust into her, over and over again, before I shoot hot jets of my cum deep inside her.

She's mine. I'll do whatever it takes to have her and keep her.

And I don't care what it costs me.

31

———

Dusty

I GET BACK to my apartment and step into the shower, where I plan to remain for at least twenty hot, steamy minutes. It's a different kind of hot and steamy than my weekend revelries, of course, and I'm almost sad to wash myself clean of him. There's every possibility the love affair between Tex and Ace is now over.

Yeah right. That's what you said last time.

And the time before that.

As I stand here under the rain shower head, which has a perfect water pressure and does its best to ease my stress levels, I mull over what I should do about my new discovery.

Should I tell Ace about Rylee?

Of course I should. Of course I will—even though she threatened to out me and Ace to the entire company, and everyone in the office will then immediately assume that I slept my way into my job.

Even so, I know I'll end up doing the right thing.

Damn these scruples. They're going to end up costing me everything.

But Ace could potentially lose the business he's spent years building, along with billions of dollars. So could Noah and Colton, who have also invested years of hard work into IE. I could never forgive myself if I didn't do everything I could to stop that from happening.

At the expense of your own career?

Unfortunately, the answer to my subconscious's question is yes.

Maybe they'll go easy on me if I save their company.

And so, after exactly twenty minutes of steam-heavy bliss, I turn off the shower and dry myself with one of the fluffy towels that were included with my furnished apartment. It's the softest towel I've ever used, along with the nicest shower I've ever had as my own, the nicest bathmat, the swankiest bedroom, and so on.

Most likely, I'll have to move out within days, once the news breaks. I'll have to bunk with Emma and hit the mean streets of New York in search of a coffee girl role. A problem for another day—or at least later on in this one.

I choose a light blue knit dress that's both flattering and professional. Standing in front of the mirror, I put on some mascara and lip gloss. I leave my hair long and loose.

Ready or not, Cash Maddox, here I come to save the day. And then to pick my way out of the rubble once I've decimated all my hopes and dreams.

I unplug my phone from its charger and notice I've missed a call from Ace. He won't be happy that I ran out on him again, but we both know it's for the best.

He's left a message. I hesitate before listening to it.

I'm expecting him to tell me that yes, it was a beautiful weekend. *The kind of amazing, in fact, that you could lose yourself in and wish for the kind of happily ever after that only happens in fictional romance novels or cheesy Netflix rom-coms.* But that it's best if we keep a low profile. I'm sure he'll tell me that he'll call me sometime once things aren't so crazy at work.

I play back the message. His low, husky voice instantly brings back a particularly vivid memory of that wicked mouth and all the things he did to me with it.

"Now you listen here, Texas. You want honesty? Well, here's some fucking honesty: I'm coming into the office now and I'm going to tell the whole company we're together. Because we are. We're *together*. I'll shout it from the fucking rooftops if you want me to. I'm addicted to you and I'm in *love* with you. Do you hear me? And I don't give a damn who knows about it. I don't care that it's happened like a runaway freight train on fucking steroids. The only thing I care about is making sure I can see you again tonight. If I have to sling you over my shoulder like a goddamn caveman and carry you through the office kicking and screaming, then I will. Is *that* honest enough for you?" There's an agitated pause. "Yes, you work for me. So the fuck what? Lots of people work for me! That doesn't mean we can't be together. The two things don't have to be mutually exclusive. I'm the fucking CEO! I own the majority shareholding of the company! *I* get to make the decisions. And here's my decision: I want you. For the first time in my life, I don't want to be half-assed about it. I'm *all in*, Texas. Now stop running from me." When he continues his rant, his voice is softer. "Yeah. Our weekend was pretty damn spectacular, wasn't it, baby girl? I loved it too. And I'm not making things harder. I'm making them easier. I don't care if my empire crumbles around me. That just won't matter to me if you're not *in* my empire. Or at least near it. I can build more empires. I've done it before, I can do whatever it takes. And as for being sorry, Tex, you fucking *should* be! But you can make it up to me tonight. You're going to be *very* sorry when I spank your sweet little ass for leaving without even so much as a goodbye kiss. So I'm going to hang up now and I'm going to come into the office and we're going to meet and talk things through. No more running. I *need* you, baby."

Wow.

A long time ago, I used to allow myself to dream about the perfect man. The kind who would say the kind of words you needed to hear exactly when you needed to hear them.

A man who would fight for you. Who would dedicate his life to you, like you see in Disney movies.

A man who would stay.

But that fantasy is something I gave up wishing for a long time ago. I honestly wish I could restore that kind of idealism in myself. I wish I could let Ace restore it, if that's the kind of thing he would even want to do.

The sad reality is that it's been too long for me. Too many years of day-in-day-out struggling. Working. Striving. Not hoping but *doing* whatever I have to do to win. Hope was never really part of the equation, so it's incredibly hard for me to hinge my future on it. The part of my psyche that might be inclined to hope was dented beyond recognition when I was four years old.

I ignore the sting behind my eyes, squaring my shoulders and getting ready to face what promises to be a roller coaster of a day.

Closing the door of the apartment, I take the elevator down to the Sky Walk. I stand there for a few minutes, staring down at the New York traffic and wondering what will become of my life.

Then I call Ace's number.

32

CASH

By the time I get to my office, I'm in a horrendous mood. I'll get my way—I have to—and see her tonight. But I have an entire shitstorm to wade through before six o'clock rolls around.

It's barely 7:30 in the morning, so I'm surprised to get to my office and find not just two of my brothers waiting for me, but all three.

They're in various chairs around my office, Noah and Colton on couches and Alexander helping himself to my ergonomically-correct desk chair like he owns the place. They're holding mugs of coffee from the machine on the bar.

"To what do I owe the astounding pleasure of being invaded by my entire family?"

"Consider it an intervention," says Alexander. The oldest of all four of us, Alex exudes a certain stoicism.

He's always shouldered the burden of our father's expectations as the oldest son like he was groomed from birth to do. Which I know for a fact wasn't easy. "You're losing your grip, Cash, that much is obvious. We're here to find out what the fuck is going on with you and to help you save your company from total annihilation."

Shit. I need coffee. "Pour me one, would you, Colton?" I never bothered with one of those cost-the-earth espresso machines with all the frothing apparatuses and whatnot. I prefer percolated black coffee straight up and plenty of it.

Noah launches straight into the inquisition. "Where have you been all weekend? Do you know how many times we've tried to call you?"

I pull out my phone and check my missed calls. "Thirty-seven?" I scroll through the most recent ones to make sure Tex isn't one of them before shoving my phone back in my pocket.

I get that I should be taking the concerns of my brothers seriously. *I'm* the one here with everything to lose. But none of it feels as important as it used to, before Tex burst into my life like a green-eyed wrecking ball, shattering everything. What matters most to me now is her. There's nothing complicated about my feelings. I want her and I'll sacrifice anything and everything to have her. I'm not happy about it, but there it fucking is.

Actually, scratch that. I *am* happy about it. Happy isn't an emotion I've had a lot to do with. Until now. Until that day on the beach when a Texan girl in a tiny little leopard print bikini strolled past my table. Now it's the only emotion I can feel. That she exists. That she's mine.

If I can figure out how to keep her and get her to stop running from me.

I take a seat on one of the leather chairs—more heavily than I mean to because I fucking miss her—and Colton puts the mug of coffee down in front of me. "Someone is distracting you at the moment and, as not only your brothers but also your business partners, we're getting some information out of you whether you like it or not."

"Who is she?" Alex asks, point blank.

Noah levels me with his blue stare. I already admitted to him I met someone in Hawaii. And despite the fact that I just gushed to Tex that I'm going to shout about us being together from the rooftops, I hesitate before opening this particular can of worms. "Someone I met. Are there any new developments?"

I don't think I've ever seen Noah this pissed off. He's usually the easy-going brother who's practically impossible to rile. But not today. "Which new developments are you referring to? The ones in which you've taken a vacation from your life at the exact same time the SEC have officially decided they're going to launch an investigation into Invested Enterprises? Or the ones in which it's only a matter of time before the press feasts on that information like vultures around a fresh kill?"

"Shit." My girl is rubbing off on me. The word almost sounds like it's got the slightest Texan twang.

All three of them are staring at me like they don't recognize me. Colton actually laughs. "'*Shit*'? That's all you have to say?"

"Fuck?" I offer. "Is that better?"

My phone vibrates in my pocket with an incoming call and I realize a second too late as I pull it out that the word *Tex* lights up the screen—and that all three of them can clearly see that. I should be feeling a thousand emotions right now that have to do with what my brothers just told me, like rage, grit, determination, whatever. The only one that registers is relief. *She got my message.*

"I have to take this."

"You can take it right here," Noah suggests.

I answer the call. "Hey."

If I didn't already have my brothers' attention, I sure have it now. And I wish I hadn't said *Hey* like I just said it. Gently. Almost hopefully.

She sounds almost breathless. "Ace, I really need to talk to you about something that happened this morning. It's important."

"Are you okay?"

"I'm fine. It has to do with…the person you suspected of the leak. I had to come into the office first thing because I forgot my key and, well, I think you'll want to hear about this. Can we talk?"

"Why don't you come up to my office now." I'll probably regret this, but I know for a fact that my brothers wouldn't leave even if I asked them to. They might as well meet the girl I'm besotted with. Since I'm determined to have her in my life, there's no way around it. And if she has some information about Rylee—something concrete that might actually help solve this whole mess—then they're going to want to hear about that too.

"Okay. I'll come now. See you soon, Ace." She ends the call.

I wait for it and Noah doesn't disappoint. "Tex?"

Fuck it. "Yes. Tex. We met in Hawaii. She left my hotel room in Waikiki without giving me her name or number. I searched for her but couldn't find her because she lied to me about being from Dallas. Then, on Friday, she turns up here as our new junior analyst. Obviously it's a bad idea to get involved with an employee and, trust me, I would avoid her if I could. But this started months ago and I'm...I think I'm—no, I fucking *know*. I'm falling for her." I run a hand through my hair agitatedly as my brothers watch me with the identical shocked look on their faces. "I'm not just falling, I already fell. Hook, line and fucking sinker."

"Dusty Rose?" Noah asks. "*That's* who you spent the weekend with? Dusty Rose is *Tex*?"

"Yes. Dusty Rose is Tex." *My Tex. Mine.*

"You dirty devil, you." Colton ruffles my hair but I shove his hand away. "Dude, you know how badly it ended last time you dated an employee. I mean, *I* do it all the time but you don't have the charm I have to pull it off."

"Fuck off, Colton."

He laughs. At least my confession has lightened one brother's mood.

But then my intercom buzzes and Hayley's voice announces, "Dusty Rose is here to see you."

All three of my brothers straighten up.

"Send her in."

33

Dusty

WHEN I WALK into Ace's office I'm surprised to find Noah there, and Colton. And another man who could only be their older brother. He's gorgeous, like they all are, but in a more corporate, serious-minded way. His suit probably costs more than my entire year's salary.

They all stand up when I walk in. All six-foot-something of the four Maddox brothers. Billionaires and the four most "eligible" bachelors in Manhattan, according to some article I read online. They all exude power, wealth and testosterone like they've been dipped in it. It's a little intimidating.

"Dusty Rose," Ace says, and it sounds strange hearing him say my actual name, "you've met Noah and Colton. And this is my other brother, Alexander. Alex, meet Dusty."

"Hey, Tex," Alexander says, grinning at Ace's feral

glare at the mention of his nickname for me, but not before taking in the look of me, slowly, from head to toe. "*Now* I get it."

"I have to say," Colton adds, "if we weren't so worried about your effect on our brother, this would all be highly entertaining. The poor boy can't even see straight."

So they know about…us. "Oh," is all I can manage.

Ace walks toward me but I take a step back. I don't want him touching me right now because the two of us are so combustible. I can't predict how I'll react to him. It's best to keep some distance.

"You want coffee, Dusty?" Colton smirks, totally reading the charged chemistry between me and Ace.

"I'd love one, thanks."

I give Ace a subtle *you-told-them?* look. At least I hope it's subtle.

"I had to, baby." *Baby?* I bite my lip but apparently he's letting *all* our cats out of their bags. "If I can't stand to let you out of my sight for more than five minutes, they need to know how insanely fucking crazy I am for you."

Wow.

Colton doesn't hold back. "It's glaringly obvious he's totally lost his marbles, Dusty. And the sparks between the two of you are practically visible. We would have figured it out."

I mean, it's not ideal, but I guess Colton has a point. And since I'm here to tell them about Rylee, once they confront her with the accusation, they'll find out anyway. Because she'll tell them.

Noah motions toward the couch. "Take a seat, Dusty. Cash said you had some information you wanted to share with us."

Colton places a cup of coffee in front of me on the table. And I'm aware of this major plot twist in my life. Only a few short months ago I was an underling's underling. Now, I have four of the most powerful men in New York hanging on my every word. And one of them is watching me like a tiger about to devour his prey in the most carnal way imaginable.

"Thank you. Yes." I guess there's no point beating around the bush. I take a deep breath, trying to center myself. "Well, as you might already know, I stayed at Ace's —uh, Cash's place over the weekend. And I'd forgotten to take my apartment key with me. I realized I'd left it on my desk when I finished work on Friday afternoon. So I came in early this morning to get it. That was just before five a.m."

"Go on," Noah urges, ignoring Colton's playfully raised eyebrows.

Here's the part where I ruin Rylee's life. Which I really don't want to do, but it's either give them the truth or watch their company burn to the ground. I either ruin Rylee's day or Ace's, and that makes the decision a lot easier. "Rylee Winters was here when I got here. She was working in one of the communal offices. As soon as she saw me, she logged off and started to leave, but not before telling me she already knew that I'd gone to Cash's apartment on Friday. She used to use the Madison Avenue entrance too."

I slide a dark glance at Ace (I can't help it) and his sapphire eyes are leveled at me. It's a look that says, *don't you dare doubt me. I already told you how I feel.*

"Dusty," Colton says, for my benefit alone, "you should know that he couldn't stand her, from day one. She made him miserable in the few short weeks they were together. But for you, he's willing to completely ignore some very real issues that have to do with the company he's spent the past four years obsessing over. Trust me when I tell you that Cash has never behaved this way before. You have nothing to worry about."

"I wasn't worried." And it's true. As always with Ace, even from that very first day, I believed him. And I believe him now. I'm speaking more to Ace than to the others when I continue, but they're all riveted. "She has someone watching that door. She said she's the jealous ex type and she keeps track of who's coming and going."

All four of them are clearly pissed off by this. It's obviously crossing a line. "That ended months ago," Noah comments.

"Bitch," Colton mutters.

"She didn't want anyone to know she was here early. She said if I mentioned it to anyone, she'll make sure the whole office knows I spent the weekend at my boss's apartment. Which means that everyone will assume I slept my way into my job."

"Then we'll set the record straight," Ace growls.

"Which computer was she using, Dusty?" Noah asks.

"The one in room 411. The room with the neon sign that says 'Don't let someone else's opinion of you become your reality.'" Somehow, it's fitting.

Noah pulls his phone out of his pocket. "I'm going to get Jared to bring up the activity records on that computer." For my benefit, he adds, "He's one of our IT guys."

As he makes the call, Ace comes over and sits next to me on the couch. He doesn't touch me, but his nearness is enough to make me want to lean in. He's so damn gorgeous in his perfect suit, which fits him like a glove and strains over his muscles. I love that I know what he *feels* like under the civilized layers of his clothing. How warm he is, how big and hard. *I love that I know the sounds he makes when he surges and comes. The bass notes of his voice when he groans my name.* "You okay, Texas?"

"Fine." But he's right. There's something unnerving about being threatened by someone you've backed into a corner. Especially when she's still pining after the man of her—and my—dreams.

"You ran out on me again," he accuses softly.

Before I can answer him, Noah puts his phone call on speaker. "I'm letting the others listen in, Jared. What are you bringing up on the activity log for 411?"

The guy on the other end of the line doesn't speak

right away but there's the sound of his keyboard clicking as he types. "An email account was deleted at 4:22 a.m."

"Deleted?"

"She's trying to erase her tracks," Alexander offers.

"She can't," Jared says. "Activity logs can't be completely deleted. They're still in the system, even though this email account is encrypted. Whoever sent it has some pretty sophisticated coding skills. It's encrypted from the back end, but I've just managed to bypass the key. The email address is officeinfo@investe denterprises.com. There are seven sent emails, all to Sanderson Fitzpatrick, dating back several months. The address they were sent to is fucm@sandersonfitz patrick.com."

"Bingo." Colton pats Ace on the back.

"Jared," Ace's voice is graveled with rage. "Can you email me those records? CC Noah and Colton. Is there a video camera in 411?"

"No, but there's one in the main office. Let's see…" Jared pauses. "…this morning at 4:44 a.m., two women were in the office. I recognize one of them but not the other. Do you want me to send you this footage?"

"Yes," Ace says. "Send me everything."

"Right. Sending it now."

Ace's, Noah's and Colton's phones buzz simulta-neously.

Ace immediately opens the email and there we are, on the video, Rylee's hair smooth and platinum, mine not even coming close to disguising the fact that I'd just spent an eventful weekend in bed.

"Thanks, Jared. We'll want to meet with you once you go through everything you've got. Can you come to my office this afternoon at one?"

"Of course. See you then."

After they've ended the call, Ace turns to Noah. "Call Rylee and tell her we have something we'd like to discuss with her. Immediately. I'd do it myself but if I go ballistic on the phone she'll never show up—and I'm not sure I'll be able to restrain myself. Tell her to come now."

So Colton refills all our coffee mugs as Noah makes the call. "Hey, Rylee, it's Noah. Yeah. Good. Listen, Cash and I would like to meet with you in his office. Yes. Now, actually. Are you free?" There's a pause as she says something to him. "No, it can't wait. No, I'm afraid it's somewhat urgent. Yes. Good. See you soon."

I stand, clutching my bag in front of me. "I should probably leave you to it—"

"Oh no you don't, gorgeous." Ace pulls me back down to the couch. I glare at him but he's pinning me with a dark look that's half stern and half...pleading. I'm not sure why, but his imploring need touches something inside me. He wants me here. "Stay." It's not so much an order as a sincere request.

I fucking need you.

I don't know if I've ever been *needed* before. This big billionaire with his suit porn and his fancy office in the

Manhattan skyscraper he actually owns…needs me. "Okay," I whisper.

Ace barely nods, then he stands. And paces.

A few minutes pass while everyone drinks their coffee and waits.

Alexander is leaning back in the swanky leather office chair, his feet propped up on the corner of Ace's mahogany desk. "I think *I* need to work here too. This is so much more fun than Maddox Enterprises."

Before anyone can respond to that, Hayley's voice comes over the intercom. "Rylee Winters is here to see you, Mr. Maddox."

We all steel ourselves before Ace goes to the door and opens it.

34

Dusty

WE ALL STAND up as Rylee walks in. Her eyes go first to Ace. But then they fixate on me and they are not friendly. I have no doubt she'll throw me under whatever bus she possibly can.

Rylee looks as gorgeous as always and I'm reminded that she's a model and an heiress. She looks every inch of both. Her cheekbones could cut glass and her lithe, waif-thin body belongs on a catwalk.

Everything about her screams money. White-blond hair hangs almost to her waist and moves like liquid. Her cream power suit and matching pumps are clearly designer and her make-up is flawless.

For a second my face flushes with the uncomfortable heat of insecurity. My dress is understated, with the slightest cowgirl flair in the suede detailing at the hem. I bought this dress in Austin and it shows. Not only that but

I'm curvier than Rylee and suddenly feel like a grain-fed heifer standing next to an exotic gazelle.

I'm an out-of-towner and, surrounded by these New Yorkers whose wardrobes are clearly sourced from Saks Fifth Avenue or wherever, I feel out of place.

Ace, who has a knack for reading my thoughts, places his hand on the curve of my hip, his thumb pressing gently. A boss wouldn't touch an employee like this. It's too familiar. It's reassurance and it's also a claim. Rylee's razor-sharp glare zeroes in on our connection and her cheeks get pink under the smooth mask of her foundation.

"So, you two are together now?" she asks icily. "Like, *together* together?"

"That's not really the concern here, now, is it, Rylee?" Colton answers. To Colton, nothing in life is to be taken too seriously. But even doused in good humor, his words are as cutting as a pickaxe.

I'm immediately struck by the band-of-brothers vibe in this room. These four men are power players. Wall Street titans. Multi-billionaires. They're also fiercely loyal to each other.

Rylee's a fool to have tried to take them down, and I think she's beginning to see that now with crystal clarity. "I *loved* you, Cash. I *still* love you." Her eyes pool with tears.

"If you love him, why are you trying to get him thrown into jail?" Alexander asks matter-of-factly. "Blackmailing him isn't the best way to get him to fall in love with you."

"He broke my heart!" Rylee cries. "I wanted to hurt him like he hurt me!"

"Did you really think you would be able to pull this off?" Noah's question is incredulous. "This is *insider trading*, Rylee. You were really willing to take us all down because Cash called it quits with you?"

"We were perfect for each other," she sobs. "He's my soulmate."

Ace runs a hand through his hair agitatedly. "We're not fucking soulmates, Rylee. Jesus Christ, what's wrong with you? You refuse to take no for a fucking answer. And now you've dragged the entire company through the mud while also jeopardizing your own career. For what? For a petty grievance. I didn't think you'd be that vindictive, I really didn't. I gave you the benefit of the doubt because I thought even *you* wouldn't go that far. Clearly I was very fucking wrong about that. But you should know that I intend to press charges and prosecute to the full extent of the law."

Rylee makes a small sound, a light exhale, like she's finding it hard to breathe. "I didn't want to do it, Cash! I just couldn't believe you could be so cold, stonewalling me like that when I loved you so much! I tried to get your attention in every way I could, but you shut me out like I meant *nothing* to you." Rylee bursts into tears. "You're *heartless*, you bastard."

"So you were willing to *destroy* me? Who the fuck *does* that, Rylee?"

I've never seen Ace this angry. Colton and Noah are also furious. Colton suggests, "I think it's time we call our lawyers, the detective who's been assigned to the case and the guy at the SEC who detected the emails. You can fill all of them in on your twisted vendetta, Rylee."

Noah begins to go through the details. "Rylee, you were seen coming out of office 411 at 4:44 this morning, which is confirmed on video surveillance footage. Your knowledge of encryption software is obviously extensive. But you might have overlooked one important detail: activity records aren't deleted just because an email account is."

Colton continues. "The activity log from the computer in room 411 shows that an encrypted email account was deleted at 4:22 a.m., precisely twenty-two minutes before you were seen vacating that office. Coincidentally, the activity log of the deleted email account shows seven sent emails, sent over the course of nine weeks, to fucm@sandersonfitzpatrick.com—the very same email address that led the SEC to launch an investigation into Invested Enterprises."

"It also just so happens," Noah adds, "that the press are dangerously close to getting a whiff of that SEC investigation. And when they *do* get a whiff, IE will begin hemorrhaging clients like rats jumping off the Titanic."

Rylee's sobbing now. Despite everything, I feel for her.

Here she is, crying, surrounded by these—rightfully—furious brothers, who are about to have her hauled off to jail.

I almost call him Ace. Then Mr. Maddox. Instead, I say, "Cash. If you give Rylee a chance to talk to the SEC herself, I'm sure this could be worked though without getting the police involved."

Ace isn't convinced. "If Dusty hadn't caught you this morning, Rylee, would you have let us all get convicted? How could you be so obtuse? Didn't you realize you'd never get away with something like this?"

"I deleted the account," Rylee pleads.

"This has been hanging over our heads for *months* now," Ace growls, "while you smugly watched us suffer."

Rylee wipes her tears. "You wouldn't even *talk* to me or give me the time of day! You were so *mean*, Cash. And now you've rebounded with *her*." She breaks down once again into sobs. "You touch her like you never touched me."

Ace sighs heavily and swears under his breath. When he continues, his rage is controlled, but barely. "I broke up with you because I didn't love you, Rylee. Either way, it doesn't justify what you've done."

I don't know why I'm trying to protect her, but she looks so heart-broken and outnumbered. "I think we can all agree that Rylee took it way too far, but if she confesses and talks it over with the SEC, this can all be worked out. It's not too late."

"I'll fix this," Rylee pleads. "I can, I promise." More tears.

But Cash is unmoved. "You'll agree to confess not only to the detective and the SEC but also to the press, if anything leaks. This is on you, Rylee. And you'll submit your resignation immediately."

Rylee nods, blowing her nose.

Noah's relief is obvious. "You'll still be lucky to escape jail time."

"She can escape jail time if you don't press charges." I'm not even sure if that's true, I'm winging this. My default mode is to always pretend like everything's fine. If you do that long enough, eventually it mostly works. "She'll confess, she'll resign and the investigation of IE won't go ahead. Rylee was obviously overcome by her emotions but if she's willing to make things right, maybe you should let her."

"I will," Rylee whispers hopefully. "*Please.*"

Cash is watching me. His expression is stormy but there's a softness behind it he saves just for me.

"So it's settled," I say, hoping like hell we can avoid more tears, fury and prison sentences. "You can contact the SEC now and Rylee will tell them everything they want to know. Then she'll submit her resignation. And IE can submit a statement to the press saying the error has been isolated, to squash any rumors and face the issue head-on. There's no case of insider trading and never has been. It's business as usual and profits have never been healthier. Done and dusted."

All four brothers are looking at me, like they're slightly bemused by my no-nonsense approach.

Colton almost grins. "Done and dusted by Dusty Rose. Rylee, do you agree to these terms?"

"Yes," she says quickly. "You really won't press charges?"

Ace glances at me before answering her. "If you stay true to your word, cooperate fully and never bother us again, I'll consider it."

"Thank you," Rylee says to him, but her eyes are on me.

Noah pats Cash on the back before heading for the door. "I'll go issue the statement. And someone give Dusty Rose a promotion."

35

CASH

THE REST of the day miraculously goes according to plan.

Rylee cooperated completely and our lawyers have convinced the SEC to let the matter drop. Because the emails were staged—with information that was confirmed to be addressed to a person who doesn't exist and was never seen by anyone except the CEO of Sanderson Fitzpatrick, who already knew it was either a hoax or something that was going to get him into very hot water if he acted on the information contained in the email—there was no actual case of insider trading.

At Tex's request, I begrudgingly agreed not to press charges. The detective was highly entertained by the "crime of passion." Rylee was fined ten thousand dollars for attempted fraud and the case is in the process of being closed.

Rylee submitted her resignation and signed a Cease

and Desist agreement to never contact me again except through my lawyers. She'll finish out the week. Even if her crime does follow her around for a while, I have no doubt she'll land on her feet. She's wily enough to bend the system in her favor. Which is fine with me as long as she's doing it far away from us.

Noah posted a press release on the company website that addressed the circulating rumors. Since then, we've had more than 17,000 new subscribers.

Done and dusted, so it would seem.

I insisted Tex stay by my side during most of the meetings. She takes the edge off my fury. Without her gentle insistence, I would never have agreed to be so lenient with Rylee, but I can agree that the compassion my Texan girl radiates has made the proceedings much smoother. First of all, she cracked the case. Second, if it had been just myself and my three brothers dealing with Rylee, somewhere down the road we probably would have regretted ruining her life and possibly throttling her.

According to Tex, our Karma has remained intact.

I watch her now, her long hair loose over her shoulders. The curves of her body under her dress. Even here in the boardroom, with its dark wood, steel-rimmed windows and hard lines, she looks so soft. So outrageously beautiful. She glows with health and sunlight, like she absorbed all that Texan sun and carries it inside her, lighting up the overcast room.

Without the fiasco hanging over our heads anymore, I

feel like I can see more clearly. She's not just gorgeous and sexy as fuck, she's everything I've ever wanted. Everything I never thought to wish for, because I was too busy working.

She's the most exquisite thing I've ever seen, inside and out. I'm not just obsessed with her, I'm in love with her. Absolutely, ridiculously head over heels. I want her in my life for the rest of time. I want to wake up with her every morning and to wrap myself around her beauty every night. She doesn't look real, she's so stunning.

She catches me watching her and smiles lightly. She stands, excusing herself from the table. "I'll head back down to the office now," she says. "Evan said we have a team meeting at four."

Every eye in the room is glued to her. Alexander has stuck with us today, more for moral support than anything. Colton and Noah are seated on the other side of the huge table, flanked by our lawyers as we go through the last of the paperwork.

I'm tempted to lunge at them all as they take in the perfection of her. *Mine.* I need her to know that. I need the whole fucking world to know that. The sooner I get a ring on her finger, the better.

"Wait for me downstairs," I tell her. "I'll come get you."

She doesn't answer, and I'm fully aware that she's wary of the office rumors. Outside this boardroom, no one knows about us yet and I get the feeling she wants to keep it that way.

I have other plans.

"Great work today, Dusty," Noah tells her. "If it wasn't for you, we might not have dodged the Rylee bullet so easily. I'm recommending to the CEO that we move you into a more senior role. There was also a reward for information about the accusation, which we'll make sure you get."

"I just did what anyone would have done," she says, her face lightly pink under the scrutiny.

"Not necessarily," Colton points out. "Not everyone would have chosen to be honest when they had something to lose."

"I could never have kept that from you all. You needed to know the truth."

"We owe you one and it's a doozy, Dusty Rose." Noah's sincerity gets my attention. But he's right.

Watching her leave without following her requires a Herculean effort. *You'll see her in an hour, you asshole.* I don't know if it's because I want to make up for lost time, with all the failed attempts at past relationships. Or if I'm just being a clingy bastard because she completely lights up every room. It's cheesy as fuck to even think it but she does: she lights up my life.

Already, it's unbearable to imagine my future without her. I realize that maybe I never felt even the tiniest glimmer of love for anyone else because she's the one I've been waiting for all along.

Even now, as she sends me one more quiet glance before closing the door behind her, the storm clouds outside the windows seem to darken. Without her, my mood instantly goes surly.

"Only a few more things to go through here, Ace," jokes Noah. "Then you can chase after her."

"Ace is *whipped*," laughs Colton.

He's not fucking wrong. "Let's get this over with."

36

Dusty

I've barely sat down in my chair for the team meeting when Lacey leans in close. "Is it true? You're fucking the *CEO*?"

"What?" How the hell did she find out? "Of course not."

But then I remember that Rylee was dismissed an hour or so before I left the boardroom, to begin cleaning out her desk. I might have saved her from prison time, but she's also out of a job and has been thoroughly dissed by the guy she thought was the love of her life. As a last gasp, maybe she decided to take one last stab at me.

"He's hot as fuck, I'll give you that much," Lacey whispers. "But *Cash Maddox*? He's a total prick. Everyone knows that. And your *boss*. Girl, you're playing with fire."

Damn it. Don't I know it.

Through the glass partition of the communal office I can see Evan approaching.

I wait for it and Lacey doesn't disappoint. "Now I know why they hired you for such a coveted position even though you're so young—I mean, I know you deserve it, Dusty, it just makes more sense now."

"It's not like that."

But the damage is done. My heart sinks and I go through the motions of the meeting, not waiting around afterward to chitchat or have a drink with the team. I'm not up for it tonight. I barely slept at all last night and it's been a long day. In fact, the whole whirlwind love affair, the early morning confrontation with Rylee and the marathon of meetings with high-powered lawyers, detectives and government officials has been…a lot. It's all catching up with me.

And with Lacey practically bursting with glee at the juicy gossip, I need to get out of here before I burst into tears in front of everyone. I don't want Ace to think I'm running again…but maybe I am. Maybe it's the only way I know how to cope with the fact that I've just self-sabotaged my entire life.

So I murmur a polite goodnight, make my way to the elevator and head home.

Back in my apartment, I take a shower to wash off the day and put on a pink babydoll nightie that I bought on a whim before I left Austin.

Collapsing onto the couch, I pour myself a glass of wine and order a pizza.

He's not going to be happy about it, but I'm too exhausted to see Ace tonight. I need to eat some pizza, drink a glass of wine and fall into a comatose sleep for a solid nine hours.

I send him a text.

> Hi Ace, I'm so glad everything worked out today. I'm going to have an early night but I'm sure I'll see you soon xx Tex

He's probably exhausted too. I can only hope my text isn't like waving a red flag at a mad bull.

I know I'm in love with Cash Maddox. And a part of me is screaming: *fight! Do whatever you have to do to keep him!* But another part of me—and she's the part that's still half sane and clearly the one I should listen to—is thinking that it might be best if we let this whole thing cool off for a while.

Over the past four days, I've started my dream job, fallen catastrophically in love, had so much hot sex I feel like a completely different person, confronted the villain in my company's almost-downfall, and played a major role in righting their multi-billion dollar ship. And to top it all off, I've ruined everything. I'll now be the butt of the office joke. I don't know how to process the tsunami of emotions.

My phone rings on the kitchen counter and my sister's name lights up the screen. "Hey, Sky."

"Hey, Dust. *Finally*, she picks up. How's the new job going?" I'm not sure I've ever heard my sister sound so upbeat. "And have I told you yet today that you're the best sister on the entire freaking planet?"

"No, you are. How's Nashville? How'd everything go? Are you still there?"

"You're not going to believe where I am. I'm in a spare apartment in Kade Tucker's house! Can you *believe* that? I *met* him! He's so freaking hot it's ridiculous. He's with someone, but a girl can always dream, right?"

"What about the audition? Did you get a recording contract? What's Roxie like?"

"Oh my *god*, Dust, I have so much to tell you. I signed a contract! Roxie is awesome. She's *so* good at what she does. She loved the new songs I've written. She has some suggestions about how to record them and we're going to be using the same producer as the Tucker Brothers. I just…" Sky bursts into tears. "…Dusty, thank you for whatever you did to work this magic. I feel like I'm living in a dream right now."

"I've always told you, Sky, I knew you were destined for greatness."

"It's all because of you."

It's actually because of Ace, of course, but it's too long of a story to explain tonight.

"Dust, I was so low after Billy dumped me and

canceled all my gigs. I didn't even want to tell you all that. He was cheating on me and I found out about it and I was about to walk out on him. You were so right about him. Men *always* leave, we know that. And I didn't listen to you or to my own instincts and I was so devastated. Again. And after that, I was on the verge of giving up. On everything."

"Sky—"

"But literally an hour later, I get a call out of the blue from *Roxie Tucker*. I mean, holy shit. At first I thought someone was playing a joke on me. She said you have a connection who convinced her to listen to my songs and to give me a chance. And then she invited me to Nashville so she could listen to me play and I couldn't believe my luck. And then buying mom's *house* for her, Dust? What the hell? Did you win the lottery or something? How did you *do* all this?"

"I—"

Bang bang bang.

Someone's pounding on my door.

Bang bang bang.

"Tex," comes the muffled command through the door. "Let me in."

"Sky, I'm going to have to call you back. I want to hear about everything. I have to go but we'll talk more tomorrow, okay?"

"Okay, Dust. Love you. Thank you so much. For everything."

I smile because I'm so happy for my sister. "Love you more. And have fun."

I end the call and go over to the door, bracing myself for Ace's reaction to me leaving and basically blowing him off tonight. I unlock the door and open it.

Six foot three inches of enraged CEO pushes through the door, slamming it behind him. "I told you to wait for me." He's carrying my pizza. "Your pizza guy was waiting by the front door." He sets the pizza box on the counter.

His tie is barely loosened and his hair is slightly unkempt, like he's been grabbing fistfuls of it. His stormy energy fills the small space like a man-hurricane has just swept in. He looks, as always, big and masculine as all hell. Hard and domineering. And, even in my world-weary state, absolutely delicious.

His gaze rakes over me, taking in my tiny nightie, my scrubbed face and my damp hair.

"The news is out," I tell him. "No doubt every single person at Invested Enterprises is currently having a marvelous time over drinks while discussing how I slept my way into my job."

"Who cares." He bridges the small divide between us and takes me into his arms, lifting me and setting me on the marble kitchen island, spreading my bare knees to stand between them. "They were going to find out anyway when I announce tomorrow that you're being promoted to a management position."

"But I don't want that. They'll just assume it's because I sucked your dick really well at the job interview." *God, I really am tired. I have no filter tonight.*

His eyes darken. "Don't talk about sucking my dick unless you're prepared to get down on your knees, Texas."

"I'm serious, Ace."

"So am I. I don't give a fuck what anyone thinks. You *didn't* sleep your way into your job, so stop obsessing about people getting the wrong idea."

"Of course I'm obsessing! I've worked too hard to get here to completely ruin everything by having a relationship with you, like...all out in the open. I need some space." I don't even know if I *want* space, I just need to say something to gain some distance here. I'm falling too hard and too fast and I know what happens next. The same thing that happens with every man who promises something: they leave. It's the story of my life. Sky's phone call only confirms it.

"Space?" He says it like it's a dirty word. "What the fuck does that mean?"

"It means I need space! To get my head around keeping both my job *and* my sanity. This is all too much, Ace. I can't see straight when you're around me and I don't want to completely lose my grip on the rest of my life!"

Even I can hear that what I'm saying doesn't make perfect sense, but Ace has no idea about what it feels like to be abandoned at a very young age by the person who was supposed to care about you more than anyone. It's not that I *don't* trust Ace, it's that I *can't*. My trust mechanism when it comes to having faith that a man will stick around got shattered a long time ago. The fresh reminder in the form of my sister's phone call has dug up all my old wounds.

Either way, Ace is doing exactly the opposite of giving me space right now. His hands are gripping my ass and he's holding my body flush against his. With my knees wide and only the tiny barrier of my cotton panties between us, I can feel that his cock is *very* hard.

My body is so attuned to his, it reacts without my consent. He smells so good. The huge ridge inside his pants rears against me and my hips barely tilt, pressing against him in a silent invitation. *Damn him.*

His thumb dips inside my panties and he slides it against my clit.

"I just told you I need space," I protest, but of course I'm already wet. He's my Kryptonite, that's well established by now. My defenses are no match for his manscent and his gruff aggression.

"If you want space then why's your pussy wet for me, sweetheart?"

"Because you make me crazy!" It's absolutely the truth and I grip the front of his jacket with my fists. I want to take out my frustrations on him. I want to make him so mad that he'll leave, like I know he will.

I know my exhaustion is catching up with me when all

my old damages rise up. At some point I should probably talk to a therapist about some of this stuff but tonight the only one who's available is Ace.

And my vulnerabilities converge in a strange direction. I want to hurt him but I also *love* him and need him and want him. *So much.* The magnitude of it all feels twisted up with heat and need. "Fine. Let me suck your big cock then, boss."

His eyes narrow at me as I push his jacket over his shoulders. I grind against him as I unbutton his shirt, kissing little licks across his chest, gently biting his nipple, which makes him flinch and get even harder. "Texas—"

But he hisses and takes a step back when I shimmy down his body to undo his pants. I push him carefully— which takes effort because he's so big and so much stronger than me—to the couch. He sits and I kneel between his spread knees, taking his huge, hot length in my hands.

I know my words and my actions don't match right now. I'm fully aware of how unhinged I feel. I want to rile him and make him as wild as he makes me.

Our eyes lock as I lick the pearl of moisture at the head, taking him deeper as I fist the heavy bulk of him. I lick and suck him greedily. Messily. I want him to come hard and quick.

"Fuck," he growls.

I ease him out a little, playing with him, flicking the

underside of his cock with my tongue. "Come in my mouth."

"Jesus Christ, Texas."

"Do it. Fuck my mouth. Give it to me."

His eyes flash with lust. "I'm not coming unless you are, baby girl. Come here."

I climb up his big body like someone spiked my wine with nympho pills, rubbing myself against his huge cock, wetting the thin cotton of my nightie. He peels off my panties and pushes my nightie up over my breasts, teasing my nipples with his rough fingers. I straddle him and grab his thickness, guiding it to my slippery pussy. My whole body feels like one big heartbeat. I slide down onto him, impaling myself by slow degrees as we both moan.

I ride him slowly at first, bouncing down onto him as I squeeze my inner muscles around him until he's murmuring the dirtiest words.

I fuck him like I'm mad at him. And I am. He's breaking my heart by being so damn beautiful. He's so masculine and I hate that about him as much as I love it. I know he's going to hurt me with it eventually and I want to hurt him first.

But my frenzy is only getting us hotter. Cash Maddox turns me into an animal.

We're staring into each other's eyes, his cock thick and rigid inside me, skewering me in slick glides. I can feel every ridge and every vein.

It's just sex, I remind myself. *Very, very good sex. You don't need him. You just love fucking him.*

He grips my hips and thrusts harder. His thumb circles my clit. The hand that's gripping my ass explores intimately, probing and gliding gently as he continues to drive in, and in.

"*Ace,*" I whimper.

"Look at me when you come around my cock," he commands.

"*Oh.*" The pleasure is centered where his fingers play, forced higher by the thick glide of his cock deep inside me. It radiates like a throbbing, blooming, white-hot explosion of stars until I'm completely consumed by it. I come so hard I can only writhe onto him. My body is locked in extreme rapture, squeezing him tightly in rippling pulls that milk his cock lusciously.

"*Fuck,*" he growls. "*Tex oh fuck…oh fuck.*" His cock surges, bucking inside me as I ride it. The warm, flooding throb of his jetting cum tips me into another rich, nearly-unendurable orgasm.

"*Ace. Ace. Oh god. Oh god.*"

I come and come, finally collapsing against him as the waves get longer and sweeter and begin to calm.

"Holy fuck, you're beautiful. My perfect girl." We're both panting.

He holds me in his arms, smoothing my hair. I can feel the moisture dripping down my thighs from the overflow.

He's ruining me, body and soul. I can feel it happening. I love him too much.

I allow myself a few more minutes of closeness. I breathe in the scent of him, that woodsmoke and whiskey blend, spiced with hot sex. Our heartbeats are in sync.

And that little mantra that's so much a part of who I am and the life I've lived whispers, *protect yourself or you'll never, ever recover from him.*

I slowly lift myself off of him, letting the gush of liquid drip down my legs. My nightie—which was bunched up over my breasts—falls back into place, barely covering the tops of my wet, bruised thighs. "Ace?"

"Yeah?"

"I meant what I said though."

"About what?" His cock is still semi-hard—it never seems to fully go *down*—all glistening and laying there innocently now but still so…impressive.

"I want you to go."

"Go where?"

"I told you. I need some time."

His low laugh is surprised and annoyed. "Time for what?"

"To think. About all this. I think we should…have some space from each other sometimes. Like now. Like… maybe you should go and then I can figure out how to handle all this."

Another deep, incredulous chuckle. "Baby girl, you just rode me like a fucking rodeo hero. I'm not leaving."

"Considering everything that happened today…I think it's best. I think you should."

"Not happening, Texas."

Some long-injured corner of me wants to lash out at him. He's trying to drag this whole thing out, to get me to fall so completely in love with him that when he walks away, my heart will break into a million tiny pieces. "What I was trying to tell you before is that I don't want us to keep seeing each other like this. Like, all the time."

Despite the insane chemistry between us and the fact that we're both still recovering from mind-blowing simultaneous orgasms, in this moment, I mean it. He can see this in my eyes and for a split second I can see that it hurts him very deeply. "Tex, I'm not fucking leaving—"

"I know you will eventually and I want you to do it now. I'm sorry, I shouldn't have let things get out of hand again tonight. I just…I lose control around you and that's the problem. I *need* my control." I hate that I'm doing this, to shield myself. I want to be the one to tell him to leave and not the other way around. I want it to be *my* decision before it becomes his. "I want you to go now," I say again.

"No. I'm not leaving." His words are measured and outraged.

I know that none of this makes sense. I know I can't see straight when I'm around him and I feel like I'm losing myself. Lines are blurred. My addled brain wants to compartmentalize. Us. The me and the him have become one thing.

So I grab a towel and dry myself. Then I find some leggings and a baggy sweatshirt from the suitcase that I still haven't even started to unpack yet and pull them on. I don't really want to lug this whole thing around New York tonight so I start shoving a few things into a backpack.

"What are you doing?"

"*I'll* leave, then."

He comes over and takes the backpack from my hands. "Stop this. You're acting crazy."

"Because I *am* crazy! That's what I mean! You make me crazy and I don't know how to slow this down."

"Then don't."

"I'm sorry, Ace." I'm heart-broken for more than one reason. "But you don't understand anything."

"I understand everything. I get that it's been a long day. I get that a lot has happened very quickly. Let me take you to bed and I'll hold you and calm you down and we can talk about whatever it is you need to talk about—"

"*No.*" This is what he does. He makes me believe him and need him. He acts like his comfort is steady and unending, like he won't ever pull it away.

I've never seen any kind of comfort that doesn't end. It doesn't just end but it ends badly. With the kind of pain I might not be able to handle.

If I let him convince me, if I let him wrap his warmth around me until I get so used to it I can't bear to be without it, then what? Then he'll take it away and I'll shatter.

The only defense I have is to create some distance now, before it's too late.

My voice sounds steadier than I feel. "Either you leave or I will." I don't mean what I'm saying as I'm saying it, but my scars are burning me. "I don't want to keep seeing you. I can't. I can't have both you and the job and I want the job."

"This is about the job?" It's not helping that he looks so hurt. It just looks wrong on him, like his usual swagger has taken a hit.

"Yes." It's partly about the job. At least I think it is.

"Fucking hell, Tex. All right, then. If it's between me and the job, then you're fucking fired. Effective immediately."

37

Dusty

"WHAT A COMPLETE AND TOTAL ASSHOLE!" I can always count on my bestie to feel my despair as though it's her own. "I mean, it's not totally unexpected though, is it? He has a reputation, after all. Grumpy and power-driven and all that. He's not exactly known for being nice."

"No. I guess not." *Except in those quieter moments, when he'd smooth my hair and kiss me softly.*

I'm in Emma's apartment sipping emergency Pinot Grigio and watching her unpack four new lamps she bought online. A few of Emma's friends are making a surprisingly good living by styling their minuscule New York City apartments and posting about it on Instagram. So Emma is making a somewhat half-assed attempt to do the same thing. I'm not sure her heart is completely in it though. "Damn it. Do you think these clash? They're all different colors. Why didn't I think of that when I was buying them?"

"It's eclectic. I think it works." I take another sip of wine. But then I set my glass on the table, wiping my tears. Wine isn't going to help me right now. I didn't allow myself to cry in front of Ace but I started bawling like a baby as soon as I got to Emma's door. And I'm not usually a cryer. The avalanche of emotions wanted out and now that it's over, I feel the tiniest bit better for it.

Emma looks up from her mountain of bubble wrap. "What did you say to him when he fired you?"

"I grabbed my backpack, told him I'd have the apartment cleaned out by the end of the week and walked out."

"Did he follow you?"

"Like a caveman dragging his knuckles, all the way down the stairs—I didn't think we should be trapped in an elevator together—demanding I listen to him and trying to grovel and talk me out of it. He even threatened the cab driver but I told him he was acting like a psycho and that he had to let me go. I finally managed to jump into the cab and I came straight over here."

"I still can't believe you left him."

I can't either.

"I still can't believe he fired you."

"To tell you the truth, I was kind of expecting it to happen sooner or later. I was skating on thin ice the whole time. I knew that the minute I saw him sitting there in his executive office."

Emma gives me a sympathetic look. "It was probably a knee-jerk reaction. Him firing you, I mean. What had you been talking about when he did it?"

"I said if it was between him and the job, I'd choose the job."

"You did?"

I nod, feeling kind of bad about it now. "And now I have neither."

"Poor Cash. That's harsh."

I know. I wish I hadn't said it.

"No wonder he was mad," she says. "He was probably just hurt."

I take another sip of wine, wishing it would help me rewind time. "I feel so terrible. But it can't really work, Em, can it? I can't have him as my boss and still be having sex with him 24/7. I'd be trying to rise above the rumors but would always feel like everything I do at work is being undermined. Every achievement would always be eclipsed by the fact that I'm screwing the boss."

Emma contemplates me for a few seconds. "You know what your problem is?"

"What's my problem?"

"You care too much about what other people think. Who cares if they have the wrong impression?"

"That's what he said too." My phone vibrates again from inside my backpack, which is sitting over by the door. I'm avoiding him, which is probably wildly immature but I told him I needed some headspace to work through all this stuff and it's true.

"You don't have to *try* to rise above the rumors, Dust. Just rise above them! Swan past them. You know what the *real* story is, that's all that really matters."

"Maybe you're right." I rub my sore, tired eyes.

"Of course I'm right. Still, I know it's easier said than done."

"I'm such an idiot."

"You're not an idiot. You're just finally getting laid properly by a prime hunk of alpha man meat and it's thrown you a little. Your emotions are on overdrive. It's understandable."

I smile weakly. "I guess so. Anyway, maybe we're just too different. He's the king of New York and I'm…not."

"You're a badass Texan power chick, Dusty Rose. You'll figure it out. Either you'll find your way back to him or you'll find a new job and I'll introduce you to all the suits I know for some great rebound sex."

"I don't want rebound sex."

"Rebound sex can be awesome."

"I don't want anyone else."

Emma rests a lamp in her lap. "He must really have an incredible dick."

"Unfortunately, he really does."

She laughs and I can't help it. I'm so strung out and exhausted, the only thing I can do is cry as I laugh with her. Tears are streaming down our faces. It's more hysterical and reactive than it is funny, but it still somehow helps.

When we finally come up for air, she says, "Hang on. I need to rewind for a second. You said…he groveled?" I can detect the tiniest bit of awe in her at the question. "Like how? What did he say?"

"He said I wasn't really fired and he wanted me to stay."

Emma's eyes round. "Why didn't you?"

I throw my hands up. "I don't *know*, Em. Because I'm insane and I was in too much of a state. I can't believe I've just thrown away my entire future after all those freaking years of hard work and lost Ace in one fell swoop. I'm the stupidest person in the world."

"You haven't thrown away your future," Emma scolds. "Don't be so melodramatic. He *groveled*, Dusty." She still seems distracted by the thought. "The CEO of one of the most successful companies in Manhattan *groveled*. I wish I could have seen that."

I wipe fresh tears.

"Dust, you're just overwhelmed because of everything that's happened to you this week. But I think we should circle back to one important detail. *Cash Maddox* was pleading with you not to go."

I sigh. He really had been…sincere. And gorgeous, of course. "Maybe I'm losing my mind. I've ruined everything."

She asks the question gently. "What are you so scared of, Dust?"

"I don't know." But I do know. And so does she.

"You're scared he'll leave." Emma knows the surface details of the old went-out-for-a-pack-of-cigarettes-and-never-came-back sob story. "It was always something you were going to have to overcome, Dusty."

"I know."

She contemplates me for a few seconds. "What else?"

"I'm scared of how *unlike* myself I feel. I've always been in control of my life. I knew exactly where I was headed and how I was going to get there. But with him…there's no control. I completely lose myself in him."

Emma's eyes get shiny. "Holy fuck. You're in *love* with him."

I don't even disagree with her. For the first time maybe ever, I tell her how I actually feel, instead of hiding from it. "It's like he's opened up a whole new universe in me that I didn't know existed. One where I'm worshipped and adored and made to feel like a goddess. It's been more than just a huge sexual awakening, it's the first time I've ever experienced intimacy on any level at all—and this is just a surreal level. I can't resist him and I never want to. But then…when reality seeps in, I always wonder if it could actually work."

"I think it will work. I think it's going to."

My eyes start leaking again. "You do?"

So do hers. "Do you know how *lucky* you are? I've never felt like a *goddess*. Damn it."

I slide down onto the floor next to her and give her a hug.

"What you need is a good night's sleep, Dust. In the morning you'll see that everything isn't as dire as you think it is and that you two are probably soulmates because no one acts like this unless they're having their entire existence upended."

"I guess I've overreacted to everything."

"You're *reacting*. Which is something you've never done before. It's a good thing." Emma places a small red cordless lamp on the coffee table and turns it on. "This actually doesn't look too bad, if you like a brothel-meets-Ikea vibe."

Emma's phone dings from where it's sitting next to her on the floor. She picks it up and studies the message for a few seconds. "What the..."

"What is it? Who's it from?"

She's distracted. Her eyes are wide and she's riveted by whatever she's reading.

"Em?"

"Um. Hang on just a sec. Holy shit."

"Who is it?"

She texts back a quick message.

"Emma, who are you texting?"

"Just someone from work."

"At eleven o'clock at night?"

"You know us editors. We work 24/7." She puts the phone down. Then, slightly more breezily than she should, she says, "Now, while I unpack the rest of these, I want you to go and take a long, hot shower. Then you're going to climb into your half of my super-luxurious bed. It even has a brand new duvet, thanks to my new side hustle. It had to look Insta-worthy."

At the mention of bed, I suddenly feel bone tired. "That sounds like heaven right now. Thank you, Em. For being the best friend there is."

"Right back atcha, honey. Are you..." She pauses, treading carefully. "I was going to ask if you're going to work tomorrow. Or did he give you notice?"

"When he told me I was fired he said it was effective immediately."

"I'll take the day off and stay with you."

"You don't have to."

"I was thinking about doing it anyway. My friend linked my Instagram account in one of her posts last week and I have, like, ten thousand new followers and four new client requests. This thing could actually work. And I can do some editing from home while I'm at it."

"Only if you want to. But I'll be fine either way. I'll be scouring the internet for another job."

"We'll see about that."

38

——

CASH

I'M NOT A FUCKING STALKER, but when you're as addicted to perfection in human form as I am, you have to take certain measures.

It's going to take a lot more than one little angel-faced meltdown to scare me away.

I know only too well that the scars we carry can sometimes flare up when we're least expecting it. My own scars are the reason I haven't looked up in four years, after all. They're the reason I've barely looked up my whole life.

Until she walked into it.

I see her tantrum as a good thing. It's emotions she needs to work through to get to the other side. And I plan on being the lifeline she needs to find her way out of whatever quicksand is still holding her back.

I'll do it as many times as it takes. I'll pull her up, take her hand, dust her off and help her find her smile again.

The angel needs me. I'm her rock now. Her shoulder to cry on. Her emotion sponge. I'll absorb her angst and beam it back to her with love and comfort and hot sex. I'm not going anywhere she isn't.

Tex mentioned she stayed with her friend Emma when she first interviewed for the job at IE. So I did some research.

I got the information I needed.

Of course I know where Emma Fontaine lives. I know she works at City Publishing Company Ltd. as an assistant editor. I even how much she makes. $54,000 dollars a year. What I'm wondering is how people survive off of that kind of income.

I know the names of the two other girls who live with Emma. Hannah Goldberg and Lauren Johnson. I found Emma's email address listed on the City Publishing website. Her phone number is listed on her Instagram profile.

The last time Tex ran from me I knew I had to take precautions. I'm so fucking in love with her she's become the sun to me, and I won't risk losing her again. I'll be groveling until the day I die if it takes that long to convince her we're meant for each other.

So I grab a cab and follow hers. Just to make sure she gets to where she needs to go safely. "Don't lose that cab in front of us." I pull a couple of Benjamins off the roll of cash in my pocket and hand them to the driver. "Make sure you don't lose that cab."

"Yes, sir."

Okay, so it wasn't the smartest move to fire her in the heat of a moment. But when she threatens to leave, she's going to have to expect me to go fucking ballistic.

She was too fired up to listen to reason tonight. But I'll get through to her. It's what I plan on spending every waking moment doing until she's got a ring on her finger and is naked and knocked up in my bed, so I figure I'll convince her eventually.

So what if she's got some hang-ups and issues. Who doesn't? I'll break through every barrier she's put up. Because she makes me crazy with lust and love and longing and it's the only choice I have.

She's mine now and until I can convince her of that I'll do whatever it takes to make sure she's safe and well taken care of. My Texan girl is not going to be wandering the streets of New York City in the middle of the night without protection.

Her cab pulls up in front of Emma's building and so does mine. I watch her buzz the intercom for Emma's apartment. I watch her get buzzed in, enter the front door and go into the elevator. "Wait here for a few minutes."

"Yes, sir. Wife giving you some trouble, sir?"

"You could say that."

I text Emma's number.

> Emma, it's Cash Maddox here. Please don't let Dusty know I'm texting you. I'm making a plan for tomorrow. She's keeping her job. She's also getting a promotion. And when she's ready, a diamond ring. I hope you'll help me. Have her downstairs in front of your building at 9 am but don't tell her why. I'll make it very worth your while. Making her wildly happy is the only thing I care about. ~CM

> And make sure Dusty doesn't leave your apartment tonight. If she does, text me immediately

I wait for the three dots and they pop up almost instantly.

> Ok!

39

———

Dusty

THE BEACH IS SO BEAUTIFUL. So warm and dreamy. I look up to the hotel patio and I see him there, like that very first time. With his dark hair and his blue eyes. He's watching me. He gets up and walks down to the beach and sits next to me, getting all sandy in his business suit. I love you, he says. The harsh sound of a ringing bell is pulling me away from him and I don't want to go. I want to stay with him. I believe him.

"Fuck," Emma moans, fumbling for her phone in the early morning light. "It's my alarm."

Ugh. I'm tired. I wish I could have stayed in my beautiful dream a little longer. By the time we went to bed last night it was after midnight.

I miss him so much. I was so wrong. About everything.

I reach for my own phone. And I remember that I don't have to go to work today. Ace fired me, effective immediately. "It's 7:00. Do we need to wake up so early?"

Emma turns on her side to face me. Her curls are wild and she's grinning, sort of mischievously. "Because we have some things to do this morning."

"What things?"

"It's a surprise."

I stare up at the ceiling. "It's way too early in the morning for surprises, Em. Just tell me."

"Can't. I'm sworn to secrecy."

I look over at her. "By who?"

She smiles and gets up. "I'm having the first shower but you're going next. We have to find you the perfect outfit."

"I'm not getting out of this bed until you tell me what you're talking about."

"You'll see," she sings, slamming the bathroom door.

Exactly two hours later, I still haven't managed to get any information out of my best friend, who's having a field day with her little secret. I'm dressed in a cute black dress that's Emma's newest purchase. She insisted I wear it. My hair hangs loose, freshly washed with some fancy European shampoo Emma was gifted because of her new Instagram following, and it looks thicker and shinier than usual. I'm wearing heels and my favorite gold jewelry. Emma did my makeup (with more free gifts) and she's good at it. It's understated and natural looking. In the mirror, I look as devastated as I feel, but the makeup sort of helps.

I have to talk to him. I need to apologize for acting

like a lunatic. I don't blame him if he doesn't want to re-hire me or forgive me, but I at least need to try to explain.

We take the elevator down and walk through the lobby to the front door of the building. I follow her out onto the street. "I really wish you would tell me where we're going," I say again. "Did you book an Uber?"

"Not quite."

It's then that a black stretch limo pulls up to the curb.

"This is our ride." She's loving every minute of this. The chauffeur gets out and comes around to open the door for us. Emma practically pushes me in.

And there's only one person I know who would be this over the top.

The limo driver closes the door. Soon we're pulling away from the curb. "Why do I get the feeling you've been communicating with the person who fired me yesterday—okay, which I possibly deserved. Tell me, Emma, I mean it."

"Okay, yes. But I think you're going to want to hear what he has to say."

"What does he have to say?"

"I don't know, but I think it's going to be good. I'm coming along to live vicariously through you. I mean, limos, billionaires, come *on*, Dust. Just go with it. You *cannot* deprive me of watching Cash Maddox grovel, girlfriend."

"What if he's done groveling? What if I've damaged everything beyond repair?"

Now that I'm well-rested and not quite as strung out, I feel calmer. But my heart aches. *Why do I have to be so damaged, by something that happened to me so long ago?* "I guess I behaved sort of irrationally yesterday."

"We've all been there, sister."

"Tell me what Cash said to you."

"Can't." Her brown eyes twinkle. "It might ruin the surprise."

I glare at her. "Traitor."

"This is *way* too good, Dust. Just go with it."

A small flurry of butterflies erupts in my stomach. "When did he contact you?"

"Last night. When I was unpacking my lamps."

"So it wasn't someone from work."

"Not exactly. Oh my god, we're here."

Once again the chauffeur opens the door for us and we climb out. A doorman is waiting for us and ushers us inside the building. Penelope is standing there.

"They're all waiting for you," she grins.

"All?"

"Yes," she beams. "Is this Emma?"

"Penelope, this is my best friend Emma Fontaine. Emma, Penelope Callahan, HR director."

"Nice to meet you, Emma. Cash told us to expect you both."

He did? Penelope is as cagey as Emma and they exchange a conspiratorial glance. The little girl with abandonment issues in me has the urge to run, but I'm done listening to her. She's been giving me terrible advice lately.

Whatever's about to happen at the top of this elevator ride is obviously going to be overwhelming, one way or the other.

I love him. I love him like that four-year-old girl on our porch that day, or the ten-year-old girl with the paper route, or the sixteen-year-old who used to hang out in the UT library could never have imagined. And I want to hear what he has to say.

We get to the executive floor and Penelope leads us to a large meeting room, opening the door.

Inside, the room is full and everyone stands as we enter.

Ace is there and for a moment, all I can see is him. He looks more gorgeous than I've ever seen him, a stormy-eyed Adonis in a perfectly-cut suit. His wild ferocity, contained as it is in his business suit is…unbelievably hot.

Even from across the room, I can detect his relief. *He's so happy to see me.* The realization opens some little fissure inside my heart. Now that I've had the few hours of distance my addled mind needed, I can see it as much as I can feel it. *We need each other. Equally.*

He's standing there at the head of the table.

I'm sorry, I want to say. Something about his expression tells me he already knows.

"Dusty," he says, almost coolly, but his gaze is fiery

and his deep voice is edged with a husky, controlled joy. He gestures to the empty seat to his right. He wants me to sit next to him.

"Mr. Maddox." It sounds weird and overly formal, but some of the most powerful people in New York are in this room.

Noah's here, and Colton. Alexander is here too. And Evan, as well as the rest of my team. Patel, who I haven't spent much time with. And Lacey, who's smiling at me. Guaranteeing that whatever happens in this room is soon going to become office folklore.

Emma and Penelope take the two empty seats between Alexander and Evan.

And I take a seat next to Ace.

Everyone sits except for Ace.

"Thanks, Emma," he says, "for escorting Dusty this morning. And it's nice to meet you."

"You too, Cash." Emma is lapping this up. "And it was a pleasure."

Ace is quiet for a few seconds as he surveys the room.

It's been twelve or so hours since I've seen him and his effect shoots straight to the pit of my stomach. *I love him so much.* I love the little wave in the thick silk of his hair. *I love that I know how it feels in my hands.* The smoothness of his recent shave is underlaid by a barely-detectable rough-ness. *I love how it feels when it scratches against my thighs.*

My craving for him is pulsing in me, along with the beat of my heart.

"Thank you all for being here," Ace says, all business this morning. "I know this is somewhat unexpected but I have some things I need to say, and since you're all going to be a part of what happens next, you need to hear them."

Ace glances down at me, his eyes a resolute, unholy blue.

"A few months ago, I took a trip to Hawaii to meet with Ty Dyson about the fund of his we purchased. After our meeting, I was sitting out on the hotel patio having a much-needed drink. It was the day after the insider trading emails were detected. And that was when I first saw Dusty. She was on the beach. She smiled and walked right past me that day, and as soon as she did, I decided to stay an extra day."

Alexander leans back in his chair and folds his arms, enjoying this. He elbows Colton. "You were right. I needed to cancel all meetings to be here."

"Told you," Colton whispers back. They both wait for Ace to continue.

Which he does. "The next night, I happened to run into Dusty at the beach bar. I really couldn't believe she was real. She seemed to me like a dream come true." It sounds romantic and it is, and I'm reminded of some-thing he said to me over the weekend.

I'm a hard-ass numbers guy without a romantic bone in my body—until that moment. You turned me into someone who wanted to fall in love. Like, hard. Deep. For real.

Even so, I'm relieved when he's light on the details of what went down that night in Hawaii. "In the morning, Dusty left without saying goodbye. She was gone and she made it very difficult for me to find her."

I glance up at him and he gives me a *naughty-girl* look, which makes my heart beat faster.

"The next two months were both a nightmare and a feverish quest. I couldn't concentrate on the impending implosion of my company—and I have to both apologize to and thank my brothers for picking up the slack—because I was too distracted by the most beautiful girl I'd ever seen, who'd vanished into thin air."

Lacey's eyes get shiny and she blinks at Ace like she can't believe the guy she always thought was an arrogant prick is gushing all these love words.

"So you can imagine my surprise," Ace continues, "when our newest junior analyst was shown to my office on Friday morning. What do you know, my Hawaiian fever dream had materialized into a living, breathing employee."

Another nudge between Alexander and Colton. "The boy is *whipped*," Colton says under his breath.

Ace slides them a glare but there's no heat in it. "I'm telling it like it is, and I wanted you to know at least some of our backstory, because I'm going to be making some changes here at IE and I want you all to know why. First things first, nothing that I say here today goes any further than the walls of this room." His question is pointed at one person in particular. "Is that understood?"

Lacey nods sincerely. "Of course, Mr. Maddox."

"Good. Because leaks will lead to immediate dismissals. I think we can all agree on that, with all that's happened lately. Second, Dusty has been relieved of her former position as junior analyst."

What? After everything he just said, he's still firing me?

But then he says, "With myself and Noah, Dusty will be helping make the decisions about her new role. We're going to be creating a position for her that suits her capabilities and her vision."

There are a few murmurs around the room. I'm as shocked as they are.

"It was Dusty who pinpointed and exposed the fraud that almost brought this company down," Ace continues. "For that reason, and because her talents are clearly being wasted in a junior position, I've made the executive decision to promote her. Let me be clear about one thing: she's not being promoted because I'm in love with her."

Emma makes a small whimper. Evan, who's sitting next to her, notices her reaction. In fact, he seems to be staring at her in a way that's sort of…rapt. Ace's romantic tendencies seem to be rubbing off.

"She's being promoted because she's an asset to IE," he says. "And—if I get my way, which I'm going to make sure I do, even if it takes me a lifetime to do it—she'll eventually, as my wife, be a co-owner of IE at the highest level."

Did he just say *wife?* is the question that fizzes through my brain at the exact same time Alexander murmurs to Colton, "Did he just say *wife?*"

"*That* escalated quickly," Colton murmurs back.

"He's lost his mind," Alexander mutters.

"So it makes sense for her to have a senior role in the company starting now," Ace is saying. "If it takes a while for me to convince her the time is right for me to close down Tiffany's for the night so she can pick out the ring of her choice, then so be it. I can be patient. But it'll happen."

The reactions around the room don't really sink in, but I watch as Emma's eyes glimmer and so do Lacey's. Penelope's hands are clasped together with emotion. Colton mutters, "*hoo, boy,*" and Alexander just shakes his head.

As for me, I don't know how to react, except to feel equal parts terror and so much love for him I feel almost stricken with it.

"And now," Ace says, "I'd like you all to give Dusty and me a moment. There are some things she and I need to discuss in private. We'll meet you in the Sky Bar in a while."

"At ten in the morning?" Noah asks, to no one in particular.

"They serve coffee," Penelope points out, and with

that everyone shuffles out of the room, some still swooning, others with much stormier looks on their faces.

Once they're gone and the door is closed, Ace sits next to me and pulls my chair so I'm facing him, between his spread knees.

His blue eyes are soulful. "I'm sorry to spring all that on you like this, but I wanted to take the everyone-thinks-I've-slept-my-way-into-my-job element out of the equation once and for all. It's not something you need to worry about anymore." Ace takes my hands. "I think I've loved you since the minute I saw you, Texas. I'm obsessed with you—in a good way. In a way that's real and monumental and has basically transformed me from someone who only thinks about work to someone who only thinks about you. And how I might be able to get you to stop running from me."

"I don't want to run from you, Ace."

"But still, you do. Every time."

"It's my default mode. My brain tells me to leave before you get a chance to. It's easier. That way, my heart can remain intact. I'm sorry, Ace."

"I get it, Tex. Your father was the kind of man who could leave. Who *did* leave."

I hold onto his hands more tightly because the words unfailingly hit that deep reservoir of emotion in me that's my earliest and most primal wound.

"Tex?"

"Yeah?"

"I'm not that man. My father was a tyrannical bastard but he was always extremely *present*, which is going to be the new normal for you. Well, at least the present part. I've spent a long time doing my best to tone down any tyrannical bastard tendencies that might have rubbed off. Anyway, what I'm trying to say is this: I'm the guy who stays, whether you want him to or not."

His handsome face is blurry now. "You are?"

"Yeah. I am. I can't guarantee that everything will be perfect every second of every day. Life isn't generally like that. I can be an arrogant prick and I'm stubborn as fuck. I like getting my way. But I can guarantee that I'll be honest with you. And I promise you I won't leave."

My face is wet with tears. "You won't?"

"Nope. You're stuck with me, gorgeous. Now, I want you to bear with me for this next part."

Ace lets go of one of my hands. He reaches into his pocket and pulls out a box. "I meant what I said about Tiffany's. When you're ready, I'm going to take you down there and you're going to pick out any ring you want and I'm going to get down on one knee and ask you to marry me. You're moving in with me tonight and we're going to take it step by step until you start to trust me and believe me, without freaking out about it every step of the way. We'll get you some therapy if you think it would help. Whatever it takes. Until then, I bought this ring when I bought your bracelet. I knew you needed time, but I don't need time, Texas. I just need you as close to me as you'll let me get. So, this is a promise ring."

He slides the giant ruby onto a very significant finger.

"I'm going to fix those broken pieces inside you, Tex, you'll see, with love and lust and by making every dream you've ever had come true."

Oh my god.

"You're going to have your own driver and I've cleared out the penthouse apartment of the employee building. It's got three bedrooms. It's empty, and it's yours. That way, you'll have a safe place to run to if you need to. Emma can even move into it if you want so you have your support team there when you need her. So there's nothing to be scared of."

Wow. He really, really gets me.

"Because you know what, Texas?"

"What?"

"I'm fucking *all in*. I'm not just in love with you, baby girl. I'm fanatically, ecstatically, *addictively* in love with you. And to be honest, I never even *thought* about falling in love before. It wasn't really on my wish list or my radar. I was always too distracted with work and with making money and with proving myself to my father. But none of that feels so important anymore. Because I can tell you this: I fucking *love* being in love with you. It makes everything make *sense*. Everything suddenly has a *reason*. And you know what that reason is, Tex?"

"What's the reason?"

"It's you, baby. It's you." He takes my face carefully in his warm hands and wipes my tears. "Please, honey, let me try."

So I do the only thing I can do. I crawl onto his lap and into his arms and I kiss him. "I want to. I want to try. I can. I will."

"You do?" His question is so deep and so hopeful.

"Yes. So much."

"Fuck yes."

Our connection started as a physical one and, like always, we can't resist each other's pull. Our kisses turn slippery and hungry and my heart aches at the sweetness of it. His hands are under my dress as I unfasten his pants and we can't get close enough fast enough.

"I hope they don't drink their coffees too fast," I gasp.

"They know not to bother us."

He positions me, pushing my panties to the side, swiping the head of his cock insistently, parting me, sliding thickly inside. I whimper because he feels safe and heartbreakingly good.

My tight body gives so wetly and so willingly as he holds me and drives deeper inside me. I slide down onto his steely girth as I inhale his warm breath, kissing him as he plays my tongue with his. He's inside me in every possible way and I can't get enough of him.

I'm already starting to come.

"I love you, Dusty Rose," he rasps, a hitch in his voice. "Trust me. Believe me. I love you so fucking much."

And so I try it on for size and it's easier than I ever expected, because it's Ace. "I trust you, Cash Maddox. I believe you."

We're gripping each other and kissing like our lives depend on it, and it doesn't take long. We both shatter at the same time, my pleasure milking his as the gushing throb of him takes me higher.

Like Ace said, life makes no promises. It has a way of throwing curveballs. But as long as we're willing to catch them, maybe sometimes we can.

I hold him close as my body worships him lovingly, over and over.

"I love you, Ace."

What surprises me is how good it feels to finally say it.

EPILOGUE

Dusty

IF THERE'S a way to request a certain Uber driver, I don't know it, but I sort of wish it was Earl who was driving us to our hotel in Waikiki. Just so I could tell him he was right about everything.

My new job title is Vice President of Creative Direction. Which sounds…kind of cool.

Like he promised, Ace and I sat down with Noah and we talked through my ideas about what I thought my strengths were for the company, what my vision was for the future of my career, and a lot of other stuff that proved to me that both of them really know their shit when it comes to building and running a business. I told them I'd love to learn how to do that too.

So we wrote out a job description that covers all the things I know how to do and all the things I aspire to learn, and they created a job for me. It's not just my dream job, it's my fantasy job. Everything is so exciting, I can't wait to get to work each morning just to get started.

Since I moved in with Ace the night he gave me the ruby promise ring, my commute is now with him in the back of his Maybach, driven by one of his team of round-the-clock drivers.

Ace also insisted I get my own office on his floor. It's not huge and in fact used to be one of the smaller meeting rooms on the executive floor, but it has a corner window with a view of the Empire State Building and it's all my own. I absolutely love it.

It's also handy that it's right down the hall from Ace's office (and has a lock on the door and also a desk that's sturdy enough to hold our weight), because he tells me he can't go without seeing me for more than an hour.

After the meeting where Ace told everyone that we were together, Evan asked Emma if she wanted to have a drink with him after work. I can't imagine two people having more different personalities, but the two of them have really hit it off.

She's the bubbly sunshine to his reserved coding geek, so it's definitely a case of opposites attract. I can't imagine what the two of them talk about, but they're planning a fourth date this week so it must be going well. Last time I talked to Emma, she told me he was "surprisingly well-endowed for a nerd." I told her that was *way* too much information but she only squealed with jubilation at her new discovery. I'm just happy she's happy.

Rylee Winters disappeared uneventfully—partly because Ace's lawyers made sure of it—and the insider trading fiasco faded out almost immediately. IE's clients and subscribers appreciated that the management had been honest and forthcoming about the incident instead of trying to hide it. If anything, the discussion around the whole thing has boosted IE's profile.

Business has never been better.

Lacey was true to her word. I was suspicious that Ace quietly offered her a bonus to talk me up because everyone in the office has been only encouraging to me about my new role. Or maybe I've just finally laid my paranoia to rest. It never helped anyway. Either way, despite the fact that I jumped from a junior to a vice president in the course of under a week, everyone I work with seems to be fine with it. Especially my boss.

Lacey and I often meet for a drink in the Sky Bar after work. She told me there's a rumor circulating that Rylee's starting her own fund and already has a lot of interest. According to Lacey, she's dating a Bitcoin billionaire. I wish her only the best. I was never the type to carry grudges, but Ace is thorough about making sure Rylee's a part of our past and has nothing to do with our present or future.

With Ace's encouragement, I did end up going to see a therapist about my "abandonment issues." I don't think I'll really need to continue with it for long. It seems very straightforward to me. I told the therapist the story, we talked about it, I told her the issue had made it hard for me to trust men, but then I'd met Cash Maddox, who changed my mind. The therapist's opinion was that I've been through the worst of it and I agreed.

With his love, a lot of hot sex and his relentless devotion, Ace cured me, so it would seem.

I was paid the reward of twenty thousand dollars for cracking the mystery behind Rylee's emails. I told them they didn't need to pay me for doing the right thing, but they insisted it was company policy.

So I gave the money to my mom. Sky doesn't need it anymore. Her recording contract is more than enough to pay for her new loft in downtown Nashville and her new, glitzy lifestyle. She'll be spending most of her time over the next few months on tour as the opening act for one of the biggest new bands in country-rock music, called the Hay Seeds.

Last time I talked to her she was dating the bass player, whose name is Luke. Unlike her past boyfriends, he sounds like a nice guy, with a close family and the kind of integrity you tend to hope for in a partner. He calls when he says he's going to call. He buys her flowers. He even wrote a song about her, that's now climbing the charts. I've never seen my sister happier.

Now that my mom's house is paid off and she has money in the bank, she was able to quit both her cleaning jobs.

For the first time since my mom got pregnant with

Sky when she was seventeen, she's started painting again, something she used to dream about being able to do. She even sold a watercolor to a local gallery.

At my insistence, my mom decided to (finally) have a dishwasher installed, which meant she needed to do some minor renovations to her kitchen. The contractor who did the work for her, whose name is Jim, asked her out. He invited her to his old house by the river that he's done up and he cooked her the best meal she's ever had. Last time I talked to her, he'd just asked her to come again next weekend. My mom even mentioned that Jim doesn't smoke. She didn't need to say it for both of us to be thinking it: *he'll never need to go out for a pack of cigarettes.*

This week is "creative" week at my job.

It's company policy to work from anywhere we choose for one week out of each month. I spent the first creative week in Ace's apartment, where we barely surfaced. I told him that some of the stuff he got creative with—in bed— might actually be illegal in some states, but he didn't seem to mind.

That week, Ace took me to dinner at his favorite restaurant. Then his limo took us to Tiffany's, after hours, where the staff brought out all the engagement rings they had. He told me to pick any one I wanted.

I chose two rose gold bands that were held together by a row of pink diamonds. As it turns out, it's the ring that matches the bracelet Ace bought for me, which I now wear all the time.

Ace said I can't have the ring just yet. He kissed me and told me he loved me, and I said it right back. But he didn't propose to me that night. He said he had something special in mind and that it has something to do with my second creative week.

For that, I chose, of course, Waikiki. Ace said he was coming with me and he'd booked us the penthouse suite, the one where we spent our very first night together. He said he couldn't handle a week without me, especially if I was on the beach in my leopard print bikini.

So now, as we check in to my favorite hotel in the world, it's crazy to think that it was only four months ago that I was here the first time.

In every possible way, my life has transformed into something that needed to be conquered or overcome or endured, to something I can only be grateful for. Somehow, Earl was right. And so was Lucas.

Ace holds my hand as we walk along the beach and we find a spot for our towels. "This is where I first saw you," he says, looking devilishly handsome in his sunglasses, swim shorts and nothing else. The man is a specimen of male perfection that I can never quite get used to. Every day, I'm amazed by him.

He's looking around for someone. "Surfer Boy is gone," he comments. "Which is probably a good thing because I'd be tempted to throttle the little punk all over again."

Ace is right. There's a new guy, with brown shaggy

hair. Maybe Lucas never came back from his trip to the North Shore.

"I'll be right back," Ace tells me. He heads to the Beach Bar.

I go for a swim, floating for a while in that blue water that's as warm as the air, wondering how I got this lucky.

When I get back to our towels, Ace is standing there, watching me walk up the beach like he's starstruck. He's holding two drinks and he hands me one. "One slushy guava cocktail for the most beautiful girl in the world." I'd raved about them to him once on a rainy day in New York.

And then, he sets his drink down and slides his sunglasses up. He takes the light blue box out of his pocket and he gets down on one knee, taking my hand.

"Dusty Rose, my Texan girl, I can't breathe if you're not near me. I fell in love with you the first time I saw you, right here in this very spot, and I don't think I'll ever recover from how gorgeous you are, inside and out. I'm fucking besotted with you. I know it's fast but in some ways it feels like I've been waiting a lifetime for you. We can wait as long as you want to get married, but I want you to have the promise I gave you, now, here, on your finger and in your heart. I love you, Texas. I love you so fucking much it takes all my effort just to function as a normal human being and not follow you around like a lovestruck puppy every waking minute of every day. Please marry me, baby girl. Please say yes."

My Ace sort of stuns me with his handsomeness as he stares hopefully up at me. I can see behind his blue eyes that there's a glimmer of vulnerability in him. He's worried it's too soon for me, and that I might not say yes.

But I'm not scared anymore. For him, I'm willing to take the risk. Because I trust him. I believe him. Most of all, I love him more than I knew it was possible to love.

"Yes."

"Yes?"

I smile at him, because he makes me so happy. "Yes, Ace. I'll marry you."

He slides the ring onto my finger, where it fits perfectly next to the ruby promise ring. He stands and lifts me into his arms. He kisses me like he's been waiting his whole life to kiss me.

The whole beach claps and cheers.

I hardly notice them. I'm too besotted with my hot fiancé. "Thank you for fixing me, Ace." My voice hitches with the overload of happiness he's somehow infused into every corner of my world.

"Thank you for letting me, angel. And for being the love of my life."

He kisses me again.

Then Ace murmurs, "Can we please go back to our room now because I've got a fucking hard-on for my new wife-to-be that won't take no for an answer and I don't want to scare away the happy vacationers."

I laugh and whisper into his ear, "I want to ride your big cock into a gilded sunset, boss."

He swears under his breath, setting me down and wrapping a towel around his waist. He holds our bag in front of his giant erection. "Whatever Dusty Rose Maddox wants, Dusty Rose Maddox gets. Forever and ever." Then he grabs my hand and pulls me up the beach.

With that, my husband-to-be takes me to bed and—between arguing with my overly arrogant lover and having hot makeup sex before the argument is even finished—we live happily ever after.

Thank you so much for reading **Billionaire Boss**. If you enjoyed this book, please consider leaving a quick rating or review on Amazon.

Want to see what happens with Dusty and Cash two—and six—years down the road? Get the FREE 20-page bonus epilogue (includes babies!) here: https://BookHip. com/SACWADP

Below I'm including the first chapter of Alexander's book, **Billionaire Grump**. Alexander is one of my favorite heroes. He's such a grump but he falls sooo hard :) Check out the **New York Billionaires** series.

xoxo,

Julie

Please come join my Facebook reader group, Julie Capulet's Romantics, where I share cover reveals, insider info and we discuss all things romance!

Sign up for my newsletter to receive my free bonus content and get access to sneak peeks and exclusive giveaways!

Visit my website @ www.juliecapulet.com

It was supposed to be a fake date.
It turned out to be true love.

My assignment is simple. I'm the fake date of billionaire Alexander Maddox for the weekend. My job: to attend a Hamptons wedding with him and convince all the heiresses and socialites competing for his attention—including his ex, who happens to be the wedding planner—that he's very much taken.

Alexander Maddox is the oldest of the four Maddox brothers, Manhattan's most eligible bachelors. He's also the CEO of his family's legacy investment empire. Loaded beyond belief. And, according to rumors, sexy as sin. But this is strictly a business arrangement.

It's also an excuse for me to get out of town for a few days. I didn't exactly *mean* to break into my estranged father's house and accidentally discover his offshore bank account details. *Or* to leave those details lying around where my hacker of a little brother with a serious vendetta might find them. He covered his tracks, he said, but we both know it was never going to be that easy.

My plan: to lay low, spend the weekend by the pool, play my part like I'm an Oscar nominee and hope the little incident blows over by Monday morning.

But my weekend doesn't go according to plan. Alexander Maddox turns out to be the most infuriating man I've ever met. And also the hottest—*so* hot, in fact, that I end up giving him much, much more than I bargained for.

When the banking incident turns out to be a tiny bit more serious than I imagined, things get complicated. But by then I've already cashed in my V-card with the sexy billionaire and made a run for it—or at least tried to.

How do I get myself into these messes? And how did I let myself get knocked up by a possessive grump who suddenly seems to think I'm his one and only?

Against all odds, I think he might be right.

Billionaire Grump is a sexy standalone billionaire romance starring a grumpy CEO and the sassy fake date he never saw coming.

New York Billionaires

Chapter One

IVY

"Are you *sure* you want to do this, Ivy? I really think you're making a huge mistake."

I'm on the train, video chatting with my best friend Cleo, my hair tied back and my baseball cap pulled down low. I can always count on my level-headed bestie to be the voice of reason. "That's definitely possible."

I came straight from yoga, so I'm wearing leggings and a zipped-up hoodie, trying to look as inconspicuous as possible.

The train isn't overly busy. It's mid-morning on a Saturday and I'm on my way from Grand Central Station out to Stamford, Connecticut. I know I'm more likely to be recognized by the groups of college students and young couples who are filling the train than if I was on an early Monday morning commuter train. Which is why I keep my cap low.

I don't mind if people want to say hi. That part of being sort-of famous is kind of cool. Most people are nice. They tell me they love my music or that they follow me on social media, they ask for a selfie, then they get on with their day. It's the silent, not-at-all-subtle filming and the stealth photography that freaks me out. I'd much rather people said something to me than try to stalk me when I'm sitting right next to them.

When I was sure no one was close enough to listen in, I called Cleo, who's been trying to talk me out of what I'm about to do since I mentioned it to her a few days ago.

"Ive? Seriously. This is a bad idea."

I chew my lip, staring at Cleo's concerned face on the screen, framed by her honey-blond curls.

"You're probably right. But this isn't about me, Cleo. I'm doing it for Josh."

"Does Josh even *want* your father at his graduation?"

"I mean, he says he doesn't. But deep down I think maybe he actually does. Graduation is a big deal. It might be nice for him to have…you know, a family."

"*We* can be his family. Found family is just as good. And in this case probably better."

"I know." I *do* know. I've almost jumped off the train at each stop we've made. "But I figure there's really nothing to lose by extending the olive branch one last time."

Cleo sighs. "You're a better woman than I am, Ive. If my dad ditched me and my sisters when we were kids so he could lavish attention all over his new family, I wouldn't have spoken to the bastard ever again."

I shrug. "Like I said, it's about Josh."

"Even if your dad did come to the graduation— which we both know is unlikely—Josh might feel more anger over the whole AWOL father thing than joy over a family reunion that we all know is too little too late. It seems to me you're just inviting drama that no one wants."

"Maybe." I pinch the bridge of my nose. "Okay, yes. But maybe if our father sees what a great man Josh is growing into, he'll realize he fucked up by walking away. If he sees what he's been missing out on, it might make him want to be in Josh's life a little more. And it might give Josh some closure. He's just so pissed off at life in general. I was hoping maybe it would help."

Cleo shakes her head. "It's wishful thinking."

"It's hopeful thinking."

I know Cleo means well, but it's easy to judge when you come from the perfect family unit, when your parents are still madly in love after thirty years of marriage and do everything they can to support everything their children do—logistically, emotionally and financially. Cleo's parents never missed a single piano recital, softball game or school play. Not to mention a single payment for the upscale boarding schools or the college tuition. "Your dad knows you're coming out to see him, right?"

"I sent him two emails."

"Did he reply?"

I pause as a group of teenagers walk past me onto the train, hiding under the rim of my hat. "Nope."

"But you think he'll be there?"

Part of the reason I'm making this trip on the

weekend is because my dad is a lawyer and he works at a law firm in Stamford. I didn't want to visit him at work. A small part of me wonders if maybe his receptionists have been given strict instructions to turn me and Josh away, if we ever happened to turn up. At least if I visit him at home he has no buffer besides his trophy wife Anita.

But who knows, he might be a golfer or something, spending exorbitant amounts of money on country club fees while meanwhile disinheriting his two oldest children.

"If he's not there after he's seen my emails, then I guess that tells me everything I need to know. All I'm doing is taking him up on his offer to 'visit anytime.'"

I cringe thinking about the lame Christmas email he sent. In January. His half-assed once-a-year attempt to keep us from being completely estranged. It's almost more of an insult than if he totally pretended we didn't exist.

Merry Christmas! I hope the two of you are doing well. Visit anytime! Dad.

She says it gently. "I think he already told you everything you need to know when he didn't reach out when your mom died. I honestly don't know how he lives with himself."

"He did reach out." With another one-liner, but still. "It's just the way he is." I don't know why I'm defending him. Cleo's right. This is probably an epically bad idea.

"Exactly."

If it was just me, I wouldn't be here. Dad didn't come to my graduation or to our mother's funeral, but he did send me an email when my debut single hit the Billboard Top 100. *That*, he cared about, apparently. "Josh is just so angry about the whole thing, Cleo. It's not healthy. I worry about it."

"He's *seventeen*, Ivy. He's a mess of angst and hormones. He's also smart and successful and he's about to start college. He's going to be fine."

"I know he is. And that's the thing. I'm so proud of him. I want our father to see what a cool kid he is."

"No thanks to him," Cleo points out scathingly. "Basically the only thing he's ever done for Josh is to donate a DNA sample."

"Ew."

She laughs. "Sorry. But seriously, your MO is and always has been to work like hell to make Josh's life easier, I get that. But he's a big boy now."

"I just don't want him hating me ten years from now when he's talking to his therapist and they're discussing why I didn't try to do more."

Cleo twirls a blond curl around her finger. "Maybe it's time for both of you to just let it go, honey, and get on with the rest of your lives."

"I know. I will let it go, I promise. After this."

Something in me is burning to tell my father face to face that we did it without him. We made it. We're successful people. Our mom and her sister did everything they could to make a life for us after he traded us in for a newer model. *They* lifted us up. And we lifted each other up. Even without him, we didn't just survive, we *thrived*.

Sort of.

"I want him to remember, even if it's for one miserable second of his carefree new life, that he left us behind. I also want to watch him squirm when he's forced to look me in the eye as he makes some excuse to miss his oldest son's high school graduation."

"Well, I wish you luck, babe. If you need some support after, come see us. We'll be back around three." She glances at her iWatch. "I better go. Sam will be back from the gym any minute and if I'm going to sell the idea of going downtown, I need to be on my A game. I might even have to resort to bribery. But call me later, okay? I want to hear how it goes."

"Of course. Good luck with the registry."

That's another thing about Cleo that puts us in different universes. Not only does she have the perfect family, she has the perfect fiancé. She and Sam met as juniors in high school and have been sweethearts ever since. They haven't set a date yet, but they're in the process of planning for their wedding, which will no doubt also be picture perfect.

It's icing on the cake that she also has a job she loves, as the assistant for Noah Maddox. He's the CFO of Invested Enterprises, one of the hottest companies in the city that literally everyone wishes they worked for.

And I'm beyond happy for my best friend. She deserves all of her good fortune.

But I also know she doesn't entirely *get* some of the grittier details of my life, because she seems to have been born under a lucky star.

I've had to make my own luck, and I have, but it's taken 24/7 of grit and hard work, every single day of my life, to get here.

We end the call, and I pull my baseball cap even lower, sliding on my sunglasses as the train slows to a stop. Stamford station comes into view.

I get off the train and order an Uber.

It's a ten minute ride to my dad's house, through streets that get progressively leafier, more manicured and lined with bigger and more ostentatious houses.

I've never been to Stamford before, or at least not that I can remember. Josh and I were both born in Bridgeport, where my parents lived together when we were very young. I have a few hazy memories of a white house. And slamming doors.

Only a few months after Josh was born, my parents went through a bitter, messy divorce. And then, after the three of us were cast out, we moved into my mom's sister's basement apartment in Bushwick, which is where we lived until around a year and a half ago, when I was able to buy our very own apartment.

Being both a bastard and a divorce lawyer, my dad was able to manipulate the child support payments into something that covered only our absolute basics, while he meanwhile married his pretty young secretary and continued to live a progressively more and more luxurious life. They have seven-year-old twin sons named Aaron and Adam who go to some elite private boarding school and who I've never actually met.

My father's neighborhood definitely has that safe, privileged family feel that the wealthy suburbs are known for.

Oh the irony.

It's not something I've ever dwelled on all that much —the kind of life we would have had if my parents hadn't split up—but this is like a cold slap in the face.

When the Uber pulls up in front of the house, it's clear that my father's house is one of the biggest and most over-the-top on the street. It's a colonial style McMansion with columns and neatly-trimmed topiary bushes. It sits on a ridge and has a nice view. Not a single blade of grass on the freshly-mown lawn is out of place.

It's the kind of house where kids could run barefoot through the sprinkler having water fights. Where you'd have backyard barbecues on hot summer days with fresh-squeezed homemade lemonade. Snowy Christmases with a real Christmas tree you went out and chose from the farm on a crisp blue day filled with laughter. Snowmen with carrots for noses in the front yard. You just *know* that, every year, the mountain of artfully-wrapped presents piled under it on Christmas morning for the excited little boys is absolutely epic.

My stomach twists.

It's the perfect place to raise a family.

Just not *all* of his family. Only his favorite half of it.

There's a car parked in the driveway, a sleek, expensive black Range Rover. Anita's car, I'm guessing. No doubt my dad drives a midlife-crisis-style red convertible sports car.

Which means it's either parked in one of the three garages or he's not here.

He *could* have parked in the garage. He probably did.

But some sixth sense tells me he didn't. It's telling me he's not here.

My heart is beating fast.

I could turn back now and keep my pride intact. I could save myself a face-to-face encounter with the woman my dad left my mom for, who I've met only once, years ago now. I could avoid the reality that he doesn't care enough about me to be here, even when he knew I was coming to see him.

How hard is it to not be a total letdown for once in your goddamn life?

I almost get straight back into the Uber and request a ride back to the station.

But I'm here now. And maybe I've got it wrong. Maybe he's inside with a fresh pot of coffee waiting, ready to listen and apologize and, for once, do the right thing.

I take a deep breath and walk up to the front door before I can second-guess myself. I raise the heavy knocker and let it slam loudly, three times.

No one comes to the door.

I wait.

I knock again.

Still no signs of life.

So, I reach for the brass door handle.

I don't expect it to be unlocked.

The door swings open.

Shit.

"Dad?" I call into the hallway. The floor is tiled with white marble. High ceilings give the place a stark feel. There's a modern (hideous) white chandelier. The walls are white, with white art and white furniture. Peering in, I can't help but notice it looks like a very up-market dentist's office. "Dad? Anita? Hello? Anyone home?"

There's no response.

I bang the door knocker again.

There's still no sign that anyone is home.

I wait probably a full minute, wondering what to do next.

Almost against my will, I step inside.

I'm rooted to the spot, not daring to go further now that I've actually strolled into my estranged father's house.

What the hell do I do now?

I can't just turn around, order another Uber and disappear back to New York. That would be too convenient for him. I want him to know I came. That I took him up on his empty promise.

From where I'm standing, I can make out the room on my left. The door is open and it's filled with dark furniture—a nice change from the sterile front hallway. Bookcases, a heavy mahogany desk, one of those leather wing-backed chairs.

Dad's home office, I'm assuming.

"Dad?" I call out once more. I told him I was coming. I knocked. I did all I could do to announce my presence.

I'm not breaking and entering. I'm his own daughter. His flesh and blood. I just want to leave a note. This isn't illegal.

And now I'm standing in his office. There are built-in shelves with books and trinkets I don't recognize. This man is a stranger who's lived a life I have no connection to.

There's a framed picture of Anita and my dad, at a beach somewhere. She's in a bikini and looks every bit of her twelve years younger than he is.

There's another framed photo, of the twin boys. I go over and pick it up, to take a closer look. As I do, of course I notice the glaring absence of *us*. I shouldn't be surprised. There's not a single shred of evidence in this office that Josh or I have ever existed. I'm so hardened to this by now, usually. But the in-your-face reminder hits me hard.

No picture of his other son, who's so smart and handsome and who's worked so hard to get into freaking Columbia. Why isn't that good enough? Why were we never, ever good enough?

You cold-hearted prick.

The boys are dark-haired with amber eyes that are very similar in color to my own. They're beautiful boys. They're identical twins and they look it. Neat haircuts and little ties. All dressed up for their photo shoot.

I place the photo neatly back on its shelf. On a whim, I take out my phone and take a picture of it. They're my brothers, after all. I'm allowed to have one small keepsake of them.

Looking around, I have a very strong urge to leave.

If I leave a note, I will, of course, be incriminating myself. Announcing that I entered his house without being invited. Then again, the *Visit anytime!* comment is the reason I'm here. With an exclamation point and everything.

And this is the last time I'll ever try. It'll be a goodbye note. A fuck-you-and-have-a-nice-life final farewell.

I check the desk for some Post-Its or note paper. There are piles of paperwork covering the desk. There's a *Finlay & Hobbs Law* mug filled with pens. I take a pen and carefully rummage to find a blank piece of paper. As I do this, a small stack of papers slide off their pile, fluttering to the floor.

Shit.

I pick them up, carefully trying to return them to the way I found them.

I can't miss the fact that the page on the top of the pile is a bank statement.

Of course I shouldn't look. It's none of my business. But the numbers printed onto that page seem to take on an almost 3D quality, jumping out at me and insisting I read them.

My father is obviously doing well for himself. That he's doing *this* well for himself and was always content to pay the bare minimum in child support for all those years suddenly grates me in a way that's new. By the time I turned nineteen, I was making enough to support Josh and me, so I set up an index fund account for Josh and let my dad's meager payments feed into that. It's not much but it might pay for a semester at Columbia.

It's the number at the bottom of the page that catches my attention. A lot of zeroes tend to do that.

Six zeroes, to be precise, with two ones in front of them. The high-interest savings account is based in the Bahamas and holds—holy shit…*eleven million dollars.*

I read it again, as if there might be some explanation on the page.

The account is in his name. There's no other conclusion to jump to. This is Roy Laine's bank account and it contains Roy Laine's money.

Eleven million dollars of it.

My heart is racing. I shouldn't be here and I definitely

shouldn't be snooping, but seeing this just about breaks my jaded heart.

I have to stop myself from ripping the statement to shreds, from pushing everything off this shitty mess on his mahogany desk and letting it crash to the floor in a pile of chaos.

How long has he had this money? Where did it come from? I mean, I'm sure he's making bank as a lawyer but this is some serious cash.

My dad is a moderately successful divorce lawyer, so he intimately knew the loopholes that would get him out of paying real child support. He went out of his way to not only abandon his family but to twist the truth and use his inside knowledge to corrupt the system—just so he could get out of doing the right thing by the people he was supposed to love the most.

The numbers are blurry now and I impatiently brush away tears.

Why did I come here? Cleo was right. This was a huge mistake.

Does he have no heart whatsoever? Did he really care so little for us that he would hide this from us to deliberately make our lives harder?

Does Anita even know about this? Is he planning a second getaway, leaving those little boys in the lurch like he did to us?

Fucker.

My emotions are raw.

I take out my phone and I snap a few more photos. Of the bank statement. The top page and several more. I make sure I'm thorough.

What are you trying to do right now?

I don't know. Nothing. I just want to make sure I didn't dream this.

Then I cover the pile back up with some other paperwork. And I scrawl a note.

> Dad,
>
> I showed up like I said I would. I came to tell you that Josh is graduating in June. He's been accepted at Columbia and he'll be starting there in the fall. It would mean something to him to know that you cared about any of the above. If you can make the effort to call me back, I could give you the details about maybe coming along to his graduation to support all his hard work and amazing achievements.
>
> Your daughter,
> Ivy

I leave the note on the white marble table in the white marble foyer of the gigantic house. Then I slam the door behind me.

ALSO BY JULIE CAPULET

I Love You Series

The Obsession Begins (free)

XOXO I Love You

XOXX I Love You More

Love You the Most (free)

Sexy Standalones

Max

Cowboy

McCabe Brothers Series

Hopeless Romantic

My Hero

Arrogant Player

Music City Lovers Series

Nashville Days

Nashville Nights

Nashville Dreams

Nashville Lights

Hawthorne U Series

Lovestruck

Paradise Series

Devil's Angel

Wild Hearts

New York Billionaires Series

Billionaire Boss

Billionaire Grump

Billionaire Devil

Billionaire Romantic

Standalone Rom-com

Beautiful Savages

ABOUT THE AUTHOR

Julie Capulet is an Amazon top 20 bestselling author of contemporary romance. She writes steamy he-falls-first romance with heart, heat and fairy tale HEAs. Her stories are inspired by true love and she's married to her own real life hero. When she's not writing, she's reading, traveling, walking on the beach and watching rom-coms.

www.juliecapulet.com

9 781968 790196